# Praise for Tori El........ Lily Wong series

"Lily Wong is gutsy, smart, and irresistible—just like *The Ninja's Blade*. Grab it!"
—**Meg Gardiner, Edgar Award-winning author of *The Dark Corners of the Night***

"With *The Ninja's Blade* Tori Eldridge turns the dial to 11. More action, more fantastic characters, and more devious twists. Highly recommended!"
—**Jonathan Maberry, bestselling author of *V-Wars* and *Patient Zero***

"An exciting mystery that takes a sobering look at the sexual exploitation of youth in Los Angeles. Readers will eagerly await Lily's next outing."
—***Publishers Weekly***

"A nonstop thrill ride!"
—**Naomi Hirahara, Edgar Award-winning author of *Clark and Division***

"Lily Wong is back and her quest for justice is stronger than ever! Buckle up for another heart-stopping ride!"
—**Karen Dionne, #1 internationally bestselling author of *The Marsh King's Daughter* and *The Wicked Sister***

"Will have you on the edge of your seat, turning pages so fast toward the end that you risk death by paper cut. If you're not reading this series, you're missing out big time."
—**Tracy Clark, author of the acclaimed Cass Raines Chicago Mystery series**

"One of the best mysteries of the year."
—***South Florida Sun-Sentinel* on *The Ninja Daughter***

"This novel explodes on every page.
An off-the-charts thrilling debut."
—*Los Angeles Review of Books*

"Readers who enjoy an action-packed adventure that doesn't
neglect character development and speaks truth about the
human condition will welcome this quirky, passionate, and
endearingly relatable protagonist."
—*Library Journal* (Starred *Review*)

"A remarkably fresh, intense thriller, and Lily Wong is one hell
of a new hero. Tori Eldridge is redefining the genre."
—**J.T. Ellison, *New York Times* bestselling author of
*Lie To Me* and *Tear Me Apart***

"Eldridge's wild ride of a first novel marries *Kill Bill*
with *Killing Eve*. Eldridge expertly mines both domestic
suspense and action thriller."
—*Publishers Weekly*

"Lily Wong is an irresistible heroine set perfectly against a
quirky millennial L.A. backdrop."
—*Booklist*

"The story of a modern-day ninja warrior following the code
of the #MeToo movement, *The Ninja Daughter* by Tori
Eldridge is as impactful as a throwing star."
—*Criminal Element*

"Eldridge has written a swift-slick PI novel that takes on sex
trafficking and social injustice with the sharpness of a, well,
ninja's blade."
—*Star Tribune*

"High drama plays out against the opposing backdrops of cozy
(scrumptious food and luxurious outfits) and gritty (fierce
riots and dangerous triads)."
—**Jennifer J. Chow, Lefty Award-nominated author of
*Mimi Lee Reads Between the Lines***

# THE

# NINJA

# BETRAYED

# THE

# NINJA

# BETRAYED

Tori Eldridge

Copyright © 2021 by Tori Eldridge
Cover and jacket design by 2Faced Design

ISBN 978-1-951709-36-5
ISBN 978-1-951709-68-6
Library of Congress Control Number: available upon request

First trade paperback edition September 2021 by Agora Books
An imprint of Polis Books, LLC
44 Brookview Lane
Aberdeen, NJ 07747
PolisBooks.com

*For Stopher, Joeye, and her Hong Kong family.*
*You've enriched my life beyond measure.*

# Chapter One

"Get your ass out here, Claire, before I tear this place down." The man's bellow was followed by the sound of shattering glass.

Billy Bodean was a mean sonofabitch with a cop for a brother and entitlement to spare. He had chased his girlfriend to Aleisha's Refuge, busted through the gate, and was now terrorizing everyone inside. Aleisha's husband, Stan, had a shotgun pointed at him through the back house window and looked angry enough to fire.

Billy hurled the chair through the broken window. The iron backrest slammed the shotgun against Stan's chest and smashed into his face. Blood splattered on his shirt.

I charged across the courtyard to take him by surprise, but neighbors shouted through the fence, alerting him to my approach. Billy turned, stumbled backwards, and threw a haymaker at my head. I ducked the wild punch, drove my palm up under his chin, and sent him flying into the jagged frame of the window.

Billy howled as glass sliced his back.

I yanked him off the frame and planted him, face down, on the terracotta tiles. As I pulled Billy's arms behind his back into a painful combination of wrist and shoulder locks, Aleisha rushed forward with a handful of zip ties—a dance she and I had done several times before.

"Can you fasten them yourself?" I asked. "That way you can tell the truth to the police when they arrive."

"We didn't call them."

"Pretty sure your neighbors did."

1

"You aren't staying?"

"Can't. My plane leaves in three hours. I gotta run."

Aleisha zip tied Billy's wrists while Stan, still a bloody mess, wrapped a phone cord around Billy's ankles.

"You all right, Stan?"

"Better once we get this piece of garbage off our property and in jail where he belongs."

A distraught woman with freckled skin and dirty blonde hair looked out the open door. Against her thigh, she clutched a spitting image of herself. "What about Kimmy? What if they take her away?"

When Billy started to answer, I stomped on his back. He shut up quick and kept his opinions to himself.

Aleisha held out her big mama arms and scooped Kimmy into a hug. "Don't you worry, hon. Stan and I will speak for you. No one in their right mind would believe you would harm this precious girl."

Aleisha and Stan didn't have any children of their own, but having grown up through rough times in Compton, Aleisha had always dreamed of running a refuge for women and children. When she married Stan, a New York Jew and former stock broker, he turned her dream into a reality.

I worked for them, extracting and rescuing abused women from violent homes and dangerous conditions. I also did whatever needed to be done to protect Aleisha and Stan. They were family to me. After losing my sister, I would do anything to protect my own.

Sirens grew louder as squad cars approached.

I stepped off of Billy's back and glanced at the unlikely couple who had become second parents to me. "Sorry to bail on you, but I gotta fly. Are you going to be okay?"

"Don't worry about us." Stan replaced my foot with his own to keep Billy planted on his stomach, then he snorted blood through his broken nose and spit. "We'll explain the situation to the police. Brother or no, there's no denying this man attacked me on our property."

I hated to leave. "Text me later?"

"We will."

Aleisha shooed me with her free hand as she hugged the frightened child. "Go. Or you'll never make it to Hong Kong."

# Chapter Two

Between yellow lights and back roads, my friend and rideshare driver Kansas got me to my North Dakota Norwegian father's Chinese restaurant in ten minutes flat. I pointed to a black hatchback with the twin golden dragons emblazoned on the doors. "Behind the delivery car is fine. How long do you think it will take to get to the airport?"

"At this time of morning and staying off the 405? Maybe twenty minutes."

"I'll be down in ten."

As I hopped out of the SUV, my father drove up in his sedan. He pulled into his parking space and called to me over his roof. "Dumpling, what are you doing here? Your flight boards in two hours. I just dropped your mother at LAX. She's already checking in."

I punched in the security code and yanked open the door. "No time to talk, Baba, got a plane to catch."

A cook looked up from the chopping block and waved a cleaver in my direction. "Hi, Lily. Why aren't you on your way to Hong Kong?" His Filipino accent took the sting out of his rebuke.

Ling slapped the dough she was kneading for dumplings and buns. "Leave her alone, Bayani, can't you see she's late?" She smiled at me. "Ng hou gap. Jing hai yiu faai." *Don't Rush. Be quick*—an idiom I would no doubt hear in abundance during the weeks ahead.

As I ran up the stairs, Baba lumbered behind me, packing the worry weight he had gained in the last couple of months. The first ten pounds had appeared after he learned the truth about my nin-ja protection work. The second ten pounds were on Ma. Her fiftieth birthday had turned her into an emotional wreck. Not because of her age. Because she had tried to impress her parents.

I snorted as I punched in the code to my apartment. I could have told her that was a losing battle.

I kicked off my shoes and hurried to the bed where I had already laid out the suitcase and clothing for my trip. If Aleisha hadn't called, I would have been at LAX on time, already checked in, and creeping through airport security with Ma.

"It couldn't be helped," I said, as Baba followed me into the apart-ment.

"What can I do to speed things along?"

"Stuff these into the case?"

While Baba packed my clothes, I took my treasured knife from my backpack. I couldn't carry the karambit through TSA, but I could send it in my luggage. My father babbled as I tried to decide.

"I'm worried about your mother."

"Yep."

"This board meeting... It's not right."

"Nope."

"She shouldn't have to go alone."

"She's not."

"I know. I just wish it could be me."

"The restaurant can't operate with *both* you and Uncle gone. You have to stay. I have to hurry."

I set the karambit on the chest beside my sister's portrait and the incense, rice, and salt I offered for her spirit. I couldn't risk Hong Kong security confiscating my favorite weapon, not when I had finally loosened the safety catch until it opened as smooth as butter. Besides, why would I need a knife? A ceremonial dagger, on the other hand, might come in handy.

I grabbed my phurba necklace and slipped it over my head. The silver pendant was barely four inches long from the crown of the wrathful three-faced Vajrakilaya to the tip of the three-sided stake. I had worn the necklace in federal courts, police stations, and airport terminals. None of their security checks ever flagged it as a weapon. No one would have guessed the pendant had been christened with the blood of my sister's murderer.

The symbolic dagger was not intended for use as a physical weapon. It was a Buddhist tool for cutting through delusion caused by the Three Poisons of Attachment, Ignorance, and Aversion. It helped me transform negative energies into positive. Many Vajrakilaya practitioners even believed a phurba could be used as a tool to subdue evil spirits. I had worn the necklace on many important occasions, including the night my sister's murderer had attacked me and on my first date with Daniel. With all the negative energy surrounding this trip to Hong Kong, it felt wise to wear it now.

Baba pressed down my clothes. "You sure you don't want me to drive you?"

"Kansas drives faster. Besides, you have twice the work to do with Uncle out of town."

Baba shrugged. "Busy hands make for a quiet mind." He held up the jade bracelet my grandfather had given me. "Pack or wear?"

"Neither."

I put the Sì Xiàng bangle in a padded jewelry pouch and stuffed it into the inner pocket of my cycling backpack. It was too fragile to wear on my wrist during travel and too precious to risk in baggage. I also needed it for Gung-Gung's cocktail party after we landed in Hong Kong.

I stuffed a fancy change of clothes into my pack and slung it on my shoulders. It was heavier than usual with my laptop and tools of the trade I hadn't had time to unpack. Baba zipped my roller bag and headed out the door. I locked up behind him and ran down the stairs.

When we reached Kansas' car, I gave him a hug. "I love you, Baba. Take care of yourself, okay?"

"Don't worry about me. Take care of your mother."

# Chapter Three

Kansas cut down the alley to Overland Avenue. It was eleven-fifteen. My flight boarded at twelve-thirty.

"Ma's gonna kill me."

"Not if I can help it."

She gunned through the yellow lights, one after another. If we caught a single red, we'd be screwed for the rest. "You looking forward to seeing your guy?"

If Kansas was trying to distract me, it worked. Just the thought of Daniel Kwok eased my tension and made me smile. "Actually? Yes." The revelation boggled my mind. After all these years, I had feelings for a guy.

"How long has he been away?"

"Twenty-two days."

Kansas chuckled. "Were you able to see him after the Big Kiss?"

"If you mean the one that Gung-Gung and Po-Po conspired to arrange, then no. They were ridiculously pleased. Daniel said they talked about it all the way to the airport. Unfortunately, he left soon after on a surprise business trip to Hong Kong."

Kansas turned south onto Sepulveda in a straight shot to LAX. "They were right to be pleased. You and Daniel make a good match."

"You think so?"

She merged in with Lincoln Boulevard and cut across to an empty lane, hit the gas, and sped through the next yellow light. The stop-and-goes—as Baba called traffic lights—seemed out to get us this morning. "I'm just going on what you tell me, and the way you blush when you talk about him."

I felt the heat rise up my neck. Damn flush betrayed me every time.

"Will you have much time to see each other in Hong Kong?"

I shrugged. "My first obligation is to Ma. This board meeting has her worried. Things didn't go well between her and Gung-Gung when he came to visit. I don't know what to expect with us staying with him and Po-Po. Besides, Daniel has his own obligations with family and business."

Kansas turned up the Sky Way ramp and followed the signs for departures. "You're flying all the way to freaking Hong Kong. If he can't carve out romance time for you, he's not worth it."

I laughed. "I thought you said we were a good match."

"Not if the boy doesn't put out."

"You did not just say that."

"The hell I didn't."

She dodged around a string of shuttle buses into the stalled traffic.

I opened my door. "It'll be faster if I run."

She popped the trunk. "Have a good time. Call me when you get back."

"Will do."

I strapped the pack onto my back, rolled my suitcase through the cars to the sidewalk, and ran. My flight boarded in fifty-five minutes. I dashed into the priority check-in line, thankful to be flying with Ma in business class, and used the wait time to shoot her a text.

Me: *I'm here.*

Ma: *I don't see you.*

Me: *Checking in.*

Her lack of response spoke volumes.

I checked my bag and raced to security where I was delayed by a long line and an over-zealous TSA officer who insisted on inspecting every compartment in my backpack.

He held up a small hank of light-weight climbing rope. "What's this?"

"I'm a sailor. I practice tying knots."

I kept skinny line in my backpack for climbing emergencies and had forgotten it was there. If I hadn't been in such a rush, I would have spared the extra ounces and left all my gear at home.

"And this?" he asked.

"Lock picking tools."

"Are you planning to commit a crime?"

"No, sir. It's a gift for my cousin in Hong Kong. He works security for a large corporation."

"I see."

Tools under seven inches in length were generally permitted in carry-on bags, but it was the security officer's call. I smiled sweetly to hide my impatience. Ma had texted me that she was already on the plane.

The officer checked the picks with infuriating care, replaced them in my pack, and slid the plastic tray down the table. "You may go."

I sprinted to the gate and waved at the attendants as they shut down boarding. "Wait! That's my flight."

She scanned my ticket and motioned me through. "You better hurry. The crew is preparing for departure."

"Thank you."

I ran down the jetway to the plane. By the time I reached Ma, I was dripping in sweat. She glanced up at me then returned to her book with a sigh.

This was going to be a very long flight.

# Chapter Four

I nestled into my personal business class pod, angled feet-to feet with Ma. We had roomy seats, triangular arm rests, pull out tables, and sizable entertainment screens that adjusted for premium viewing. A sprig of white orchids decorated our console. Partway through the flight, the attendant converted our seats to beds and sprayed our pillows with botanical mist. Between the almost sixteen-hour flight and sixteen-hour time difference, we would arrive at the end of the following day. Both of us had the tops of our beds raised so we could finish our drinks.

I sipped my chrysanthemum tea. "Do you always travel like this?"

"Don't you remember?"

"Our trip with Rose was a long time ago, but I don't remember the airline being quite this fancy."

"I suppose it wasn't back then. But, to answer your question, yes, HKIF always flies me business class. I paid extra to have you beside me."

"That was nice of you." I'd experienced more pampering in the last six hours than I had in the last six months combined. "Do you mind if I keep my light on? I don't want to sleep through the luxury."

"Whatever you prefer, Lily, as long as you feel refreshed for the party tonight. It's important that we both make a strong impression."

"Why didn't we fly in yesterday?"

"Because your grandfather neglected to tell me about the party until last night."

"On purpose?"

She sipped her chardonnay. "I have no idea."

As she stared off in thought, I surfed the net for Hong Kong news. Ma and I would land in a hotbed of discontent. I wanted a clear understanding of what to expect.

Ever since the Hong Kong government had announced the extradition bill that would enabled fugitives to be transferred back to China, pro-democracy citizens had protested. So far, over 1,400 people had been arrested in 2019.

I opened a recent article from Amnesty International demanding a "prompt and independent investigation."

"Are you reading about the protests?" Ma asked.

"Yep."

She sighed. "Yet another reason why this surprise board meeting shouldn't have been called. Did you know the airport was shut down in August? Almost two hundred flights were cancelled. If the protesters target HKG again, we could be landing in mainland China."

Ma had a point. Last month, more than five thousand protestors had descended on Hong Kong International Airport and shut down all the flights after a weekend of violent clashes between protesters and riot police.

"At least we're not taking the MTR," I said, searching for a bright spot to lighten her mood.

Ma groaned. "The activists are disrupting city operations to draw attention to the cause, but what is MTR supposed to do about it? When they shut down vandalized stations, the protesters get angrier. When they add more trains to accommodate surges in protest traffic, China-owned media hammers them in the press."

"Good thing Gung-Gung is sending a driver for us."

"Indeed." She sipped her wine. "Is anything bad happening now?"

"You heard about the march last Sunday?"

"The one near Gung-Gung's offices? I read that it turned violent."

"Kind of an understatement. Tens of thousands of peaceful protesters were hit with tear gas and water cannons."

Ma sighed. "And protesters hurled bricks and gasoline bombs at government buildings. It's not as cut-and-dried as you might think. We're going to have to be very careful about what we say during this visit. I can't afford to antagonize anyone on our board of directors."

The Amnesty International report mentioned a *disturbing pattern of reckless and unlawful tactics against people during the protests*. I decided not to mention it. Ma had enough conflict in her life without adding another to the debate.

"Have you practiced your Cantonese?" Ma asked.

"Ever since Gung-Gung dropped the bomb about your surprise meeting."

She raised one eyebrow.

"What? I figured you might want company."

She smiled. "I'll steer the conversation to English when I can. Some people will be stubborn. Others won't speak the language."

"I'll be fine. I understand more than I can speak. If I run into trouble, I'll smile and nod."

"You're a good sport, Lily."

She sipped her wine and frowned. Creases of worry marred her beautiful skin.

"Would you like my chrysanthemum tea?"

She reached over the partition and squeezed my hand. "Actually, I would. The wine was a bad idea. I should be drinking a cooling tea if I want to sleep."

I passed her my hot tea. Having grown up in Hong Kong, Ma usually paid attention to the Eastern medicine practices of yin-cooling and yang-heating foods and drinks. Tonight's exception did not bode well for her state of mind.

When she finished the tea, she lowered her bed and covered her eyes with the sleeping mask provided by the airline. "Good night, Lily. Wake me when they serve breakfast."

I put in my earbuds and watched video footage from a disturbing August incident when the Hong Kong Special Tactical Squad, known as Raptors, stormed onto an MTR train at Prince Edward station.

They sprayed the passengers with pepper spray and beat them with batons. The passengers weren't protesting, vandalizing, or setting fires. They were only riding the train.

I paused the video on an image of a man cowering on the floor, shielding a terrified woman, and pleading with the Raptors to stop. What were we flying into?

I pressed the call button for a cup of hot water and took out a satchel of highly caffeinated Asaam tea.

# Chapter Five

Ma and I hurried through the terminal to the nearest Cathay Pacific business lounge, stylishly appointed with its own tea house, noodle bar, and yoga sanctuary. No Vinyasa yoga for me. Our flight had arrived at 6:40 p.m. Hong Kong time. Gung-Gung's business party began in twenty minutes.

We passed on showers and changed directly into our cocktail dresses, both smartly chosen for their wrinkle-free fabrics. Ma's lake-blue dress hugged her figure in classic cheongsam style with modern Western flair. I wore the same little black dress I'd worn on my first date with Daniel Kwok, minus the flat ankle-high boots.

Ma frowned at the sturdy flat sandals I pulled out of my pack. "Didn't you bring a decent pair of pumps?"

"We're traveling."

She sighed as though my excuse was the lamest thing she had ever heard.

I shrugged and heaved on my backpack, thankful I wouldn't have to teeter through an airport on spiky heels. Ma, on the other hand, glided through the terminal with quick and graceful steps. Since Ma lived and worked in the US with a green card permanent-resident status and retained her Chinese citizenship and Hong Kong passport and identity card, we split up at immigration. She breezed through the returning citizen line well ahead of me and was in the process of hiring a porter at baggage claim when I immerged.

"I can handle it, Ma. You only have one suitcase, right?"

"Are you sure? It's awfully heavy."

"I'll be fine." I waved off the porter, thanked him in Cantonese, and collected our luggage from the conveyor belt. As promised, hers weighed a ton. Even so, I handled both rolling cases and my backpack with ease. By the time we exited baggage claim and spotted Gung-Gung's driver in the arrival hall holding up a sign that read Violet Wong, I was very happy to have worn my practical sandals.

"Welcome to Hong Kong," he said in English. "My name is Mr. Tam."

"Pleased to meet you. I'm Violet Wong and this is my daughter, Lily." She glanced at the restroom. "Would you excuse me a moment?"

"Of course, Madame. Take your time." Mr. Tam smiled at me. "If you wait here for your mother, I will take the luggage and load it in the car."

"Sure. That'd be great."

"May I take your backpack?"

"I'll hang on to it."

He nodded and hurried through the crowd, out one set of doors as a group of men in black T-shirts entered through another. They assembled quickly and raised their signs. Most were written in traditional Chinese but the two in English read: *Five Demands, Not One Less*, and *Reclaim Hong Kong, Revolution of Our Times*.

"Gayau! Gayau!" They chanted in Cantonese, pumped their signs, and waved at travelers.

When I competed in Wushu, we had yelled, "Jaiyou!" in Mandarin to cheer each other to victory. Both words meant *add oil*, the Chinese expression of encouragement and support, a way to tell people to keep going and be strong.

Foreign passengers hurried out the doors. Locals paused to record the demonstration on their phones. A handful of transit officers in blue short-sleeve shirts marched in from customs and shouted for the protesters to disband. Rather than wait for the situation to escalate, I circled around the protesters to find Ma.

"Join the struggle," a man yelled, in Cantonese. "The time is now to liberate Hong Kong."

When I didn't answer, he shoved the handle of his sign toward me.

I shouted, "Gayau," and pumped my fists so he couldn't wedge the sign into my hands.

The transit police made another futile attempt to disband the protesters then hurried out the way they had come. Reinforcements? Riot gear? I didn't wait to see.

I ran around the commotion and jumped to see if I could locate her over the crowd just in time to see my mother emerge from the restroom. When I jumped again, she was gone.

I threaded through the protesters, elbows in, hands up to protect my ribs and face. Travelers and transit personnel pressed in from the sides. The center mass between me and Ma had compacted.

Transit police shouted through bullhorns, this time geared up with full-face helmets, plastic shields, and batons. "Disband immediately."

I called Ma's name. She answered from somewhere in the mob. I angled my arms like the prow of a ship and cut my way through the crowd, guided forward by flashes of her lake-blue dress. When I reached her, I turned her back toward the restroom.

"My God, Lily. What's happening?"

"Are you okay?"

"Yes."

"Into the last stall."

"Why?"

"The protesters are fighting back, but that could change if the cops hit them with pepper spray.

"Pepper spray? They aren't allowed to use that indoors."

"You want to count on that? Now, can we, please?" I gestured down the corridor. "We'll be safer away from the entrance."

"Where's Mr. Tam?"

"He took our luggage to the car."

"Fat lot of good he is."

"Don't worry. This will be over soon."

"It better. Gung-Gung's party has already begun."

In the commotion I'd forgotten all about our tight schedule. Although I didn't want Ma to be hurt, I understood her concern. The board members and clients of Hong Kong International Finance were expecting to see her at this party. I doubted any of them would consider an airport incident as an adequate excuse for her absence.

"I can get us through safely if you want to leave."

She exhaled with determination. "Please."

"Okay. Grab onto my backpack and don't let go."

I reached behind me to make sure Ma was there, then I flowed between the obstacles like water and made it to the shore.

# Chapter Six

Once we were out of the traffic congestion caused by dou-ble-parked transit cars and frantic travelers, our car ride smoothed onto a broad highway across a flat island, desolate except for a few squat buildings up ahead. As we approached the bridge to Lantau Is-land, the first twinkle of civilization appeared, strips of light that grew into towering walls of radiance.

Hong Kong housed its dense population in tight clusters of high-rise apartment blocks. Lit up for the night, they lined the entrance onto Lantau Island like a platoon of brilliant sentries. This was only the beginning. Although the New Territories, which included Lantau Island, covered over eighty-six percent of the Hong Kong Special Ad-ministrative Region, half of HKSAR's 7.5 million people lived in an area smaller than the smallest Hawaiian Island.

The sentry lights ended and we plunged into darkness.

"I wish I could see the hills," I said.

Mr. Tam shrugged. "They are only green. The lights will be much more impressive across the bay."

"When will we reach it?"

"We have already. Keep watching on the left."

True to his word, the highway dipped, and a fairyland of shim-mering lights appeared across Tung Chung Bay. Battalions of high-ris-es and commercial buildings rimmed the island in gold and sparkled in the dark, unpopulated hills. The view vanished, the road widened, and highway ramps swooped overhead, followed by a teaser of bay lights, and the widest, brightest toll station I had ever seen. After that, darkness and anticipation.

I leaned forward in my seat. "Wow."

Mr. Tam chuckled.

Golden brilliance peaked like waves in the night sky as we drove onto the suspension bridge that connected Lantau to tiny Ma Wan. A second bridge crossed a longer stretch of water to Tsing Yi Island. Through the lighted suspension cables, shipping lights and coastal cityscapes of the main landmass of the New Territories could be seen.

"This is incredible. How many bridges are there?"

"In all of Hong Kong? More than one thousand." He noted my surprise in the rearview mirror. "Not all as big as this. But still, very impressive."

"I'll say."

Ma patted my shoulder. "Lily, sit back and leave Mr. Tam alone." She handed me a lighted mirror. "And use this to fix your face."

"What's wrong with it?"

"You need lipstick and blush. And for God's sake, brush your hair."

I looked at her more closely, eye makeup perfect, lips bold and red, hair newly swept in a high twisted chignon. No one would ever guess she'd been caught in a protesting confrontation with the police. "You look…beautiful."

She offered the barest smile and nodded toward the mirror. "And so will you."

I peaked at my reflection and grimaced. Tangled hair, smudged makeup. Time to pry my eyes from the spectacle and fix this mess.

"How long until we arrive?"

"Fifteen minutes," Mr. Tam replied.

"Yikes. No way that's enough for me to look decent. "

"You have time," Ma said. "Just—"

"Be quick?" I asked.

"Exactly."

Once we hit the Tsing Sha Highway and the glorious view disappeared, it was easier to concentrate on Ma's compact. I took care of the basics then used the glaring light of the tunnel to reapply my eyeliner and lipstick. I was combing my hair when the tunnel ended and the urban cityscape began. Since Hongkongers drove on the left-hand side of the road, I had a perfect view of the container terminals before we soared into the sky onto Stonecutter's Bridge.

Two blue spires shot from the bridge's deck like Jedi lightsabers, their glow spilling onto the web of cables that reached down and out to support the bridge. Below, container cranes flocked like birds on the edges of the channel shores bathed in brilliant gold while blue-tinted sky rises blanketed the land. The waterways glistened with reflected light.

"And people think Los Angeles is crowded."

"Yes," Mr. Tam agreed. "Mr. Wong complained about your terrible traffic after his visit."

"Did he say anything about my driving?"

Mr. Tam smiled and shrugged.

As we sped along the elevated highway over the ports and treatment centers of Stonecutter's Island, I reached into my backpack for Gung-Gung's bracelet. I slipped it out of the jewelry pouch.

"I wondered if you had brought it," Ma said.

"Seemed wise."

"Good idea. He'll check."

A corridor of brightly-lit high rises illuminated the four curving segments of jade as I fastened the bracelet to my wrist. Each segment was in a different color to correspond with the four celestial creatures—red phoenix, white tiger, black tortoise, and a blue-green dragon close to the color of Ma's dress. Gold links joined the segments and let the creatures move.

When we drove through a glaring tunnel, I caught Ma examining her own celestial protectors carved into a single imperial jade bangle. The deep translucent emerald was more elegant than my four-colored jade and suited her perfectly.

"You'll do great," I said. "The Sì Xiàng will look out for you."

She patted my hand and sighed. "I wish I had your confidence. I don't relish arriving an hour late."

As if hearing her concern, Mr. Tam sped up an off-ramp onto another elevated cement road with Victoria Harbour on the right and sky-scraping hotels on the left. He circled around and pulled in front of the tallest building of them all.

"The party's here?"

Ma nodded. "Your grandfather rented one of the Tin Lung Heen private dining rooms in the Ritz. Yet another reason we should have arrived on time."

"I drove as quickly as I could, Madame Wong."

"It's not you, Mr. Tam. Our flight arrangements would not allow us to arrive any sooner."

She glanced at my backpack and frowned. "Is it all right if Lily leaves her luggage in the car?"

"Of course, madame."

I put it on the floor, out of sight.

"It will be fine, Lily. We, on the other hand, will not."

# Chapter Seven

The elevator door opened on the one-hundred-second floor of the Ritz-Carlton Hotel where a hostess waited to escort us to the Hong Kong International Finance private party.

"Welcome to Hong Kong, Mrs. Wong," she greeted us in English. "How was your flight?"

"Very well, thank you," Ma replied. "Have they seated for dinner yet?"

"About fifteen minutes ago. The first course has been served, but your father has saved both of you a place at his table."

She opened the tall wooden doors and showed us into a living room-style lounge appointed with elegant contemporary Asian décor and a stunning view of Hong Kong Island. Glassware and appetizer platters covered a marble coffee table and cocktail tables positioned at the windows—remnants of mingling guests.

The hostess looked up from the empty platters. "Chef prepared appetizers of his signature chilled shredded abalone with jellyfish in sesame oil. They seemed to be very well received."

Ma nodded with approval. "I'm sure they were."

The hostess smiled in acknowledgment and gestured to the adjoining room where a round banquet table sat below an inverted dome chandelier. A second table could be glimpsed to the side, both surrounded by a rich leather club chairs enveloping animated guests.

Gung-Gung sat in the host's seat on the far side of the table, facing the entrance, with his guests on either side in order of importance.

The two seats across from him and closest to us were empty.

He rose when he saw us cross the threshold and addressed his guests in Cantonese. "My daughter and granddaughter have just arrived from Los Angeles." He switched to English. "Did you have a good flight?"

"It went very smoothly." Ma replied in Cantonese, even though she had assured me she would steer conversations to English. "Are we late for dinner?"

"Oh, no." He continued in English. "We've only just tasted the first course. I had them serve you in the hopes that you would arrive."

Ma glanced at the small-plated masterpieces, a little less elegant for having sat overly long on the table, and replied, pointedly, in Cantonese. "How thoughtful."

The guests at both tables watched the exchange and nodded every time Ma spoke. Either they only followed her side of the conversation or they approved of her language choice and accent.

Gung-Gung conceded the language battle and introduced his honored guest in Cantonese. "You remember Mr. Cheung, our most loyal client, and his wife Chung Yi."

"Of course. Very nice to see you again."

He gestured to the couple beside them. "And this is Mr. Fong, who has joined us most recently, and his wife, Lai Kun."

Ma bowed to each of them. "I'm very pleased to meet you. This is my daughter, Lily."

My grandmother waved. "Come here, Lei Lei." She spoke in English, rescuing me from the awkward situation.

"Hello, Po-Po." I squeezed her hand but didn't offer a kiss as I would have done in private.

"Why you so late? Sit down. Your food melts. Next course comes soon."

Ma bowed to her mother and offered a tight smile. She didn't appreciate being called out for lateness in front of an audience. Instead, she switched to Cantonese, greeted the man seated beside Po-Po, and introduced him to me as Gung-Gung's original partner.

23

Derrick Lau was in his late seventies and had a chic, playboy quality about him as though he'd stepped out of the pages of a fashion magazine. He wore a slim-cut suit the rich color of maple syrup that warmed his skin and made his brown eyes shine almost as brightly as his bleached-white teeth.

"It's good to see you again, Violet. This is my friend Melanie. Melanie, this is Violet Wong, she runs the Los Angeles division of HKIF."

The stylish younger woman bowed her head in greeting. "I've heard many good things about you, Mrs. Wong."

"It's very nice to meet you, Melanie. Please call me Violet. You look well, Derrick."

"Not at all, but please…sit and eat. We can catch up later."

Ma introduced herself to the banker seated beside Melanie and returned to our side of the table. Gung-Gung had placed Ma in the farthest seat away from his number one client and his largest shareholder and seated us both next to wives.

Ma whispered to me in English. "Thank goodness for Derrick."

I nodded. Without his introduction, Gung-Gung's guests wouldn't have known she was even part of the company. We'd been here less than five minutes and the evening was already spiraling down the drain. I tried the chilled pea paste with foie gras and sighed. At least my taste buds would be happy.

I gobbled the rest before the servers could collect my plate. Ma tasted each creation then set down her fork as if she'd had all the time in the world to enjoy the delicacies and had eaten enough. As the banker's wife chattered about all the sites Ma should see during her visit to Hong Kong, I focused on the pan-fried crab claw.

"Would you care for wine?" a server asked, in English.

"May I have tea?"

"Of course. Lung Jeng, Tik Guan Yum, or Wong Fu?"

"Tik Guan Yum, please." Although I loved Dragonwell and chrysanthemum, Iron Goddess Oolong seemed like a better choice for the evening, in taste and spirit.

"Have you visited before?" Mrs. Fong asked, in careful English.

"Several times, but not in the last seven years."

"Oh. That's a long time to be away from family."

I didn't want to explain how my sister's murder had intensified the tension between my grandfather and parents, or how Gung-Gung expected me to make things right. It didn't matter that my father had given his daughters Ma's surname instead of his own. Gung-Gung needed me to marry a man who would do the same. Only a male descendant bearing the Wong family name would make up for Ma's disobedience and Baba's transgression.

"It has been a long time," I agreed. "But my mother comes every year for the board meetings."

"Oh?"

"She's the Los Angeles director of HKIF."

"Ah." Mrs. Fong passed this information to her husband. Apparently, neither of them had heard Derrick Lau's comment to Melanie.

Ma squeezed my hand beneath the table in thanks and raised her voice, ever so slightly, as she shared American media trends with the banker. Mr. Fong leaned in to hear. By the time we had all enjoyed the hot and sour soup and pan-fired scallop with salmon roe and asparagus, everyone at the table was listening to my mother.

Gung-Gung interrupted. "No more business talk. Tonight is for enjoyment and to celebrate the recent achievements of my honored guest."

Everyone at both tables stopped what they were doing and raised their glasses.

"Mr. Cheung, my honored guest, I will down my glass, but you may finish at your leisure. Cheers."

The toast broke the attention away from Ma and directed it to Mr. Cheung, who threw the attention back to Gung-Gung by honoring him as the host.

"That was petty," I whispered to Ma.

She smiled as if I had said something delightful. "Wasn't it?" With that, we kept to ourselves and ate our bamboo fungus in peace.

Between the garoupa filet and the chilled milk pudding with

black truffle dessert, an elderly man with silver hair and a stooped posture came over to say hello from table two. Raymond Ng was a close family friend of Gung-Gung's and Ma's kai ba or "agreement father," the equivalent of a secular godfather. As Gung-Gung's other original partner in HKIF and the third largest shareholder, Raymond Ng had been seated in the host position at the second table.

Ma rose and greeted him in Cantonese. "Hello, Kai Ba, are you well?

"Very well, Shun Lei. And you?" He used Ma's legal Chinese name, which, although beautiful, had a submissive meaning she didn't like. It translated as *moving smoothly without a hitch*, or more directly, *to obey and follow*. Ma preferred the nickname Po-Po had given her for the violet flowers Ma had loved as a child.

"I'm doing well, surprised to be in Hong Kong at this unusual time."

Raymond Ng waved his hand dismissively. "You know how the board is. Things come up."

"Do they?"

He smiled at Ma and addressed me in English. "Hello, Lily. You have grown into a beautiful young lady. It seems like only yesterday you were chasing Mah Lik around our yard."

During our last visit, Rose and I had fallen in love with Uncle Raymond's frisky Shiba Inu, a rarity in Hong Kong.

"Is he still as swift as his name?" I prayed he was still alive. Hong-kongers didn't like talking about death and dying, which was probably why Uncle hadn't offered condolences to us.

"Very energetic. It's hard for me and Auntie Lan to keep up with him. Maybe you can take him for a run when you visit."

"I'd love to."

Ma shifted so her back was to the others. "Kai Ba, can you tell me anything about this meeting? I would like to be prepared."

"I must thank your father. I'll see you at the office on Monday. Enjoy your dessert, Lily."

Ma forced a smile and sat. "Did you hear that?"

"Yep."

"It's not my imagination?"

"Nope."

"Do you have any suggestions?"

I appraised the guests at both tables. Aside from the London Director, all of the men lived in Hong Kong. Whatever was going on, Ma was the outsider. Was that why Gung-Gung kept speaking to her in English—to accentuate the difference?

A battle of languages wouldn't win this war. My mother needed to remind these people of her birthright. She needed to prove to them she was the most qualified person to expand in the West and, one day, take over as CEO of Hong Kong International Finance.

I squeezed her hand and infused my words with intent. "Remind them who you are. And win."

# Chapter Eight

Once the last guest had left, we said good-bye to the one-hundredth-second floor and returned to street level where Mr. Tam waited to drive us to Ma's childhood home.

"You girls sit in back," Gung-Gung said. "I'll sit up front with Mr. Tam."

Po-Po charged in and wiggled her way across the back seat to the far window. "You sit here, Lei Lei. My bottom is too big for the middle seat."

I laughed and crawled in beside her. Ma followed, silently. Other than complimenting Gung-Gung on the dinner party, she hadn't said a word.

Mr. Tam circled out of the Ritz-Carlton, drove up a six-lane thoroughfare, and headed toward a twenty-lane toll station for the Western Harbour Crossing. On a Saturday night, lines of cars filled every lane.

"How are the streets this evening?" Gung-Gung asked in English, as we entered the tunnel toward Hong Kong Island.

"Quiet. The big disturbance is at Yuan Long MTR station. I haven't run into any protests in Tsim Sha Tsui or Central. The only sign of trouble was at the airport when I picked up your daughter and granddaughter."

"At the airport? Did they shut it down again?"

"It was a small protest, but Madame Wong was caught on the other side of the scuffle."

"Define scuffle."

Mr. Tam shrugged. "Transit police and batons. Your granddaughter escorted her out safely."

Gung-Gung looked at me in surprise. "Are you okay?"

"I'm fine. It wasn't that big a deal."

"Really?" He looked back at Mr. Tam. "And where were you during all of this?"

"Taking their luggage to the car. I'm very sorry, Mr. Wong. I won't leave them unattended again."

"I should hope not. Were you injured, Shun Lei? Is this why you were so late?"

I glanced at Ma with her head leaning against the window. She had either fallen asleep or was intentionally ignoring him.

"Ma's fine. Mr. Tam's excellent driving made up for the slight protesting delay. Honestly, we arrived as early as our flight could allow."

I didn't mention the short notice about the party. Neither did Gung-Gung.

He fixed his gaze on the tunnel lights ahead. Ma remained still. Po-Po snored softly. I picked my backpack off of the floor and retrieved my phone. When Mr. Tam glanced at me in the rearview mirror, I nodded my thanks.

I checked my phone for messages and found one each on Facebook, WeChat, and WhatsApp. Since Hong Kong had open internet access, it was easier and cheaper to communicate through various apps than to pay for international cellular service. Aleisha preferred Facebook and had updated me about the man who had stormed the refuge this morning—or rather yesterday morning. Things got a bit confusing with Hong Kong sixteen hours ahead.

Aleisha: *Hi, Lily. Hope your flight left on time. Cops arrested Billy. We took Claire and her daughter home, packed Billy's stuff, and put it in short-term storage. His lawyer can deal with it. Claire filed for a TRO. All is well. How's Hong Kong?*

Me: *Arrived on time. Ready for bed. Great news about Claire etc. PS: Food here is awesome.*

Aleisha: *Glad to hear it. Fatten up and sleep well. Stan and I are off to check on Claire.*

Me: (thumbs up emoji)

Baba messaged me through WeChat because we had used it on our family trip and because it was now the only messaging app allowed in mainland China, where his lead cook was visiting family in Shanghai. Baba chatted with Lee Chang through WeChat every day. Although Uncle spoke English very well, the automatic translation function came in handy.

Baba: *Off to bed. Thinking of you. Hope the flight and dinner party go smoothly. Let me know.*

I smiled at the animated sticker of a steamed bun blowing kisses and sent one of my own.

Me: *So cute! But now I want char siu bao. LOL! Are you eating breakfast? The flight was great, very posh. Small protesting disturbance at baggage claim. No problem. Dinner was delicious…and complicated. Gung-Gung introduced Ma as his daughter (not the L.A. director) and Raymond Ng wouldn't tell her anything about Monday's board meeting. (Some Agreement Father he is!) Only Derrick Lau was supportive. All in all, an inauspicious beginning.*

Baba: *Hello, my dumpling! Glad you made it safely. Finished breakfast hours ago. Up with the roosters, dontcha know. Don't like hearing about a protest, but glad you're okay. H.K. food is always delicious. Sad to hear about Shaozu and Raymond. What a surprise to have Derrick stand up for Vi!*

Me: *Right? Worse yet, Gung-Gung and Raymond are both calling her Shun Lei!*

Baba: *Sigh. That won't end well. How's she doing now?*

Me: *We're in the car. She's pretending to sleep.* (Animated sticker of bunny snoring under the covers)

Baba: (animated sticker of green creature pounding floor with laughter)

Me: *We're driving up the mountain. I'm getting car sick. I'll message more tomorrow. Love you!*

Baba: *Okay. Give your mother a kiss on me.* (animated sticker of bunny blowing heart kiss)

WeChat stickers were the best.

I opened my last app and stared at the icon with Daniel's handsome face. Like most Hongkongers, he preferred using WhatsApp because it was the global leader and because their end-to-end encryption kept the Chinese government from spying.

Daniel: *Welcome to H.K. Sleep well. See you tomorrow.*

The message had come in during dinner. I sent a thumbs up emoji and shut off my phone.

Queasiness wasn't the only reason I wanted to stop texting. The night view from The Peak was astounding. Between the high-rise apartments built into the hillside and the dense coastal cityscapes below, we were hit by walls of light every time we rounded a bend into an open segment of road.

"You like the view?" Gung-Gung asked.

"It's stunning."

"I've worked hard all my life to live up here." He sounded melancholy rather than boastful. "Maybe one day, you will too."

I pondered his meaning. Would he leave me his house? Did he hope I would marry someone like him who would work hard to support me in such a grand lifestyle? I doubted he meant I should work hard so I could buy a house on The Peak for myself. If he didn't give Ma credit for her accomplishments, he wouldn't expect greatness from me. Even so, his melancholy tone troubled me. Gung-Gung was eighty-one years old. I didn't like how frail he had become.

The city lights vanished as we turned off the winding access road and onto less busy streets with housing complexes on both sides. Some were only a few stories high, but many soared to the stars in clusters along the hillside. Mr. Tam turned onto a narrow, downhill road and into the covered carport for an older, four-home complex.

"Time to wake up," Gung-Gung said, hopping out of the car with reassuring agility.

Po-Po's eyes popped open. "Are we home so soon?"

I nudged Ma awake.

She really *had* fallen asleep and was sighing from exhaustion. "Jet lag's getting to me."

Gung-Gung opened her door. "Come, Shun Lei. A good night's sleep with refresh you for the morning."

"How about the afternoon. We don't have anything planned, do we?"

"No. You may sleep as long a you wish."

As she followed him inside, I waited by the trunk for our luggage.

"It's in the house, Miss Wong. I believe Bao Jeh has already unpacked the suitcases for you and your mother."

Bao Jeh was from Guangdong Province and had lived with my grandparents for the last ten years, cooking, cleaning, and ordering groceries from the market across the street. Her name was pronounced with a low lilting pitch that meant treasure rather than the high flat pitch for the buns and dumplings I loved to eat. The "Jeh" was tacked on as an honorific meaning elder sister. From what I remembered of Bao Jeh from my last visit, she was as precious to my grandparents as her name described.

"That's very kind of her and thoughtful of you to leave my backpack in the car."

"I could tell it was important to you, Miss Wong."

"Call me Lily."

He smiled but didn't nod. "I will be available tomorrow if you need a ride."

# Chapter Nine

I gaped at the stacks of cardboard boxes, plastic crates, and sewing baskets stuffed into Ma's childhood bedroom. Needlepoint kits, yarn, fabric, rug-hooking projects, crocheted baby blankets, and other crafting paraphernalia overflowed onto the window sill, desk, and chair.

"You can't be serious," Ma said, in Cantonese. "How is Lily supposed to sleep in here? There isn't any bed."

"It's behind the boxes," Po-Po said. "Bao Jeh cleared it off before she went to sleep. She unpacked Lily's clothes and hung them in the closet behind the towels and blankets. She even cleared out the top drawer in the dresser."

"What dresser?"

"The one under the quilt."

"It'll be fine, Ma. Nice and cozy, right Po-Po?"

"Exactly. You can share the bathroom in the hallway with your mother."

I threaded through the obstacles and fell onto the bed. "See you in the morning."

I woke later than expected and found everyone downstairs, drinking tea in the walled-in garden beside the koi pond. Crumbs on the empty plates gave hints to the breakfast I had missed.

Ma looked up from her phone. "Did you sleep well?"

"Like the dead. And you?"

"Soundly at first, then up at dawn."

"You want milk toast?" Po-Po asked, as Bao Jeh brought another cup and poured more hot water in the teapot.

"I do. Good morning Bao Jeh," I said in Cantonese. "It's good to see you."

My grandparent's housekeeper was a trim woman in her forties with veiny hands. "Jo sun, Lily."

I switched to English. "What are you reading, Gung-Gung?"

He glanced up from his phone. "More bad news."

"What happened?"

"Sixteen weeks of civil unrest. What good is it doing? Disrupting our transportation, interfering with business, antagonizing Beijing. This is not the way. The protests last night were because a pro-Beijing law maker decided to clean up those so-called Lenin Walls. Who cares about flyers and post-it notes? Let the pro-democracy supporters have their benign art displays. This violence and disruption must end."

Ma flashed me a warning look then sipped her tea.

Gung-Gung returned to his article. "Do you have plans for today?"

"Not sure. What do you recommend?"

"I'm an old man. I don't know what young women like to do."

"Why don't we relax?" Ma suggested.

I poured a cup of tea and sipped it as I strolled over the koi pond bridge. Orange and white carp swam through the green water beneath branches of low spreading pines. When I reached the ivy-covered wall on the other side, I returned on the stone walkway that ran along the other edge of the garden. The whole trip took no more than twenty-five steps. I'd only been awake a few minutes, and I was already antsy to explore.

"There's a trailhead at the end of this road, isn't there? Maybe I'll hike down to the Aberdeen Reservoir."

"That trail is too steep," Po-Po said in Cantonese. "Walk around the rest garden where I do Tai Chi with the ladies. It's so peaceful there."

"I'll save that for when I can go with you, okay?"

"Don't worry about Lily. The reservoir hike is less than a mile. She runs ten times that distance just to avoid driving a car."

Po-Po waved me back to the table. "Come eat."

Thick white toast drowned in butter and slathered with sweet condensed milk. A diabetic's nightmare. I was two heavenly bites in when my phone pinged with a message.

Daniel: *Are you awake?*

I gobbled the rest of the toast and typed while I chewed. *Barely. Milk toast is helping. Any plans today?*

Daniel: *Hoping to see you.*

Me: *Excellent! The old folks want to relax at home. Maybe a hike?*

Daniel: *Or Peak Circle Walk?*

Me: *Ooh… even better.*

Daniel: *I have a family thing in Kowloon this evening and need to catch the bus straight from The Peak Tower. My uncle can give us a ride there, but I can't get you home.*

Me: *No problem. It's an easy run.*

Daniel: *LOL! Okay. Pick you up at 1pm?*

Me: (thumbs up emoji)

When I looked up from my phone, all eyes were on me. "What?"

"Who were you texting with such a big smile on your face?" Gung-Gung asked.

"A boyfriend back home?" Po-Po added.

Ma smirked. "Or maybe Daniel?"

"Daniel Kwok?" Gung-Gung said, full of excitement. "Well, that's good news. You can spend the day with him."

Po-Po nodded. "And your mother can stay home with us."

I glanced at Ma. "You don't mind?"

"Not at all. I could use the rest."

"Okay." I gobbled the second piece of sweet, sticky toast and wiped my fingers on a sheet of Tempo tissue, a disposable handker-

35

chief used by every person in the city.

"Take the pack of Tempo with you," Po-Po said. "Take mine too."

I inhaled the jasmine scent and smiled. "Thanks, Po-Po. I better change before Daniel arrives with his uncle."

Gung-Gung looked alarmed. "His uncle is coming *here*?"

"Just to pick me up. He's giving us a ride to the tower."

Po-Po beckoned to Bao Jeh. "Clean up this mess and prepare a fresh tea for our guests. I have to put on my face."

"They're only picking me up."

"So you think. What if they stay?"

Gung-Gung stood and followed Po-Po into the house. "Your grandmother is correct. We must be prepared to entertain."

Ma rose with a sigh. "I'll put on a dress."

"Wait. Why is this such a big deal?"

She blinked in surprise. "You don't know? Daniel's uncle is Derrick Lau."

# Chapter Ten

Bao Jeh served tea in an open family room in sight of a formal dining table surrounded by chartreuse-velvet chairs. The two areas were defined by recessed ceilings—circular over the dining table and square above the couches and cooking cabinet. Bao Jeh stood with her back to the television, raised the steaming kettle from the built-in burner, and poured hot water into a ceramic teapot. The presentation was both homey and elegant.

"We don't want to intrude," Mr. Lau said, as Po-Po offered him a selection of petit fours and scones.

"We are delighted."

"Well, maybe a quick cup of tea. I need to drive Daniel and Lily up to Sky Terrace so they can get on with their date."

Gung-Gung pulled out his phone and spoke with someone in Cantonese. He smiled at me and switched to English. "Mr. Tam is filling the car with gas at the station down the road. He'll be here in five minutes." He turned to Mr. Lau. "Now you can stay and enjoy a relaxing Sunday afternoon."

"Want to wait outside?" I asked.

Daniel nodded. "Great idea. So nice to see you all."

"Have fun," Po-Po said, brushing her hand to shoo us out of the room.

I kissed Ma on the cheek and whispered in her ear. "You good?"

"Fine."

"Okay." I straightened up. "Nice to see you again, Mr. Lau." I grabbed my backpack and hurried Daniel out of the room before anyone could change their mind.

When we rounded the corner into the entryway, Daniel caught my hand and pulled me into a kiss. When we finally parted, he grinned at me like a kid who'd raided the cookie jar. "What do you say we find Mr. Tam and get on with this date?"

I laughed. "Yes, please. But first…Derrick Lau is your *uncle*?"

"Yes. Why? Is that a problem?"

Daniel didn't just come from a good Hong Kong family, he came from one of the best.

"No. I mean, I don't think so. Why didn't you tell me before?"

He shrugged. "You don't seem to have much interest in your grandfather's business. I didn't think you'd even know who Derrick Lau was. Besides, you already know my parents and brothers live here and that I work for Mandarin Group Realtors in Los Angeles. We haven't had much time for a full family history."

Daniel was right. We'd only been on a two dates, four if I counted Ma's fiftieth birthday party a month ago and the ambush dinner at my parents' home a month before that. Even if he had brought up Derrick Lau, I wouldn't have cared.

"Okay, Mr. Kwok, you're off the hook for now. But I'm going to want to hear more about this family of yours."

I led him out the front door and into the communal walkway of the housing complex. Of the four three-story homes, my grandparents had the premium location with the best angle of view. It also afforded them the closest parking spot in the garage where we found Mr. Tam standing beside Gung-Gung's black Mercedes.

"Good morning, Miss Wong. Where do you want to go?"

"Up to the tower, please. We're going to walk around The Peak."

"Ah. It's a good day for the view, not too smoggy."

As we drove the short distance up mountain, Mr. Tam received a call. He answered quietly, but his Cantonese grew louder as the conversation progressed. "Jing, listen to me. I don't care. Be smart. You have to…" He grunted in frustration and put down the phone.

"Is everything okay?" I asked in English.

He heaved a sigh. "Daughters can be troublesome."

"My mother would agree."

"You are being kind. I suppose every parent feels this way."

"Only those with daughters," Daniel teased.

I poked him in the ribs.

"What? You're the one who always says what a lousy daughter you are."

"Oh, no," said Mr. Tam. "I saw what Lily did at the airport. Only a good daughter protects her mother like that."

"What happened at the airport?"

"Nothing," I said. "Besides, we're here. Time to walk." I leapt from the car like a dog eager for a run. "Thanks, Mr. Tam. We'll be a few hours. May I call you later?"

"Of course. I'll make sure I'm nearby."

Buses pulled up to the curb, releasing both locals and tourists. Some headed into the futuristic entertainment complex for shopping, dining, and gaping at the view, others, like us, headed for the pedestrian roads that circled the summit. Since most of the walkers headed toward Lugard Road for a counter-clockwise route, Daniel and I, took the first left onto the Harlech Road Fitness Trail. We could walk against the flow and bypass the hawkers waving real estate flyers and selling fruit and drinks to tourists.

Within fifty yards, Daniel and I strolled on a quiet jungle road, lush mountainside on our right and trees, anchored to the cliff below, towering over us on the left.

"This is the most relaxed I've felt in...I have no idea."

Daniel chuckled. "For someone who claims they're not ambitious, you lead a very busy life."

I shrugged, unwilling to share my ninja exploits so early in our relationship. I had waited years before telling Baba, and I still hadn't fessed up to Ma.

"About this family of yours..."

He shrugged. "What do you want to know?"

"Let's start at the beginning. I thought you had grown up in Los Angeles, but you call yourself a Hongkonger. Where were you born?"

"In Los Angeles while visiting my father's sister. My mother thought she had another month in her pregnancy, but I came early."

"So, you're a U.S. citizen?"

"I am—the only one in my family, aside from my aunt who became a naturalized citizen a few years after marrying. I grew up in Hong Kong, but my parents sent me to stay with my aunt in the summers so I would become comfortable in the U.S. My brothers stayed here."

"How many brothers do you have?"

"Two, both older."

"What about the two-child law?"

"It was a policy not a law, my parents only received government benefits for the first two children. I was a hardship for them, both financially and socially. When my parents ignored the Two Is Enough campaign to have me, many of their friends disapproved. I was the extra son they should not have had. My U.S. citizenship set me apart even more."

"That must have been hard."

He shrugged. "Some families wanted their children to know me since I might grow up to have special privileges."

Gung-Gung's meddling interest in my dating habits was becoming clearer. If Daniel's parents had an embarrassing excess of sons, they might be more amenable to having Daniel take on the Wong family name if he and I ever married.

"You have a complicated history."

"Doesn't everyone?"

I thought about Rose. "Maybe. But yours is definitely unusual. Is that why you're so ambitious? To prove your worth?"

"Maybe." He laughed. "Probably. My father and brothers all sell and lease apartments for a residence community in Tseung Kwan O with fifteen towers and almost six thousand units."

"Whoa, that's huge."

"Not compared to Mei Foo Sun Chuen. That has ninety-nine towers and can house up to eighty *thousand* people. This is Hong Kong, don't forget, the most vertical city in the world. Anyway, it was too depressing to follow my brothers, selling and leasing apartments that were barely 400 square feet. So, I moved to Los Angeles where I could work for my father's friend and sell beautiful houses and buildings."

"Are your brothers married?"

He nodded. "Two children each."

"You're the rebel. No wonder I like you."

"Have you heard enough? Because I'm tired of talking about my family."

"Almost. What about Derrick Lau?"

"He's my mother's eldest brother. Her side of the family is much more successful than my father's. She's counting on me to turn that around."

"Sounds like a lot of pressure."

"No more than the average Hongkonger. You know how it is. Study, study, study. Work, work, work."

I spotted a fitness park ahead with high, middle, and low bars. "What about play?"

Daniel smirked. "Not a high priority. Besides, that looks more like work to me."

I grinned. "Not the way I do it."

I ran to the park, leaped for the high bar, and pulled myself over the top. Feeling secure in my balance, without the laptop in my backpack, I cast out my legs and came back with a full hip circle around the bar.

Daniel stared up at me, perched over the high-bar with my arms straight and my legs hanging down. "How did you do that?"

His surprise made me eager to impress. I cast out again, all the way this time, straightening my body from wrists to toes, and swooped toward the ground. When I reached the bottom, I shot my legs up to the bar and kipped back into my perching position.

Daniel laughed. "Okay. Now you're just showing off."

41

"Not quite," I said, then cast out again, swooping in a full arc, and released my hands for a back-flipping dismount. I landed on the fitness park's cushioned all-weather mat and basked in Daniel's astonished delight and the simple thrill of flying through air.

"I've never seen you like this," Daniel said.

"Like what?"

"Carefree."

I'd grown up tumbling on trampolines and swinging on gymnastic bars to augment my Wushu training. All of it had complimented my Chinese martial arts and had given me an edge in competition. It also came in handy during my ninja rescue and protection work. That said, I rarely did any of that just for fun.

"Maybe we both need to play more often."

Daniel took my hand. "I could get behind that. Just maybe not on high bars."

We resumed our jungle stroll past gazebos, park bench lookouts, and even several homes down the slope behind graffitied gates or up narrow driveways against the hill. It was hard to imagine residents driving along a road barely suited for a Mini Cooper, but apparently they did. The cliff steepened and the trees lowered for a panoramic view.

I leaned against the railing and took it all in. "I'd forgotten how stunning this is."

Verdant green, blue harbor, packed high rises. The Kowloon coast across the harbor was just as crowded, with cargo shipyards extending into the water. Barges, tiny from this distance, clustered off the docks while speed boats trailed lines of white wake-water in slashes.

Daniel joined me at the railing. "There's no place in the world like this."

"Would you ever want to come back here to live?"

"It depends where fortune leads me. Right now, Los Angeles is looking pretty desirable."

He leaned in for a kiss at the same moment an adorable Chihuahua darted up the road. It slipped between the railing on the uphill side, peed against a rock, then slipped back onto the road. Behind it, two middle aged women hurried forward calling for the dog to stop and come. The rascal paused for a second then bolted around the bend. All was well until the women shouted for help.

# Chapter Eleven

We ran up the cantilevered road until we spotted the women hanging over the railings on either side.

"What happened?" I asked in Cantonese.

"Our dog ran through the bars and fell. We don't see her anywhere."

The other woman wailed as she stared down. "Aiya, Siu Siu, our sweet little mouse. Where have you gone?"

"She went in through here?" I pointed to the bars on the uphill side of the road where solid ground fell away into branches and leaves.

"How will we get her out?"

I took off my backpack and climbed over the railing onto the last bit of solid ground where hill met road.

"Lily, are you crazy? What are you doing? You could slip under the path and fall down the cliff."

I grabbed the railing and side-stepped until I felt the drop in the ground. "I'll be okay."

Hanging onto the bars, I lowered myself through the tops of the plants until I hit the earth. I let go with one hand and grabbed onto a sturdy branch with the other.

Daniel kneeled on the pavement and looked down at me through the leaves. "Do you need a hand?"

"Maybe later." The hillside sloped under the road with a yard of headroom before it dropped into a cliff. "I'll be right back."

I let go of the railing and crawled under the road into the dense growth. "Siu Siu…come 'ere, girl. Here, Siu Siu."

The Chihuahua whimpered up ahead. I followed the sound, exchanging one branch for another to keep from sliding down the steepening hillside. "Where are you, little mouse?"

The dog barked then whimpered, as if the effort might have hurt.

"Are you okay?" Daniel called from above.

"I found Siu Siu."

"Be careful. Don't risk your life for a dog."

"It's a little late for that."

I let go of a branch and slid to the base of a tree growing at an angle from under the cantilevered road. Its trunk and branches reached for the sky on the view-side of the railing. A couple yards to my right, the Chihuahua whimpered, trapped in the roots of another tree.

"Daniel?"

"Yes?"

"In my backpack, you'll find a short hank of climbing rope."

"Why are you carrying around rope?"

"Long story." I didn't have time now to fabricate an explanation. "Unwind it then tie one end to the top of my pack and the other to the railing on the left side of this tree." I bounced on the trunk to shake the branches. "Can you see it?"

"Yes."

"Good. Make sure your knots are secure."

"Um…okay. Hold on a second." A minute later, Daniel lowered the backpack.

"Make it swing."

"Like this?" The backpack swung near and away but not close enough to reach.

"A little more."

As I climbed up the slanted tree trunk, the drop below me increased to fifty feet. "Okay. Let the rope swing on its own." I caught it, passed the rope under the trunk to my other hand, and shimmied down the trunk. All I needed now was the dog.

Using roots and branches to keep from sliding over the edge, I crawled to Siu Siu. She licked my hand and whimpered. I made a nest for her in my backpack, pulled her out of the hole, and stuffed her inside. "Be calm, little mouse. You're almost free."

I zipped her in and crawled back to my tree. "Daniel, I have Siu Siu in the backpack. In a moment, I want you to pull her up."

I climbed up the trunk then eased the precious bundle over the side. When the pack swung away from me into open space, Siu Siu yipped and whimpered. "Pull her up."

As Daniel raised the pack, I studied the hillside to see if I could go up the way I'd come down. Some of the plants had uprooted during my slide. The soil around them had sloughed away. I considered the tree. If the branches had been stronger near the top, I might have climbed them to the railing. As it was, the flexible branches would bend me away farther over the cliff—assuming they didn't snap.

"I have the dog," Daniel yelled.

"Good. Tie the rope to the other railing and toss the end under the road. And, Daniel?"

"Yes?"

"Tie a knot at the end to give it some weight."

A few moments later, the knotted end of the rope bounced down the hill and settled a yard out of my reach. I braced my feet against the base of the tree and jumped up the slope, grabbed the rope, and slid until the slack tightened and yanked me to a stop.

"Are you okay?"

"Yep."

I pulled myself up, hand over hand, across the slick soil. The slope was steeper here than where I had descended, but soon I reached a solid patch of hill where I could dig in my feet. A few pulls later, I reached the edge of the road and Daniel's outstretched hand. I climbed over the railing, looking considerably worse for the wear.

"Are you alright? You could have been seriously injured. I can't believe you did all of that for a dog."

"You don't like dogs?"

"Of course I do, but not as much as I like you."

"That's sweet, Daniel. But I wasn't doing anything I couldn't handle. You saw me on that high bar. I'm more capable than you think."

"I know. It's just…" He handed me my pack with a shaky smile. "Can we go back to dinner dates?"

"Dinner? After all of this, I want lunch."

# Chapter Twelve

Our scenic loop returned Daniel and me to the plaza stairs between The Peak Galleria and Sky Terrace 428.

"Do you want to shop?" Daniel asked.

"Not really."

"Eat?"

"Always."

We turned away from the mall and entered The Peak Tower, oddly named since it was only a few stories tall. Additional floors cascaded down the hillside. Mostly, it served as a pedestal for the massive Sky Terrace viewing platform 428 meters above sea level.

Daniel looked at the directory. "What do you feel like eating? Bubba Gump's popular."

"How about Hong Kong Day?" I could eat at an American chain back home, but I'd only get deep-fried peanut butter French toast or scrambled egg in curry sauce in an authentic cha chaan teng. As it turned out, we didn't get either.

Every tea restaurant has its own specialty. I ordered the Silver Tooth Pork Noodles, served with a tall crispy noodle island sitting in a pond of delicious mushroom gravy. Daniel chose a cold sticky-rice bowl with shrimps and scallops swimming in a winter melon broth that was almost too beautiful to eat. I passed up my intended yuen yeung milk tea and ordered a thick red bean smoothie: The classic sweet red bean paste was my favorite addition to boba teas, mochi, ice cream, and dessert dumplings. I'd never had it in a smoothie. Daniel ordered chocolate. Both drinks were served in a round goblet with an upturned bottle of Vitasoy suspended from a plastic holder attached to the rim. The presentation was almost as awesome as the distinctive taste.

After rinsing our forks and spoons in the water glasses provided for that purpose—only tourists drank from the water placed on the table or, God-forbid, asked for ice water to drink—we dug into our meal.

After devouring half the plate, I slurped in a noodle and smiled. "I'm envious of you."

"Why's that?"

"You've been eating like this for three weeks."

"The food would have tasted better with you here."

I stole a scallop off his plate. "Think so?"

He laughed. "Providing you let me finish any of it."

I wiggled the scallop at the end of my chopsticks and popped it in my mouth. "Where are you staying? With your parents or brothers?"

"Neither. Their apartments are too chaotic. I'm staying with Uncle Derrick."

"Really? That's interesting."

"If by interesting you mean elegant and roomy, then yes."

"Have you been working a lot?"

"The first two weeks. It's calming down now. Meetings, mostly."

"But not this week?"

He smiled. "Not enough to keep me from seeing you."

I hid my goofy smile with a long pull of red bean smoothie.

"Want to switch?" He slid over his chocolate. The warmth from his mouth lingered on the straw.

With one type of hunger satiated and another inflamed, we left the cha chaan teng and strolled past the air-conditioned gift shops to the bus stop outside.

"Sorry I can't take you home. I'm catching the 15 to Central then an Uber to Kowloon."

"I understand. Would you like me to ask Mr. Tam to take you?

He'll be here soon."

He frowned. "It wouldn't be right to impose. Besides, you should get home and spend time with your grandparents. Will you visit other relatives while you're here?"

"I would assume."

He took my hands in his and rolled his thumbs across my skin. "Think we can squeeze in another date?"

His simple caress made my breath quicken and my belly warm. "Mm-hmm."

"Dinner, this time, somewhere as beautiful as you."

I brushed a chunk of dried mud from my shirt. "You have a strange idea of beauty, Mr. Kwok. But at least you're easy to please."

"Tell that to my mother."

"Hey, that's my line."

He laughed then kissed my hands. "There's my bus. I'll call you later."

I had a goofy grin on my face until I saw the strained smile on Mr. Tam's face. "Everything okay?"

"Fine, fine." He paused. "Why...do I look worried?"

"Little bit. Is your daughter protesting?"

"How did you know?"

"What you said on the phone earlier about not wanting her to go and to 'be smart.'"

"I don't know what to think. I feel as she does, but I don't want her near the police. A young woman was shot with in the eye a beanbag last night. What if the same happens to Jing? She's only seventeen."

"Where is she now?"

"Shopping in Nam Cheong. I don't think she's buying clothes. Shopping is code for protesting. I think she is causing trouble."

"How far is Nam Cheong?"

"In Sham Shui Po, across the bay in West Kowloon, maybe twenty-five minutes."

"Then let's go find her."

"No, no. This is not your problem. I will drop you off on my way."

"You can try." I leaned forward. "Trust me, Mr. Tam, I have a lot of experience tracking down missing girls."

His eyes squinted as he studied me for qualities he had missed before, turned back around, and started the car.

"Have there been protests in Sham Shui Po before?"

"Several. Mostly in front of the police and MTR stations."

"Are there shopping malls nearby?"

"Dragon Center is very close."

"Okay. Let's head for the mall, in case she actually *is* shopping. If she calls or texts with a new location, at least we'll be closer to her than we are now."

# Chapter Thirteen

Mr. Tam turned off the Kowloon Highway and onto Yen Chow Street, a busy six-lane road that cut through an older section of Hong Kong where sleek modern high rises gave way to a mishmash of retail centers, mid-rise building, and mangy apartments with first-floor shops. Air conditioning units jutted from filthy windows like warts on a body already scarred by water pipes and wire laundry racks. Wet clothes and sheets sagged from balconies as dresses and underwear fluttered from telescoping poles—an immodesty born of tiny apartments and expensive electricity. Only a few modern spears shot up from Sham Shui Po.

This was the working-class reality of Hong Kong, not the spacious green hills of The Peak with fancy apartment complexes and koi pond-gardens.

Traffic clogged as we approached the pedestrian bridge, packing us between double-decker buses and irate drivers who laid on their horns.

"I thought you had laws against honking," I shouted to Mr. Tam.

"Excessive honking, yes. But the drivers are protesting."

I covered my ears. "Where's the mall?"

He pointed to the black glass building on the other side of the pedestrian bridge. The Dragon Center was the second largest shopping center in West Kowloon and had its own ice skating rink, arcade, and out-of-commission rollercoaster. The place was massive. If thousands of protesters had gathered inside, how would I ever find Mr. Tam's daughter?

My iPhone vibrated with an AirDrop message: *HandsNFeet would like to share a message.*

"I just received an AirDrop message from someone called Hands and Feet."

"Hands and Feet is protester code for people on the ground. Phone service overloads. They communicate with AirDrop and hand signals. Your phone must be within range. Accept it and see what it says."

I opened the message, written in a confusing mix of English and phonetic Cantonese. "Preparing for magic. Rain expected. Be prepared." I shook my head. "What does it mean?"

"Someone will set a fire. They expect the police to retaliate with pepper spray. They're encouraging everyone to wear masks or bring umbrellas. Do you have this?"

"No. But I have something close." I opened my cycling pack and took out a black spandex neck gaiter.

I pulled it over my head and around my neck, then opened a selfie photo Jing had recently posted on Instagram. She was wearing a yellow shirt, white shorts, and a hot pink surgical mask. Her bright eyes gazed upward as she posed with her hand beside her mouth, fingers spread, as if calling to her friends. I'd seen the popular pose in many H.K. social media feeds. Five fingers stood for the five pro-democracy demands—full withdrawal of the extradition bill, commission of inquiry into alleged police brutality, retracting the classification of protesters as "rioters," amnesty for arrested protesters, and universal suffrage for elections.

Cute teenager or cautious pro-democracy activist?

"I'll get out here, Mr. Tam. Will you snap a photo of me and send it to Jing? Tell her I'm your employer's granddaughter from Los Angeles and that I ran out of your car to join the protest. Tell her you're worried and to look out for me."

I hopped out of the car, tightened the straps on my pack, paused for a photo, and ran.

Horns blared from the gridlocked traffic as pedestrians hurried to and from the Dragon Center entrances. Most of the people heading for the mall wore black shirts and shorts. A few men toting heavy cameras, microphones, and backpacks wore reflective yellow vests. Most wore face masks to safeguard against germs in the crowds.

I raced through the entrance doors expecting chaos and was instead met with thousands of peaceful protesters.

The massive polygon-shaped lobby was ringed by nine floors of shops and restaurants with escalators zigzagging to the top. Banners with traditional Chinese writing hung from the railings with slogans I couldn't read. People crowded the balconies and escalators to watch the main event below, blocked from my view by a thick ring of observers. Some sang. Most spoke quietly amongst themselves. Shoppers meandered around the edges, unconcerned. Whatever was happening in the center of the lobby appeared to be peaceful.

Inside the ring of observers, dozens of protesters in black shirts and shorts folded origami cranes while others held up the middle of a long paper chain that draped down from one balcony and up to another. I turned in a circle and scanned the crowd on every level for a girl with a hot pink mask and a bright yellow shirt. If Jing had been on the edges of the balconies, holding paper chains, riding the escalators, or making cranes, I would have spotted her, but there were thousands of people in this mall, most of them hidden from view.

I messaged Mr. Tam: *Any news?*

He responded immediately: *Just a thumbs up after I sent your picture.*

Me: *Ask where she is.*

Mr. Tam: *Third floor.*

Me: (thumbs up emoji)

I ran up the escalators, first one then the next, as protesters shouted into stores and pasted stickers on various storefronts. No one vandalized any property, but emotions were growing hotter. When an angry group of protesters entered the mall below, the noise and intensity levels grew.

I sprinted across the third floor, searched for Jing's bright yellow shirt, and found her quietly pasting stickers on a storefront window.

"Are you Jing Tan?" I asked in Cantonese.

"Are you the American?" she replied in English, lowering her bright pink mask. "Baba said you wanted to join our protest."

"I do. But things are heating up on the first floor. There might be trouble."

Jing's eyes lit up with excitement. "Really? Let's go see."

She ran to the balcony and squeezed between spectators. The angry group had taken over the middle where the origami folders and paper-chain holders had been. They spread out an enormous red flag, squirted it with water, sprayed it with paint, and stepped on it with their dirty shoes. One boy shined a laser pointer at the yellow stars as if that might burn them out of the fabric.

I tugged on Jing's arm. "Let's go."

"Why? It's just getting started."

She grabbed hold of the railing and chanted slogans as the flag-desecrating activists broke into splinter groups and painted protest slogans on the floor and mall directory. Others ignited a fire in a trashcan.

Protesters shouted a warning about police. "Yau Gwai Ah!" *Ghosts coming!* Others yelled, "Be water!" to remind everyone to stay flexible and scatter. A new group of men dressed as protesters attacked *actual* protesters and threw them on the ground. As they did this, police in riot gear stormed the mall.

People on the edges of the commotion screamed, scattered, or raised their phones to record the clash. Those caught in the center tried to flee but were beaten back with plastic shields and batons. Anyone resisting was thrown to the ground, knees on backs, arms wrenched behind shoulders. What had begun as a peaceful protest with paper chains and origami cranes had devolved into a riot.

I grabbed Jing by the straps of her backpack and yanked her away from the railing. "Where are the stairs?"

"I don't know."

I looked around for signs, then spotted one with a staircase symbol in the distance. "There. Go."

Shouts echoed up the mall as we ran against the flow of protesters and shoppers, foolishly heading for the escalators. I hurried Jing down the stairs.

"Where's my dad?" she asked.

"On the street, in a car."

When we hit the lobby level, I yanked her away from the main entrance and shoved her toward the side of the mall where I hoped to find an emergency exit. Behind us, paper chains fluttered in the air.

I charged for the exit, shoved my hands against the cross bar, and bolted out the door. Jing followed me into the garage, panting with exhaustion and fear.

I called her father on the phone. "We're out. Where do we go?" I listened a moment then headed for the street.

Jing hurried to keep up. "Wait. I thought I was supposed to be looking out for *you*."

# Chapter Fourteen

We zipped away from Sham Shui Po along the elevated highway, stories above the bustling streets, into a corridor of buildings so dense no daylight passed between them.

Mr. Tam glanced at his daughter. "Your mother will be angry if I don't take you home."

"Can't we go to your apartment? Please, just for a little while?"

"I have to drive Lily home to her grandfather's house."

I leaned forward between their seats. "I don't mind. I'd be happy to see where you live."

Mr. Tam scoffed. "It's not The Peak."

"Come on, Dad, she should see how the rest of us live. Besides, Mommy will give me a hard time about the protest."

"She should." He glanced at Jing. "Fine. But if she wants you back at her place, I must obey."

Mr. Tam drove down a ramp into a neighborhood congested with commercial and residential buildings.

Jing pointed to a parking spot on the curb. "Lily brought you luck."

He swerved into the space and turned in his seat to face me. "You sure you want to come in? Because I can always take you home."

"It's fine."

Across the street, men unloaded crates of live chickens from a cage-framed delivery truck. Feathers puffed into the air as the clucking birds flapped and pecked. Other delivery trucks, painted with produce, waited along the curb. "Is that a wet market?"

Jing nodded. "You can buy everything in Yau Ma Tei Market—fresh produce, butchered meats, live seafood, even incense. It comes in handy for shopping. Want to check it out?"

Mr. Tam looked at our expectant faces and shrugged. "I could use more fruit."

Jing and I ran across the street before he could change his mind.

"If you want souvenirs later, the Jade Hawker Bazaar is down the street. Cheap stuff, but fun."

I followed Jing into a noisy pink warehouse jammed full of independently run stalls. The rubber grate floor had been recently hosed and giant fans blew from the rafters between rows of florescent lights. Ducks hung beside slabs of meat over fish on ice or live seafood in tanks. Chickens clucked at one stall while shoppers scrutinized bok choy and pomelo at another. The scent of fragrant produce mingled with the musk of ceremonial incense, stacked high in red-wrapped tubes, boxes, and packages. Dried strings of sweet lap cheong sausage hung above bins of dried abalone, fungus, and beans.

Mr. Tam marched down the aisle past several produce stalls to the one of his choice and examined the fruit. "You girls want anything?"

Jing turned to me. "Do you like wah mui?"

"Dried preserved plums? Definitely. But I like the dried lemon peel even more."

She led us to another stall with canisters of plums, lemons, and ginger dried or preserved with a distinctive combination of licorice, salt, and sugar. The salty-sour scent reminded me of trips to L.A. Chinatown with my sister Rose.

Jing and I filled a few small bags then followed Mr. Tam across the street to his apartment building. The elevator clanked as it ratcheted up and stopped on what would have been the fourteenth floor. In this building, we landed on the eleventh, avoiding Britain's unlucky thirteen and Hong Kong's even more unlucky four and fourteen, numbers which sounded in Cantonese like "death" and "certain to die." Hoping for a long and lucky life, we exited into a corridor barely wide enough for the three of us to walk side-by-side, then paused for Mr. Tam to unlock the metal security gate and front door.

The space was tight, with an alcove kitchenette on the left, a bathroom on the right, and just enough floor space for me to throw one cartwheel between a two-seater sofa and a small television console. The back half of the apartment was elevated by a foot-high wooden platform, which, on closer look, was actually a sturdy cabinet laid on its back with the doors blocked by a futon, rolled against the louvered windows on the sidewall, and a short square table and floor pillows occupying the center. An open-shelved storage unit was wedged behind the bedroom/dining/storage platform against a second set of louvered windows.

Mr. Tam closed the security gate but left the front door open for ventilation. Even with all of the windows open, the apartment felt hot. "Anyone want lychee?"

"I do," Jing said, jumping onto the platform and plopping onto one of the cushions. She dumped the bags of dried and preserved fruit on the little square table and popped a wah mui into her mouth, sucking on the salty sour plum with loud smacks. "Want one?"

"Mind if I wash my hands first?"

"Over here." Mr. Tam said. "The other room is where I sleep."

A quick look showed me a full-sized bed crammed in the tiny room with clothes overflowing from a closet and hanging on hooks. The bathroom was just as cramped with barely enough room to open the glass door to a shower where a mop, bucket, and other cleaning items sat on the floor beneath suction-cup racks for shampoos and soap. Hanging towels, washcloths, and storage hammocks hung from every bit of wall space, and the sink was lined with toiletries.

When I was done, I returned to Jing and sat cross-legged on a cushion, as I often did when visiting Sensei back in Los Angeles. Aside from this one similarity, Mr. Tam's cramped apartment could not be more different from the minimalist perfection of Sensei's home.

I considered Jing's salty-sour dried plums and opened the bag of preserved lemons instead, pulled one apart, and placed the gooey mess in my mouth. Something truly magical happened when you buried a lemon in salt and fermented it in the sun.

Jing smiled. "Ever put preserved lemon in 7-Up? Dad, do you have any 7 for haam ning chat?"

"No. Just Coke."

Jing shrugged at me. "Usually we use preserved lime, but since you like the lemon, why not?"

"I'll try it at home."

"You want hot coke and lemon?" Mr. Tam asked.

"Hot water's fine for me," Jing answered.

"Me, too."

Jing laughed. "How very Chinese of you."

Growing up with Ma taught me the anti-intuitive cooling effects of drinking hot water on a hot summer day. Although if tea had been offered, I would have jumped at the chance. I could use a boost of caffeine now that the protest adrenaline had receded.

"Well, I am half."

"Yeah…but not really. You're from Los Angeles, right? It's not the same."

Culturally speaking, she was correct, but I got tired of the yellow on the outside, white on the inside banana argument. Being raised in America did not lessen my ethnicity. Genetically speaking, my half Chinese was just as authentic as hers.

Mr. Tam saved me from the debate with glasses of hot water and plates of pineapple buns, named for their cracked crust that resembled the fruit. "Hot from the bakery. Eat."

He returned his serving tray to a wall rack beside the front door and stood in front of the kitchenette sink drinking his hot water. The police raid had upset him, but he didn't want his daughter to see.

I picked at the crunchy top of the bolo bao. "Have you protested before?"

"I have. It's important to have a voice." She picked up her bun, but didn't eat. "This was my first time with the police. I didn't expect to be so…scared."

Mr. Tam scoffed. "How do you think *I* felt? You're seventeen. You should be at your mother's doing your homework, not rioting in malls."

"I wasn't rioting."

"Really?" he answered in Cantonese. "Because video footage was AirDropped to my phone. I saw what was happening inside before the police arrived—vandalizing property, starting fires in trashcans, desecrating the People's Republic flag."

She glanced at me and encouraged him back to English. "I only pasted stickers on the windows of Beijing-friendly stores. I didn't desecrate anything."

"Maybe not, but other protesters did."

I held out a hand to calm Jing. "I've marched in protests before. Most of them remain peaceful, but they can change quickly. What happened at the mall was a classic example of escalation."

"What about the police?"

"Same thing. You can't control the reaction of others, especially not agitator cells and excessively forceful LEOs."

"Leos?"

"Law enforcement. My point is, every protest has the potential to turn into a riot, which is why your father was worried."

Jing glanced at her dad then ran to give him a hug. I thought of Baba. Seven-thirty at night in Hong Kong was still four-thirty yesterday morning in Los Angeles. Even an early riser like him would still be snoozing in bed.

My phone chimed with a WeChat message.

Ma: *Are you still with Daniel?*

Me: *Nope. In Kowloon with Mr. Tam.*

Ma: *The driver?!*

Me: (laughing emoji) *Yeah. Visiting markets and eating bolo bao.*

Ma: *Huh. Well, Bao Jeh made five spice ribs and hot and sour soup if you want leftovers.*

Me: *YES!*

Ma: *Okay. Don't be too late. And remember, Mr. Tam is Gung-*

*Gung's employee. Don't get too friendly.*

I closed my phone as Jing turned on the television and squished next to her father on the couch to make room for me. Mr. Tam carried over the low table and covered the surface with drinks and snacks.

Not too friendly? Too late for that.

Jing flipped through the TV channels and found the one she wanted. "Come and sit. The show's about to start."

# Chapter Fifteen

My second morning in Hong Kong began earlier than the first. If I hadn't set an alarm and put my phone—and snooze button—out of reach, I would have missed it entirely. The fifteen-hour time difference made it hard to fall asleep and even harder to wake.

I rolled off the narrow bed and staggered between the boxes and crates. Ma's childhood bedroom, now Po-Po's craft room and storage, was ridiculously cramped. Space was tight in Hong Kong, even in a fancy home like this. At least it was better than sleeping with Ma.

I wandered out the door in search of caffeine and found it in the kitchen surrounded by my family bickering in Cantonese.

"You must know something about this meeting," Ma said. "What aren't you telling me?"

Gung-Gung shrugged and swept back the soaking tea leaves with the lid of his gaiwan cup. "You will have to wait like everyone else." He sipped the brew through the crack between lid and cup, uncovered it, and added more water to the leaves. "Good morning, Lei Lei. You want tea?"

"I do."

Ma switched to English and turned her annoyance on me. "When did you get in last night?"

"Not so late, but everyone was already asleep."

"That's because we're old," Po-Po said, in Cantonese. "Did you have fun with Daniel? What did you do?"

"Never mind that." Ma switched back to English and shot me a warning look so I wouldn't say anything about my field trip with Mr. Tam. "Lily needs to have her breakfast and get dressed."

"She's coming with us?" Gung-Gung asked.

"I didn't bring her across the world to leave her at home. I'm going to take her to lunch after the meeting."

I slapped peanut butter on the buttered toast, drizzled condensed milk over the top, and stuffed it in my mouth.

Gung-Gung frowned at Ma. "The meeting could last a long time."

"Are you saying it will? Because, so far, you haven't told me a damn thing."

"Violet," Po-Po exclaimed.

"Sorry, Mama, but it's true. Ba is keeping secrets from me, and I don't like it."

I gulped my tea and slathered a second piece of toast.

Gung-Gung slid his tea bowl to the center of the counter, done with breakfast and with Ma. "I hope you packed something appropriate to wear, Lei Lei. We leave in thirty minutes."

I gobbled the remainder of the toast and washed it down with another cup of tea.

Ma heaved a sigh and drank daintily. She'd already put on her face and was dressed in a sophisticated muted-rose pencil dress and ivory jacket. Before we walked out the front door, she'd exchange her house slippers for matching pumps.

"Guess I better get dressed."

"I'll go with you. I want to see what you brought."

We entered her childhood bedroom-turned-storage closet, single file so as not to topple any of the towers. "I can't believe she put you in here. The guest room bed is big enough for both of us if you want to share."

"It's fine, Ma."

"If you say so. Let's see what you brought."

Bao Jeh had hung my charcoal gray slacks in the closet beside an athletic blazer made from the same spandex-polyester blend. Like most of my wardrobe, the gray-on-gray outfit was wrinkle free and allowed total freedom of movement.

"And the blouse?"

I took out one of my nicest stretchy black tees.

"Absolutely not."

I held out a white button-down blouse—also made of wrinkle-free stretchy material. "How about this?"

She sighed. "You'll look like a secret service agent, but I suppose that's a step up from looking like a hoodlum."

I changed quickly and tossed my pajamas on the bed. "You going to be okay?"

She shrugged. "Do I have any choice?"

"Nope."

She smiled and smoothed the side of her chignon. "Tie back your hair and keep your makeup to a minimum." She paused at the door and looked back at my outfit. "You know what? I'm glad you're wearing that. They should know the Wong women are not to be trifled with." It was an uncommon and unexpected compliment.

I took the bare essentials from my cycling pack and slipped them into the zippered pockets of my pants and jacket. Hair plaited and makeup applied, I met Ma and Gung-Gung at the front door where Bao Jeh had unpacked our shoes.

Ma frowned at my choice of footwear. "At least you're not wearing your luggage."

I had given up the hated backpack, but if she wanted a show of force, the flat ankle-high boots were non-negotiable.

Mr. Tam waited beside the sedan with the passenger-side doors opened. He bowed his head in greeting then walked around the car to open a door for me.

"Was Jing's mom angry?" I whispered.

"Only with me."

We exchanged secret smiles and got in the car. No one said another word until we descended into the skyscraper jungle of Central Business District.

"You've never been to my offices, have you Lei Lei?"

"No. Are they in one of these towers?"

"Not just *any* tower. HKIF is inside Two International Finance Center, the second tallest building in Hong Kong and the same height of the former World Trade Center."

I craned my neck. Pristine skyscrapers and futuristic pedestrian bridges blocked my view. Everything looked clean and expensive. As we drew nearer to the harbor, space opened to reveal an observation wheel, half the size of the London Eye, then we turned left onto the paved driveway for an impossibly tall glass tower.

Gung-Gung hurried out of the car and marched toward the revolving glass and chrome doors beneath the words and characters, Hong Kong Monetary Authority.

Ma set a calmer pace. "I refuse to be frazzled by your grandfather. If he wants to take a lift without us, so be it." But with eighty-eight floors—minus the inauspicious numbers—even Gung-Gung had to wait.

As we packed into the elevator, Ma leaned close to my ear. "Your grandfather was right about how long this might take. If you get bored, go next door to the IFC mall. I can always meet you there."

I slipped my hand into hers. "I'm not going anywhere."

I didn't know what corporate bullies she might face or what I could possibly do to protect her, but if my presence emboldened her spirit and made her enemies monitor their behavior, I would stand guard over my mother all day long.

She glanced at Gung-Gung and squeezed my hand.

# Chapter Sixteen

The doors opened inside a central area with a lounge, kitchen, and restrooms, surrounded by businesses with what I assumed would be stunning views. The glass conference rooms along the interior gave the floor a spacious and airy feel while strips of frosted glass shielded those inside the conference rooms from the people passing by. It was an interesting blend of transparency and privacy.

As we approached HKIF, the receptionist greeted us with a smile. "Jou san, Wong Sin Sang."

"Good morning, Katie," Gung-Gung responded in English. "This is my granddaughter, Lily, she will be waiting while her mother and I are in meetings. Try and make her comfortable."

"Yes, Mr. Wong."

Gung-Gung led us into HKIF, with the glass conference room on our right, two sets of two-person desks in the center, and two private offices against the window. Of the four employees, all greeted Gung-Gung, but only two of them greeted Ma. The view could be seen through the glass walls of two executive offices. The one on the right was set up with an L-shaped desk and chairs. Gung-Gung's office, on the left, was furnished with modern chairs and sofa around a low, sleek table. Both of the glass doors were open.

"What happened to your desk?" Ma asked.

"The work I do is handled better over pots of tea."

I glanced at the bar in the corner of his office and wondered what kind of tea came in whiskey bottles.

"You may wait in here, Lei Lei, or in the front with Katie. There's a kitchen and bathrooms near the elevators.

"Don't worry about me." I plopped myself in a chair with a partial view of the conference room, pulled out my phone, and checked my messages. Seeing that I was already engrossed, Gung-Gung and Ma left me alone.

I adjusted my position so I could watch them greet the arriving board members. I recognized several of them from the dinner but only knew the names of Gung-Gung's main partners—the dashing Derrick Lau and Ma's agreement father, Raymond Ng.

Katie arrived with a tray of tea and biscuits and set them on the coffee table. "Is there anything I can get for you?" she asked in English.

"This is great thanks. Have you worked here long?"

"Three years."

"This is my first time meeting the people my mother works with. Could you help me with the names and positions?"

"Of course. Your grandfather is the owner, CEO, and Chairman of the Board. Kenneth Hong is the COO and Hong Kong Director."

"Which one is he?"

"Speaking with Derrick Lau just inside the conference room."

Despite being decades younger and wearing an almost identical black suit and crisp, white shirt, Kenneth Hong had none of Mr. Lau's sex appeal. While Gung-Gung's partner sported a silver stubble beard and wavy mane to match, Kenneth's chinless face was as flat as his hair.

I nodded toward a portly man with a black toupee and a mid-thirties geek who had just arrived. "Who are they?"

"Mr. Lee is a local banker and Mr. Wen is an American I.T. specialist working in Hong Kong." She pointed to the man behind them with a cheery, yet confident demeanor. "Mr. Zhao is an international corporate recruiter from Canada."

"A headhunter?"

"Correct. They are advisory board members from outside the company."

"Advisory board?"

"They consult and sit in on board meetings when they can. They don't vote. Out of consideration, meetings are held in English when they are present. The other HKIF voting board members are your mother, Raymond Ng—the other original partner and major share holder—and London Director Cecil Chu."

"Where is he?"

"Sitting at the table. Mr. Chu always arrives early with an armload of files. He's a very…diligent man."

I stood to see over the frosted privacy glass and spotted a man hunched over his files with thinning hair and a dull gray suit.

Amidst all the gray and black, my mother shone like a queen in her muted-rose and ivory suit.

"If you need anything else, please don't hesitate to ask."

As Katie left me to check on the board members, I slipped out of Gung-Gung's office in search of a better place to spy. The employee workspace in the middle of HKIF plus the frosted privacy strip on the glass made it hard to see what was happening inside the boardroom and impossible to hear. I hoped to have better luck from the hallway looking in.

Since all of the offices on this floor shared a similar floor plan, I settled myself inside a stone-façade nook between the glass conference rooms of HKIF and its neighbor. I leaned against a wall, rested my ear against the HKIF conference room glass, and pretended to scroll through my phone.

"Any other old business?" Gung-Gung asked in English. When no one answered he said, "Good. Then let's move onto the purpose of today's meeting. The chairman yields the floor to Raymond Ng. Go ahead Raymond, the floor is yours."

The older man cleared his throat. I imagined him sipping water during the long pause. Was he a nervous speaker or discomfited by what he was about to say?

"Well," he began. "As you all know, we would like to increase our client reach in the U.S. So far, all of that has been through the Los Angeles office, headed by Los Angeles Director, Violet Wong." He cleared his throat again.

"But the world is very different from when Violet first took office. A younger generation is influencing American attitude, practices, and politics. In order to remain relevant and expand properly, we need a fresh approach."

Ma interrupted. "I'm happy to discuss my 'approach' with you in a private meeting, Raymond, but I hardly think a board meeting is the appropriate time for area-specific conversation."

"Let him finish, Violet," Gung-Gung said, followed by another uncomfortably long pause.

"Normally, I would agree with the Los Angeles director," Raymond said. "However, the leadership of our U.S. expansion is not something that can be discussed with…existing leadership."

"What are you suggesting?"

"I am only casting a brick to attract jade," Raymond said, reverting to proverb. "It is my hope that our younger board members can speak more eloquently to this issue. Mr. Zhao, perhaps you have insight to offer as a corporate recruiter."

"I don't understand where this is coming from," Ma interrupted. "The Los Angeles branch has always performed exceptionally well. Just this year, I've brought in significant investors. Our chairman has met one of them and can tell you about the esteem in which I am held."

I imagined Ma shooting daggers at Gung-Gung. During his visit to Los Angeles, my grandfather had intentionally gotten Ma's biggest client drunk after he didn't kowtow to Gung-Gung as the owner and CEO of HKIF. They drank so many shots of baiju that the man had passed out on Ma's patio in the middle of her fiftieth birthday bash. Ma had been livid.

"I did meet an enthusiastic client," Gung-Gung admitted.

"*Enthusiastic*? Rudy Leong invested ten million dollars in his first three months working with me. And he is only one of my *enthusiastic* investors."

"One or two loyal investors is not enough to expand into a new generation," Raymond persisted.

Another man, possibly Derrick Lau, chimed in with a mature and confident voice. "Our company was built on a handful of loyal clients."

"I would still like to hear from Mr. Zhao," Raymond Ng insisted.

"It's always good to hear another opinion," the other man agreed.

"Mr. Zhao, *you* have the floor," Gung-Gung said, in a forceful voice, no doubt trying to reinstate order in his boardroom.

The younger man spoke in a clear and energetic voice. "The new generation of millionaires analyze investments by a different metric and value system. To understand them, we must first…"

I pulled my ear from the glass as a security guard marched across the corridor.

"Why are you standing here?" he demanded in Cantonese.

"Um…I was tired of sitting in my grandfather's office."

"If you want to stand, do it inside *his* office, not out here. People are complaining."

I followed his glance to the boardroom next door where several irritated corporate types glared at me over their frosted privacy glass.

"Oh. Right."

He waited for me to move and followed me to Katie's desk. "Please make your guest comfortable in your own area."

"I will, security guard," she responded in Cantonese, then switched to English for me. "If you would wait Mr. Wong's office, I will bring you tea."

She offered a tight-lipped smile and waited for me to obey.

I channeled my mother and nodded regally. "Thank you, Katie. That would be lovely."

# Chapter Seventeen

When Ma stormed into Gung-Gung's office, she was anything but lovely.

Gung-Gung followed her in and shut the door.

She whirled to confront him. "Why didn't you tell me this was coming?"

"Because Raymond came to me in private. This is a serious matter. He wanted to propose it properly to the entire board."

"I'm your *daughter*."

"But you are *his* director."

"He's not the only one who owns this company. Cecil, Kenneth, and I all own two percent each, Raymond owns ten, Derrick thirty, but you have the majority—fifty-four percent. Are you actually going to vote against me?"

Gung-Gung shook his head and stared out the window. "The situation is not as simple as you believe."

"Then, by all means, please explain."

Gung-Gung glanced at me, slouched in the chair, trying not to be noticed so they wouldn't ask me to leave.

"Don't worry about her. Tell me what you have to say."

Gung-Gung came over and sank onto the couch with a sigh. "You want so much, Shun Lei, you always have, ever since you were a little girl. Nothing satisfied you, not pretty dresses or ballet lessons or all those parties your mother threw for you. Remember them? The other girls were so jealous. You had everything." He shook his head with a laugh. "But none of that mattered because you always wanted more."

Ma stared at Gung-Gung, sealed tight, giving away nothing.

"The other mothers gave yours a hard time, did you know that? They said you thought too much of yourself. They told Yu Ying to teach you humility and graciousness. Can you even imagine her shame?" He scoffed. "Your mother lost her standing among her peers because of your lofty opinion of yourself."

"She never told me this," Ma said, her voice trembling behind an iron mask.

"Of course not. A candle illuminates others, yet destroys itself."

I stifled a gasp, shocked by Gung-Gung's wounding words. Even if what he said about Po-Po was true, why tell this to Ma now when she was already hurt and vulnerable?

"Po-Po seems alive and well to me," I snapped, angered by his cruelty.

Gung-Gung glared. "You have no place in this conversation, Lei Lei."

Ma found her voice. "Do I? Because my memory of my childhood does not match yours."

She poured herself a glass of water, took a sip, and set it on the coffee table. "I remember ballet…and also the lessons in art, music, English, French, cooking, math, debate, etiquette…horseback riding…and every other skill you felt a young lady ought to know in order to attract an executive husband and breed a suitable heir to the HKIF *empire*." She spoke this last word with distain. "And in all that time, I never once heard a discouraging word from Mama or a solicitous inquiry from you."

"You make it sound like a hardship."

Ma laughed. "Did you think it was fun? I had no time to breathe. You scheduled every moment of my life—school, tutoring, lessons, parties, family obligations—I can't remember a time when I just played."

"Some children would be appreciative."

"Some children like time to be a child."

Gung-Gung heaved himself from the couch and marched to the window, staring at the view. When he had himself under control, he turned back to Ma.

"I apologize for nothing. I gave you the best of everything. Why shouldn't I have expected the best of you in return? You say I scheduled every moment of your life? Why not? Beauty without sophistication only appeals to men of poor character and meager opportunity. Lazy girls grow up to marry lazy men. I wanted you to excel in life *and* in marriage."

Ma shook her head. "Why does everything come back to this?"

"Because you cannot separate yourself from family, no matter how hard you try."

Ma sighed. "I've never wanted to separate myself from you. I only wanted you to respect my choices."

Gung-Gung sat on the couch and poured tea for each of us and then himself. Was he signaling for a truce?

"Baba isn't lazy," I said, unwilling to let this go without defending my father's honor.

Gung-Gung nodded and drank his tea.

When we finished, he stood and brushed the creases from his slacks. "We have a few days before we reconvene for a vote. You're not stir-fried octopus yet. There is no point in worrying about the outcome."

"I would worry less if I knew you would fight on my behalf."

"You know I will."

"Do I?"

Gung-Gung smiled. "Why don't you take Lei Lei to a nice lunch. Go shopping. Have dessert at Lady M's. I'll take care of this. Now, if you'll excuse me, I need to speak with Kenneth about other matters."

Gung-Gung walked out of his glass office and into Kenneth's.

Ma fixed her gaze on me, etiquette preventing her from spying on the men behind me through the glass wall. "Well, that was illuminating. Shall we go have lunch?"

"Don't you want to do something?"

"Like what?"

"I don't know…confront your kai ba, talk to Derrick Lau, rally the support of the other board members—*something*."

"That's not how it's done. The motion was placed. Arguments were spoken. It would be inappropriate of me to rally support. Gung-Gung's right, it's best to leave it in his hands."

I followed her out in silence.

HKIF was a nest of vipers. Ma's agreement father had struck first. I wasn't about to do nothing and wait to see who attacked my mother next.

# Chapter Eighteen

International Finance Tower Two was the spear of an impressive development that included the IFC Mall, IFC Tower One—half the height of tower two—and the Four Seasons Hotel. The inside of the mall gleamed with four sweeping stories of polished steel, creamy marble, and brightly lit stores.

"This is even cooler than the Dragon Center."

Ma looked at me suspiciously. "And how would you know that? You didn't go there yesterday, did you?"

"What, me? I was roaming the markets in Yau Ma Tei." I didn't want to admit to being in the Dragon Center in case Ma had heard about the protest.

"Yau Ma Tei? What were you doing *there*?"

I shut my mouth and glanced at the walkways over head, criss-crossed like a space station in a futuristic movie.

*Yeah, Lily. What* were *you doing there?*

"Um…someone told me the jade market was a good place to shop for souvenirs."

"Ha. Bunch of junk. I hope you didn't waste your money."

"Nope. Didn't spend a thing."

I was high stepping through the truth like a Riverdance revival. "Where should we shop?"

"There's a Parisian store on the third floor that carries chic fashion. Maybe we'll even find something for you."

Parisian chic? Not likely.

"Sure, Ma. Whatever you want." This outing wasn't for me. If it made her happy to watch me try on clothes, I'd play supermodel all day long. "Everything is so clean, like we could eat off the floor."

"Please don't."

"I'm kidding. But, seriously, they must spend a fortune on floor polish and glass cleaner."

"If only they would do the same for the smog and the soot."

She had a point. Hong Kong was a city of extremes—dirty and spotless, grossly rich and heartbreakingly poor, innately casual yet deliberately chic, like the knit skirts and flowing slacks in the white-framed showcase for Claudie Pierlot. Definitely not my style. Fortunately, Ma was too busy outfitting herself to worry about me.

I checked the apps on my phone and found a Facebook message from DeAndre, a first-year college student who worked at Baba's restaurant. It had been sent twenty minutes ago.

DeAndre: *You hear about your dad? Crazy, right?*

I lowered my phone as Ma returned from the cash register with a branded cotton tote full of her purchases.

She eyed me dubiously. "Is everything okay? You look as though you bit into a lemon."

I forced a smile. "All good." Or so I hoped.

"The shop next door is closer to your style. Let's see if we can find you a dress."

I slipped behind her and typed furiously: *What happened to my dad?*

DeAndre: *Shit, girl. You don't know?*

Me: KNOW WHAT?!

DeAndre: *Don't yell at me. I'm just keeping you informed.*

I swallowed my anger and took off the caps. *Know what?*

DeAndre didn't answer.

I followed my mother into the brightly-lit, black-framed shop. She headed for a neat display and held up a long flowing sundress. "How about this?"

"For you or for me?"

"You, of course."

I made a face.

"Fine. But I know there's something in this store you'll like."

I checked my phone for a response. If I hadn't been concerned about alarming her, I would have interrupted DeAndre with a call.

Ma sorted through sweet floral dresses and moved onto a new rack. "These jumpsuits could pass for dresses. Maybe you'd like one of these."

"Uh-huh."

My phone chimed.

DeAndre: *Sorry about that. My sister's freaking about a missing brush. Don't know why she's up in my business. Not like I need a brush for dreads.*

Me: *What about my dad?*

DeAndre: *Right. He passed out in the kitchen and hit his head. I took him to the hospital. Came out looking like Frankenstein.*

Ma held up a flared jumper with pieces cut out at the waist, like flaps needing to be reattached. Had Baba's head looked like that?

She glanced at my horrified expression and sighed. "Don't be so dramatic, Lily. It was only a suggestion. Besides, it might look interesting on."

"Um…I'll look over there." I dodged behind a clothing rack.

Me: *What happened? Is he okay?*

DeAndre: *Yeah, he's good. He overheated while cooking and fainted. Said he didn't drink enough water. But he closed the restaurant.*

The last time Baba had closed Wong's Hong Kong Inn was when Rose had been murdered. Like all of us, he had been too grief-stricken to work. I came home from UCLA and the three of us huddled together in our family house, gone cold without the warmth of my sister's vibrant energy. In time, Baba had found solace in the restaurant, Ma in work, while I intensified my ninja training so I could hunt down my sisters' killer.

"Lily, are you all right?" Ma asked, holding a short wrap-in-the-front jumper with stems of white peonies on black rayon.

I forced a smile and hurried across the room to take it. "This looks nice. I'll try it on. See what else you can find."

Once in the dressing room, I hung up the jumper, sat on the bench.

Me: *Where is he now?*

DeAndre: *At home.*

Me: *Alone?! With a possible concussion?*

DeAndre: *Don't get in my face. I offered to stay, but he kicked me out. You know how he is...stubborn...like YOU!*

Me: *I'm going to message him. Don't go away.*

DeAndre: *I'm not going anywhere. I'm buried in pre-calc.*

I opened my WeChat app and sent Baba a cute animated blob waving its shapeless little hand. When he didn't respond, I went back to DeAndre.

Me: *Are you sure he seemed okay?*

DeAndre: *Yeah. He looked fine. If he hadn't sent everyone home, he probably would have gone back to the restaurant. Not that I would have let him!*

I sent another WeChat sticker to Baba, this one with a panda peeking out of a box then took off my jacket and hung it on the dressing room hook.

Me: *He's not answering.*

DeAndre: *You want me to drive over there?*

Baba's delivery guy and protégé worked so diligently at his studies and dreamed of running his own restaurant. I hated to disrupt his homework by having him drive all the way to Arcadia. Maybe I could ask Mrs. Chin to walk over and make sure he was okay. I checked the time. Noon in Hong Kong was nine at night in Los Angeles. Baba's neighbor might be preparing for bed.

Me: *You sure wouldn't mind?*

When DeAndre didn't immediately respond, I pulled off my shirt. I was half way out of my pants when my phone chimed with a WeChat message.

Baba: *Hey, Dumpling. Are you having fun?*

I sagged with relief and messaged DeAndre to hold up.

Ma knocked on the door. "How does it look?"

I glanced in the mirror at my disheveled state—jacket on the hook, shirt on the floor, black stretch slacks hanging from my hips. "Working on it."

I typed into WeChat and ignored my mother's response.

Me: *Hey, Baba. Everything okay?*

Baba: *Why wouldn't it be?*

Me: *A friend messaged me that the restaurant was closed.*

Long pause.

When I didn't see the typing signal, I peeled my pants over my boots and tossed them on the bench. I had one foot in the shorty jumpsuit when my phone chimed again.

Baba: *Had a little accident.*

I wanted to scream. Little accidents didn't require shutting down restaurants and a trip to the ER.

Me: *Oh yeah? What happened?*

Baba: *Overheated in front of the woks. Too long without water. Fell over and hit my head. Small cut. Tiny bit of blood. No big deal. Don't tell your mother. I don't want her to worry.*

Ma knocked on the door. "Do you have it on yet? How does it look?"

I stepped into the other leg and got caught at the thighs. I had forgotten to untie the sash.

"Honestly, Lily. Has it been so long since you've worn a dress that you've forgotten how to put one on?"

"It's a jumpsuit."

"Oh, for goodness sakes. Do you need help?"

"Nope. I've got it."

I untied the sash with one hand and messaged DeAndre with the other: *Baba said there was only a tiny bit of blood.*

DeAndre: *TINY? It looked like a freakin' crime scene.*

I messaged Baba: *Define tiny bit of blood.*

Baba: *You know how head wounds are. Bleed like crazy. Not to worry. I'm fine. How's your mother?*

I pulled the jumpsuit over my hips and shrugged on one of the sleeves.

Me: *Did you go to the ER? Did they do an MRI? What did the doctor say?*

Baba: *Calm yourself. I'm fine. The doctor stitched me up and checked for signs of a concussion. Superficial wound. No need for an MRI. Told me to take it easy for a day. If I notice symptoms, I'm to call my internist. But I feel fine. How's your mother?*

Me: *Hold on. What about sleep? Aren't you supposed to have someone with you? I can send DeAndre over to spend the night.*

Baba: *Absolutely not.*

Me: *Then I'm going to call later tonight and wake you up. If you don't answer, I'll send paramedics to pound on your door.*

Baba: *Fine. I'll answer, but this is ridiculous. Now...how's your mother?*

I knew my father well enough to know when the door had closed.

Me: *I'll tell you later. We're shopping.*

Baba: *SHOPPING?*

Me: (Laughing emoji) *Yep. She's dressing me up like a doll.*

I stuck my arm into the other sleeve and wrapped the sash to close the front.

Baba: *I'm sure you look beautiful.*

Me: (heart emoji) *Actually, it's kinda fun.*

Baba: (smiley face emoji)

I ran my thumb across his tiny picture, wishing I could see his face.

Me: *Are you sure you're okay?*

Baba: *Yep. Good as new.*

Me: *Where are you now?*

Baba: *Crawling into bed. It's late. Kiss your mama on me. But don't trouble her with this. She has enough on her plate without piling on my accident.*

He sent a bunny blowing kisses.

I sent a marshmallow guy doing the same. Then I messaged De-

Andre and told him he could stay home and study.

"Do you need me to zip you up?" Ma asked.

"Nope. I got it."

I set down my phone, smoothed the silky rayon, and hurried out of the dressing room.

Ma stared at me in surprise.

I checked the V-wrapped front in case I had forgotten to fasten something important. "What?"

Her face softened into a loving expression. "Nothing. You look beautiful."

I turned to the mirror and gaped.

"Do you like it?" she asked.

The graphic impact of white peonies on black added toughness to the otherwise delicate fabric, which hung like a skirt with the casual practicality of shorts. The mid-thigh length, half cuffed sleeves, and open Mandarin collar gave the jumper a polished Asianesque flare. My mother had managed to find an outfit that was bold, feminine, casual, and chic.

"I love it."

She smiled with satisfaction then glanced down at my boots. "This could work, but not with those."

"I thought you wanted me to actually *wear* this outfit. I won't last an hour if you bind me in a strappy designer sandal."

She held out an open shoe box and grinned. "Try these."

Inside, were a gorgeous pair of black ankle-high boots with a sturdy one-inch heel.

"Whoa."

"Right?"

"Yeah."

I sat on an ottoman and tried them on. The leather felt as soft as gloves while the structure of the boot with its arch and laces held my feet firmly in place. I double buckled the stylish band around my ankle and twirled in front of the mirror into a tough-girl pose. "What do you think?"

Ma nodded. "It's very…*you*."

I threw my arms around her and squeezed. "Thank you. I love it." I picked up the box and saw the price. "Oh my God, these boots are four hundred dollars. You can't buy these."

"Why not? Quality comes at a price. If you had a more lucrative job, you might be more willing to pay."

I twisted around to check the price tag on the jumper. It was only a hundred dollars less. I had paid top dollar for my racing bike and weapons, but spending this kind of money on clothes and shoes seemed indecent.

"What about your job?" I asked.

Ma shrugged. "I may not be the Los Angeles director next week, but, right now, I can most certainly afford to buy my daughter a gift."

I nodded. This wasn't only about me. This was my mother's declaration of personal power and confidence.

"Go change," she said. "We'll have lunch at Crystal Jade. I'm craving their Szechuan peanut with chili oil noodles."

"Yum. But don't you want me to wear this?"

Her eyes twinkled as she grinned. "Oh, no. This outfit is for your next date with Daniel."

# Chapter Nineteen

After a delicious lunch of pulled noodles and Shanghainese soup dumplings, Mr. Tam drove Ma and me up The Peak to Gung-Gung's home. While Ma checked her messages, I studied Mr. Tam in the rearview mirror. His jaw was tense with worry. I tried to catch his eye, but he focused only on the road, very different from our previous excursions.

When he parked in Gung-Gung's garage and retrieved our shopping bags from the trunk, I whispered for him to wait then turned to Ma.

"Do we have afternoon plans?"

"No, do whatever you like. I'm going to relax and visit with my mother."

I smiled at Mr. Tam. "Give me a lift across the bay?"

"I will."

"Great. I'll be right back."

Eight minutes later, I returned to the car in a T-shirt, shorts, athletic shoes, and my trusty backpack. I hopped in the front seat with Mr. Tam.

"What's going on?"

"My ex-wife called looking for Jing. She cut school."

"Is this normal behavior?"

"Not at all."

"Think she's at a protest?"

He shrugged. "I haven't heard about any."

I brought out my phone and messaged her on WhatsApp: *I'm free for the day. Want to hang out?*

Jing: *Yes! In Mong Kok with friends. Want to come?*

Me: (thumbs up emoji) *Send the address.*

Mr. Tam watched me in surprise. "She shared her contact info with you?"

"Yep. In between the wah mui and bolo bao. She's at Lo Yi Faateng on Shantung Street. Do you know it?"

Mr. Tam started the engine. "It's a retro café in an old tenement building across from the MacPherson playground. The kids love it because it's so hard to find. That and free Wi-Fi."

"Okay. Let's see why your daughter's cutting school."

The playground was actually a fenced in soccer field with covered brightly-colored bleachers on one side, surrounded by a hodge-podge mix of multi-purpose buildings. Mirror-glass spears, pastel-painted apartments, decrepit cement blocks with dingy small-paneled windows were packed together in a timeline of modern infringement on a weathered past. Mong Kok—Cantonese for *Crowded Corner*—teemed with shoppers, gawkers, and residents.

On my last trip, Ma had led Baba, Rose, and me down Goldfish Street, Flower Market Road, and the Bird Garden where the serenade of hundreds of songbirds had made Rose squeal with delight. We had browsed through the street stalls and eaten fried fish balls in broth. We had laughed to watch the cooks snip flaps of beef, tripe, and squid with scissors into bowls the way we would snip paper for a collage. Mong Kok had filled our young eyes with wonder and our bellies with steaming comfort.

Although my wonderment had mellowed, my wariness had intensified. Even insulated in the car, I felt the press of strangers and the potential for criminal activity. Years of rescuing women and children had opened a curtain that could never be drawn. For me, the busiest district in the world was a labyrinth of hideouts, getaway routes, and disinterested human obstacles. I'd never be able to look at Mong Kok through the innocent filter of childhood.

"Don't look," Mr. Tam said, as we drove along the thirty-foot high playground fence.

"Don't look at what?"

"Across the street. Jing is standing on the sidewalk with her friends."

I snuck a glance across the lane of opposing traffic. Lucky for us, Hongkongers drove on the left side of the road or we would have passed right beside them. "They look kind of old for high school kids."

"I agree. Why is my daughter with them?"

"Don't worry, Mr. Tam, I'll find out. Drop me at the corner. I'll walk back from there."

I crossed the street and walked back toward Jing, sizing up her friends as I closed the distance. The three of them stepped down in height like a set of stairs, all with short black hair and trim physiques. The tallest and shortest wore glasses. The middle-sized person had spiky hair, dangling earrings, and extreme makeup. All three looked to be college age, which made them notably more mature looking than Jing. Beside them, her soft cheeks and bangs made her look like a child.

She waved and called my name. "You made it," she said in English. "These are my friends, Kris, Nate, and Matthew. This is Lily. The restaurant opens at three. It won't be much longer."

"Nice to meet you."

After the obligatory nod of welcome, Matthew, the shortest of Jing's friends in the slim-rimmed glasses and a button-down blue cotton shirt, resumed his discussion in English, presumably for me. He looked oddly formal and reminded me of someone I couldn't quite place.

"If we're going to be recognized as a significant contributing force in the pro-democracy movement, we have to bring in the numbers. Jing, how are you doing with your classmates at Poly U?"

*Poly U?* Jing was still in high school.

She glanced at me then checked her watch. "Aiya, it's three o'clock. Let's go upstairs and sit down." She bolted through the steel door between appliance and audio shops and vanished up the dark stairway. Her friends followed, leaving me behind to ponder her lie.

Mr. Tam pulled up to the curb. "Is she okay?"

"Yeah. Her friends are pro-democracy activists. They think she's in college."

"That's not good."

"Don't worry. I'll see what she's up to."

"Thank you. I have to pick up your grandfather at work. He wants to go home. Will you be okay? I can come back later."

"No need. I'll find my own way."

I hurried up the sweltering stairway, eyes lowered for signs of rot or rats. The F.D.A. would have had a field day with this entrance. I could only pray the restaurant maintained a cleaner kitchen.

When we stopped on the second floor, I understood the appeal. The quirky café was furnished like a super cool sixties' apartment. The designers had kept the bare bones of the tiny flat but opened the doorways to create an open space with a suggestion of nooks. In place of the standard tables and chairs, conversation areas were created around antique sewing machines, student desks, end tables, TV tables, and a metal counter that ran along the open crank windows. Random items from the past were sprinkled here and there: a standing scale and a classic old fridge. What really set the mood were the street-art murals of notorious dictators in ridiculous scenarios.

As Jing and her friends settled around a Formica coffee table with clipboard menus, paper cups, and an aqua free-standing reading light, I admired Kim Jong-Un hula hooping in a red bow tie and black Mary Jane shoes. On other walls, Osama Bin Laden skipped rope in a bunny-eared turban while Muammar Gaddafi rode a flying tricycle with the birds.

I took a seat on a metal chair beside Jing. Her three friends sat across the coffee table, on a floral settee.

Kris, the tallest guy with the black-frame glasses, T-shirt and shorts, addressed me in English. "You're American?"

"Yep. Los Angeles."

Nate looked up from the menu and sent his earrings swaying against his neck. "Do you live near Hollywood?"

"Close enough to bike. Have you been there?"

"Not yet, but I've acted in student films and in both of our pro-democracy videos."

Matthew waved for service. "Don't worry about America. Focus on improving conditions here. This is the important work, not acting. What does everyone want?" Matthew looked up at the server. "Hazelnut latte and tiramisu."

"Tiramisu," said Kris.

"Strawberry shake," said Jing

Nate smiled at me. "They're all sugar addicts. I'll have rose tea and onion rings."

I glanced at the menu, filled with surprisingly elaborate Italian entrees and decadent drinks and desserts. "Osmanthus tea for me."

"The protest last night was a mess," Matthew continued. "I couldn't find any of you. Were our people even there? We have to organize ourselves better so we can make our contribution known."

"What happened last night?" I asked.

"There were protests in many districts. The biggest was outside Mong Kok police station. That's where all of us and our teams should have been."

Nate grimaced. "So we could get arrested or shot in the face with bean bags? The police lights were so strong a man drove his car into a bus. Five people were arrested. I'm all for democracy, but I want to promote it with films and art and peaceful demonstrations." He nodded at Jing, who had brought out a sketch pad to create her own version of the Bruce Lee mural with him shouting while bouncing on a rubber hopper ball. "Jing's art is amazing. We need more of her flyers in the Hin mural style."

Jing smiled but kept her eyes on the page, pleased yet embarrassed.

Matthew nodded. "We also need to march in the front lines. We need to be seen and recorded doing our part. We need to be interviewed. How else will we gain the notice of heroes like Joshua Wong and Nathan Law."

"And don't forget Agnes Chow," Nate said. "Jing looks so much like her, she could play her in a movie."

I typed Joshua Wong's name into my phone and came up with a photo of him meeting with Nancy Pelosi in Washington D.C. a few days earlier wearing a pressed blue shirt, slim-framed glasses, and brushed-forward hair similar to Matthew. Joshua Wong, Nathan Law, and Agnes Chow had founded a pro-democracy political party in 2016, after years of student activism. All three looked very much like Matthew, Kris, and Jing. Only Nate stood out as his own person.

"It doesn't matter what we look like," Matthew said, dismissing his own copy-cat appearance. "What matters is what we say and who is able to hear it. Who can join me at Queen Elizabeth Stadium this Thursday for the community dialogue with Carrie Lam?"

"I'll join you," Kris said, stabbing his fork into the tiramisu that had just arrived. "But the audience has already been selected. How will we get inside?"

"It doesn't matter. We'll hold our own rally outside the doors. Nate and his film friends will bring lights and cameras. Jing will make flyers with our names and logo. Five hundred copies. Get your friends at the college to distribute them."

I smirked at Jing. "Need help rallying those *college* friends?"

"Um, sure. That'd be great."

"And we need art for Saturday. Something different that speaks to the occasion. Make it clean so it looks good on flyers."

"What's happening Saturday?" I asked.

"It's the fifth anniversary of the start of the Umbrella Movement. We have permission from Central for a protest and have already begun decorating the amphitheater in Tamar Park with political art. I want a thousand copies of Jing's satiric art plastered across the walls and walkways."

"You arranged this?"

"Of course not. There will be thousands of protesters. But we need our own presence."

Jing glanced at the murals. "Maybe Hin would contribute."

"We don't need Hin. You have more talent. With confidence and exposure, you will become famous in your own right."

My phone pinged with a message from Mr. Tam asking about Jing.

"It was nice meeting all of you. Good luck with the protests." I placed thirty H.K. dollars beside my cup and smiled at Jing. "Matthew's right about the art. Keep it up."

# Chapter Twenty

Once out of the grungy tenement, I headed for the Mong Kok MTR station, down busy one-way streets. People flowed through Crowded Corner with skilled precision, disrupted only by the abrupt actions of tourists who didn't understand the rules.

Don't stop. Don't block. Don't crowd.

Locals didn't squeeze into tiny shops without purpose, nor did they add to the noise pollution with boisterous conversation. They waited outside and kept their voices low so there would be room for others to shop and think. In a city this congested, no matter how independently-minded its citizens, Hongkongers acted in the best interest of their community.

If only the same could be said of my grandfather's company. From what I had overheard at HKIF, some of them would be more than happy to kick one of their own to the street.

I opened a chat and dictated a message to Ma. *Having fun with Po-Po?*

I took her silence as a good sign. When Ma relaxed, she put her phone away. When she was agitated, it was in her hand, ready to fire. I frowned as a third possibility occurred to me, that my message had gone unnoticed because Ma was comatose in a stress-induced nap. Which reminded me to call Baba.

He answered on the third ring, sounding sleepy but coherent. "Hello, Dumpling. I'm fine. Good night." Then he hung up.

At least he responded.

I thought about Ma. There was something suspicious going on. Perhaps, a surprise visit to HKIF would give me a clue.

I hurried down the stairs into the MTR station and bought an Octopus card at the kiosk. After loading it with money, I swiped my way through the turnstile and used the card again to purchase a rice ball with pickled radish and a bottle of water. My phone pinged with a message as I followed commuters down the stairs. I didn't stop moving until I had arrived at the platform and was out of the way.

Daniel: *Thinking of you. Want to meet for dinner?*

Me: *I'd love to.* (smiley emoji) *But I should stay with family. Tomorrow?*

Daniel: *OK. How about brunch?*

Me: *Yes!*

Daniel: *See if Mr. Tam can drop you at Repulse Bay. I'll send the address. It's close to The Peak.*

Me: *Running distance?*

Daniel: *LOL! Not that close.*

I boarded the train and squeezed into a spot against the opposing doors. *What time?*

Daniel: *10am?*

Me: (thumbs up)

Daniel: (smiley face with hearts)

I stared at the emoji, pleased and perplexed. While adorable, his smiley face with hearts made my thumbs up seem gruff. I scrolled through my selection of emoticons, vacillating between various expressions. Should I match his smiley face with hearts or step it up with a clean, universal symbol of love? By the time I worked up the courage to send a simple red heart, I had arrived at my station, and the opportunity had passed.

I followed the bustling crowd through the immaculate Central Station, then power-walked across the elevated steel and glass walkways to IFC Tower Two.

Gung-Gung's receptionist looked up at me in surprise. "Lily. How nice to see you again."

"Hello, Katie. Is my grandfather here?"

"So sorry. He left an hour ago."

I pretended to be disappointed. "May I check his office. I might have dropped my phone in that comfy chair of his."

"Of course."

I waved my hand as she started to rise. "Don't trouble yourself. I know the way."

I passed the employees sitting at the two two-person desks and entered Gung-Gung's empty office. Next door, Cecil Chu, white hair and face etched with worry, chatted with Kenneth Hong, the nerdish COO with the recessed chin. Although the London Director looked considerably older, I guessed him to be mid-sixties under stress. After pretending to find my phone in one of Gung-Gung's chairs, I went next door and knocked on the open door frame.

They stopped speaking in Cantonese and looked at me in surprise.

"Hi, I'm Violet's daughter, Lily. I left my phone in my grandfather's office. I just wanted to say hello before I left."

Mr. Hong beckoned me inside and switched to English. "Please, come in. We didn't get to meet you at the banquet. I'm Kenneth and this is Cecil Chu, he's in from London for the meetings."

Mr. Chu nodded in greeting and turned away. Annoyed or shy?

I focused my attention on Kenneth. "It's nice to finally meet you and put a face to my mother's praise."

"Oh?"

"Yes. She speaks so highly of you and the way you've been running things for my grandfather."

Kenneth's eyes widen with delight. "Would you like refreshments? I have water, or I can ask Katie to bring us tea."

"Water would be great. I spent the afternoon in Mong Kok and feel a little dehydrated."

"It's very hot this time of year. The IFC Mall is much more comfortable, and we have many appealing shops right here on the island. Isn't that right, Cecil?"

The London director huffed in agreement.

Kenneth smiled brightly enough for both of them, his eager eyes magnified by the thick lenses of his glasses. "Will you be here long, or do you have a husband and children to return to?"

I glanced at his ring finger and saw the tan mark and indentation where a wedding ring had rested for years. "Nope. It's just me. I'll be here with Ma for the week."

He handed me the glass of water and held onto it a moment longer than necessary. "Then you'll have many opportunities to dine in our excellent restaurants."

"I certainly hope so. I'm pleased to meet you as well, Mr. Chu. My mother has also spoken very highly of you." I kept my tone respectful and offered a slight bow.

The London director met my eyes for the first time, armor eased, ever so slightly, by my formal address.

"I've always wanted to visit London," I continued. "Especially with its past relationship to Hong Kong. It must have been a very exciting time for you between the Sino-British Joint Declaration and the 1997 transfer of sovereignty."

Mr. Chu adjusted his glasses and inspected me more clearly. "It was. When your grandfather opened the London Office and put me in charge, Hong Kong was still a British colony. Once Britain and China declared their intentions, confidence was lost. Tens of thousands of Hong Kong residents emigrated, many of them to the U.K. We were fortunate to capitalize on that influx."

"We?" I tilted my head as if I didn't quite believe him. "I think you're being modest. My mother says your office handles all of HKIF's European clients just as she looks out for the United States and Canada."

He thought for a moment then nodded. "Your mother has learned and accomplished much in twenty-five years."

"I'm sure she will appreciate hearing this."

Kenneth held up the pitcher of water. "May I pour you more? Certainly, you are very hot."

I suppressed a laugh at his awkward phrasing then caught the twinkle in his eyes. Was Gung-Gung's divorcé director hitting on me?

"I should go. Sorry to interrupt."

Mr. Chu shook his head. "Don't apologize. It was a pleasure to meet you."

"I agree," Kenneth added and extended his hand for mine. "I hope you'll come in again."

"Thank you. I'd be interested to learn more about what you do." I let him squeeze my hand longer than was necessary then offered a polite bow to both men. "Mr. Chu, you have the advantage of knowing the island as a local and a visitor. Can you recommend a good hotel for my friend? She'll be here on business, early next year."

He shrugged. "Everyone stays at the Four Seasons, but I prefer 99 Bonham, four stars, moderately priced."

"Thank you. I'll pass that along."

As I exited the offices, Katie looked up from her desk. "Did you find your phone?"

I smiled. "It took a while, but I found exactly what I needed."

# Chapter Twenty-One

When I returned home, I found Ma lounging in the family room, a little tipsy, while Gung-Gung and Po-Po watched news footage of yesterday's protests. Her words rolled out lazily in greeting. "Hello, Lily."

"Hey, Ma. How's it going?"

She nodded toward the television and shrugged. On the screen, protesters set fire to the People's Republic flag, destroyed property, and tossed tear gas bombs at police.

Gung-Gung muttered in Cantonese then snorted in disgust. "These radicals destroy everything to grasp an unattainable goal."

I thought back to their visit in Los Angeles and our political conversation over Ma's mahjong table. "I thought you told me not to believe the news footage because we're never being shown the whole picture."

He pointed at the screen. "What is hidden does not change what is seen."

"But it does. What if this riot began with paper cranes and quiet singing? What if a handful of activists changed the tone of hundreds, whipped into violence by police dressed as protesters?"

"You don't know this, Lei Lei."

"Neither do you, which is exactly my point."

He snorted again. "It doesn't matter. A mouse cannot bully a lion. China will bite off their heads. All of us will bleed."

I opened my mouth to describe my first-hand experience at the

Dragon Center mall, then shut it just as fast. What difference would it make?

"You want cake?" Po-Po kept her eyes glued to the screen and motioned to the tea tray where only crumbs remained. "Turn it up, Shaozu, I can't hear."

Ma downed the rest of her wine. "I'm going to take Lily out to dinner."

"Good," Gung-Gung said.

"Go," agreed Po-Po.

I swallowed my guilt. Was this how Ma had spent the afternoon, ignored by her parents? I shouldn't have let her come home alone. I should have followed Baba's advice and looked out for her. I checked the time: quarter past six, 3 a.m. in Los Angeles. Almost two hours had passed since I called Baba. Should I call him again? Had the fall given him a concussion? Was the wound more serious than he had led me to believe? Now I had *two* parents to worry about.

I sent a message to Mr. Tam requesting a ride then followed Ma into the kitchen where she informed Bao Jeh about our plans in rapid Cantonese. I caught something from Bao Jeh about cold food for later.

"Fancy or casual?" I asked, as we headed for our rooms.

"Whatever you want. I just need a break from them."

"Have you had a chance to speak with your kai ba?"

She shook her head. "I wouldn't know where to begin. I feel so betrayed."

"Call him. Maybe he'll open up to you in private."

Ma leaned against my doorway as I changed out of my shorts. "I would prefer facial cues and body language."

"Then let's visit him in person."

"What, you mean now?"

"Why not?"

"It would be terribly impolite."

I pulled on a fresh shirt and stretchy slacks. "Blame it on me. Where does he live?"

"Deep Water Bay."

"So they have restaurants in Deep Water Bay?"

"Of course."

"Then we'll drop in on our way to dinner and say you wanted me to meet your kai ba's wife."

"I don't know."

"Well, *I* do. You can't hide in this house for the next four days, drink wine, and pray everything will work out while Gung-Gung's original partner removes you from the company. We have to get to the bottom of this, and that means starting at the top."

# Chapter Twenty-Two

Ma fluffed the cellophane wrap and bow as Mr. Tam drove us through the hills to the south side of the island. She had brought California dates to give as special gifts. Her thoughtfulness would be noted.

She fidgeted in her seat and smoothed her aqua silk blouse and tan slacks as we drove up the cement corridor to Raymond Ng's townhome complex. "I hope this isn't a mistake."

I squeezed her hand and hoped the same. Bad enough Ma's agreement father had rebuffed her at the banquet and motioned against her at the meeting, if he rejected her in his home, the rift would be too deep to repair.

"You can't give up without a fight, and you can't fight what you don't understand."

Ma sighed. "When did you become so wise?"

I opened my calendar app and starred the date.

"What are you doing?"

"Memorializing the date you called me wise against the next time I do something foolish."

"Ha. You think I'll care?"

"Nope."

We shared a laugh.

"But seriously, Ma, it'll be okay."

She patted my hand in thanks.

The security gates were open, so Mr. Tam drove into the complex plaza and parked in the carport between elevated townhomes above and another row of townhomes below. From the graceful aesthetics and drop-dead view, I guessed each unit ran in the double-digit millions.

Ma crinkled the cellophane. "This is so rude. We should at least announce ourselves through the intercom."

"And give him the chance to turn us away?" I got out of the car. "We attack with dates and defend with courtesy. Trust me on this, Raymond Ng will invite us into his home."

Fortified by my conviction, we headed down the walkway to Mr. Ng's townhouse, wedged between identical mansions with stone pillar façades and glass-walled rooftop gardens. While only a couple of yards separated the buildings, each appeared to have a sizable deck in front and a bit of property cascading below.

Ma took a breath and rang the bell. A dog barked. Voices spoke. When the door finally opened, it wasn't Raymond Ng that answered but a short, round woman with white hair and wide eyes.

"Violet?"

"Hello, Auntie," Ma greeted.

"What are you doing here?" Mrs. Ng asked in Cantonese. "Aiya. Is this your daughter?"

"Neih hou, Auntie Lan."

"Bah. Call me Ah Ma," she continued in Cantonese. "I'm too old for auntie." She rattled off a paragraph too quick for me to catch directed at Ma and to whomever was behind her in the house. Husband? Maid? Dog? I couldn't keep up.

She beckoned us inside and gushed over the present Ma gave her. I caught the words "pretty," "kai ba," and "pleased."

A yapping Shiba Inu skidded around the corner, toenails clacking on the marble, and triggered another unintelligible spray of Cantonese from Mrs. Ng.

I knelt on the floor to greet the dog. "Hey, Ma Lik, did you miss me?"

He dodged my arms, circled once, then ran to his master who had entered the foyer. Mr. Ng commanded the Japanese hunting dog to sit, which he did for all of two seconds then raced up and down the stairs on his slim, graceful legs. When he skidded to a stop in front of me, I caught him by the collar and petted his reddish-gold coat.

"Have I forgotten an appointment?" Mr. Ng asked Ma in English.

"You have not. Lily and I are having dinner at the bay and stopped by to say hello to Auntie Lan."

"She brought a gift, Wai Yan," Mrs. Ng interjected in Cantonese. "Isn't it pretty?"

Ma shrugged. "California dates. I remembered how much you liked them during your visit to my home."

Mr. Ng smiled, caught by the thoughtfulness of Ma's gift and the reminder of her past hospitality. "Do you have time for a cocktail or tea?"

"We don't wish to disturb your evening."

He shrugged. "We've eaten, you're here, and Ma Lik has remembered his friend. You must stay."

The fox-like dog wagged his curled tail in agreement.

Ma nodded. "If you insist, tea is fine."

Mrs. Ng dashed off to the kitchen muttering something about chrysanthemum, cooling, and…prostate health?

I picked up Ma Lik, afraid he'd snub me again if I let him go, and followed Mr. Ng and Ma around the gold lattice screen into a spacious living room. Ivory leather couches, one long and two short, formed a U that faced the patio deck and stunning view. The sun had set during our journey, but the sky mingled orange and indigo over the island and bay.

As Mr. Ng motioned us to the best view couch, Ma Lik scrambled out of my arms and ran outside through the open gap between the glass doors.

"He's not allowed on the furniture."

I nodded. "It's good to have rules."

Mr. Ng raised brows so thin they were almost as bald as the shiny crown of his head. "Most young people would not agree."

"I grew up with Ma. She runs a tight ship in family and business."

Ma followed my lead. "It's true, you know. I've built strong legs in Los Angeles to support a wide expansion. My clients are loyal for good reason. You've always been very complimentary of my work, Kai Ba. Why are you pushing me out?"

"Is this why you came? To challenge me in my own home?"

"I'm not challenging, I'm asking."

"I can't talk about this."

"Why not?"

"It's not proper, Shun Lei. You should not have come."

"We're family."

"I'm your boss."

"You're retired. Besides, you've never taken an active part in running HKIF. Why are you interfering now?"

He stood up, walked to the doors, and stared through the glass at the darkening sky. "I apologize for hurt feelings. Life is hard. Expectations bring unhappiness."

"If they're unreasonable, perhaps, but I've been doing an exceptional job for twenty-five years. I was running Los Angeles for seven years before Kenneth was even hired. Now, he's CEO and you're trying to oust me from the company? Why?"

Mr. Ng called to his wife in Cantonese, asked about the tea, offered to help, then left the room before she answered.

Ma sighed. "That was poorly done—me not you. I'm too emotional for this conversation. We should go."

"Emotion is exactly what's needed." As the Ngs returned, I pulled Ma into a dramatic hug.

"What's wrong?" Mrs. Ng asked in Cantonese, as she set down the tray.

"Nothing, Ah Ma. Just reminding my mother that she's loved."

"Everyone loves Violet, especially her kai ba. Isn't that right, Wai Yan? He brags about her more than he does our own children. Sometimes, I think he loves her more than he loves them." Her eyes crinkled with delight. "Shaozu better watch out or Wai Yan will—something something—Violet and never let her go."

"Bong gaa?" I asked.

"Kidnap," Ma explained.

Mrs. Ng poured the tea. "If he had his way, Violet would be running her father's—"

Mr. Ng waved his hand for her to stop. "Enough of this, Lan. Let's enjoy our tea so they can go to dinner."

Had Mrs. Ng been about to say *company*? From the twitch in Ma's brow, she had assumed the same.

"I have leftover rice and fish if you're hungry."

"We're fine, Auntie."

"Butter flower," she exclaimed in English, and hurried out of the room.

I looked at Mr. Ng. "Butter flower?"

"Her favorite cookie."

I sipped my tea and considered Mrs. Ng's disclosure. If her husband had wanted Ma to become CEO, why was he trying to sabotage her career?

Ma set down her cup. "What's going on?"

Mr. Ng shrugged and answered in proverb. "A ghost hits her head, and trouble spills out."

"Maybe I can help."

"How, by falling on your sword?"

Ma grimaced. "I'd prefer another way."

"So would I. Believe me, Shun Lei, replacing you gives me no pleasure."

"Then why do it?"

"I have no choice."

"Everyone has a choice."

"Only children say such things."

"First a ghost and now children? Who else will you blame to avoid telling me the truth?"

Mr. Ng groaned. "You're a stubborn as an ox."

"No, I'm as fearless and quick-witted as a monkey. Isn't that what you always told me? People born in the year of the monkey are good at business because we work harder and smarter than our competitors. All my life, you have challenged me to grasp the highest fruit. What has changed to make you chop down the tree?"

Ma Lik growled and barked outside, hidden by the darkening twilight. The barking grew louder and more insistent.

Mr. Ng called through the open doors. "Ma Lik! Gwo lei, Ma Lik!" He looked back at us. "Wild animals roam the hills. I hope it's not another pig. They're quite big."

I joined him at the glass. "Do you have a stick or a broom?"

"Maybe a rake on the side of the house?"

I sprinted up a spiral staircase too slim and treacherous for a boar. Whatever was on the rooftop deck with the little Shiba Inu, it wasn't a pig.

# Chapter Twenty-Three

The lights from the terrace above bathed the roof in a bluish glow. A figure towered over the dog. Ma Lik scrambled to his feet. The intruder kicked. Ma Lik tumbled across the deck.

I sprinted forward, circled the rake over my head, and launched a lateral Yoko Men strike to the back of the intruder's head. Using ninjutsu push-pull leverage, I struck with the handle again and swept out his legs with an Ashi Barai strike to the calves. The high-low combination stunned his mind and landed him on his hip. I yanked the staff behind me for a third attack.

Ma Lik leapt for his throat.

The man rocked back onto his forearm and stomped.

I launched the rake in a wide circle over the tumbling dog and into the intruder's face, but he must have seen it coming because, at the last moment, he ducked the prongs and grabbed the staff. I yanked. He yanked. When he did, I lunged forward and raised the handle of the rake. Since he was still holding on, it raised his arm just enough to open his ribs for my kick. I expected bone crunching contact. Instead, he skipped to his feet and elbowed my shin.

My leg throbbed and my confidence wavered. Not only was the intruder larger and stronger, he was skilled. I'd need every sneaky trick in my ninja arsenal to win.

He dropped the rake and lunged for my throat. I knocked his arm off course, grabbed his wrist, and slammed the handle of the rake against the back of his locked arm. Rather than dislocating his elbow or planting him on his belly, he rolled over his shoulder, grabbed my wrist, and sent me flying over his head. With my hand trapped and my body too high off the ground to roll, I torqued into an aerial cartwheel and landed on my feet. The momentum yanked him forward and planted him on his face as I had tried to do before.

My win didn't last. The rake had flown out of reach and Ma Lik had returned to bark and nip. Before I could grab the dog, the intruder yanked him by the collar and stuffed his head under his arm as he rose.

"Put him down."

The man grinned and dangled Ma Lik behind him, twisted his body like a discus thrower, and prepared to launch. With no time to stop the man, I bolted to intercept the dog.

Arms extended, mid-leap, like a volleyball player blocking a spike, I crashed into Ma Lik in a tangled frenzy of nails and teeth. We hit the railing and crumpled onto the deck. Desperate from fright, Ma Lik clawed new wounds on my already bleeding arms and scrambled away.

The intruder yanked me to my feet.

I grabbed his wrist and shoved off the deck so he wouldn't rip the hair from my scalp. The added force of my jump took him by surprise and knocked him off balance, but not enough for him to let me go.

If I'd had a second to recover from saving Ma Lik, I could have turned this around. But even after I elbowed the intruder in the face and kneed him in the groin, he twisted like a discus thrower and launched. As my legs flew from his body, I grabbed his wrist with both hands. Suspended in the air, I saw it all: Ma Lik nipping at his legs, the deck bathed in light, and a scorpion tattoo, claws open, tail aimed at me.

I sailed over the glass railing and slammed against the house.

Sliding on sweat, I clawed at the intruder's dangling arm, the glass, anything to stop the inevitable fall. With nothing to save me, I kicked off the wall so I wouldn't fall backward and break my neck. I hit the awning and tumbled over the edge. When I caught the last wooden slat, I thought I had survived, but my legs kept swinging. I lost my grip and fell.

The Ngs and Ma screamed as I hit the patio, flat on my back, arms slapping the deck to disperse the shock. The entire altercation had happened in a flash.

# Chapter Twenty-Four

Ma rushed to me as the Ng's shouted in Cantonese.

Ma Lik barked from the roof, too injured or frightened to chase the intruder down the spiral staircase. I had one more chance to catch our attacker. I couldn't let him escape.

I rolled onto my feet, dodged Ma's caring embrace, and sprinted to intercept. By the time I chased him to the walkway, he was gone.

I jogged up to the gate and searched the parking area. I didn't expect to find him, but I needed time to gather my thoughts. The invader had been inordinately skilled. Who was he? What did he want with Raymond Ng? Why had he fought a dog when he could have fled?

Where had I seen that scorpion tattoo?

When I heard Mrs. Ng shout for Ma Lik, I ran back to the patio and stopped Mr. Ng from going up the spiral staircase. "I'll get him." The last thing we needed was for the old man to slip and break a hip.

When I reached the top, Ma Lik cowered and limped away. It broke my heart to see him scared of me, but after I had struck him in the air and pulled on his legs, I understood. The dog didn't know I had saved his life. He only knew I had caused him pain.

I knelt on the deck and cooed soothing words, hoping to calm his fear and earn his trust. As I did this, I scanned the roof. Unlike their neighbors, the Ng's hadn't decorated their roof deck with furniture. They probably hadn't been up here in years. I peered through the bluish glow for anything left behind. If the intruder had brought equipment, he had taken it with him.

Ma Lik limped into my arms. "You're such a good boy. I'm sorry if I hurt you." I kissed the furrow between his pointed ears and received a lick of forgiveness in return.

Once down the stairs, Mrs. Ng snatched him from my arms and whisked him into the house while Mr. Ng shot rapid questions at me in Cantonese. I ignored him and studied Ma, hands clasped in a fist at her mouth. I touched her gently on the shoulders, afraid she'd crumble if I pulled her into a hug.

"Ma? Are you okay?"

She bit her knuckles and shook her head.

I pulled her into a hug. "I'm not hurt, Mommy. I'm fine."

Her chest heaved with a sudden intake of air then calmed. I hadn't called her Mommy since Rose and I were little, before the care-free joys of childhood had collided with my mother's middle school expectations. Saying the word now triggered emotions I didn't have time to feel. It must have done the same with Ma because she pushed me away at arms length and took a long, steadying breath.

"You're bleeding."

"I know."

We followed Mr. Ng into the house and found Mrs. Ng in the family room, cradling Ma Lik on a coral-pink over-stuffed couch. Either family room furniture was considered dog friendly or tonight's near-death event had superseded the rules.

I heated water for tea as Ma asked Mr. Ng for first aid supplies. By the time they returned, I had retrieved Mrs. Ng's tray of cookies and cups from the living room and replaced the cooled water in the teapot with hot.

"Sit down, Lily, and let me clean those wounds."

I placed the tray on the lacquered coffee table and sat on an ottoman in front of Ma. The scratches on my arm were deep. One of Ma Lik's claw-marks needed tape to hold the wound closed. The worst of the pain came from the bruise on my hip where I'd smashed against the house and a general ache from landing on my back. My training had kept me from slamming my head.

Mr. Ng muttered in Cantonese and poured himself two fingers of whiskey.

"Who was that man?" Ma asked in English.

"No one. Nothing. You and Lily should go. He was a robber. That's all."

I shook my head. "He wasn't here to rob you."

Mr. Ng scoffed. "How would you know?"

"He had no tools."

"Maybe he left them on the roof."

"Nope. I checked when I brought down Ma Lik."

"Then he was scouting the area."

"I don't think so."

"What *do* you think?" Ma asked me.

"I don't know. Spying?"

"Why would anyone spy on me?" Mr. Ng sounded more nervous than indignant. He drank his whiskey, poured another shot, and drank that too.

Ma tossed the bandages on the table. "You tell us, Kai Ba. You've behaved strangely ever since we arrived."

Mr. Ng sat on a porcelain barrel, an uncomfortable seat for an uncomfortable man.

I glanced at Ma Lik, sleeping in Mrs. Ng's lap. When the commotion broke out, he had barked for a full minute before yelping in pain. Why hadn't the intruder fled?

"Are you in danger, Uncle?"

"What? No." His eyes darted to his sleeping wife.

Ma saw it, too. "Why don't we return to the living room and let her rest."

"Good idea." I picked up the tea tray. After the whiskey Mr. Ng had consumed, he could benefit from butter flower cookies and tea.

"No. You need to go. Lan and I are tired. We're not young anymore. You have visited long enough."

I set down the tray. Whatever was bothering him would not be revealed tonight.

Mr. Ng ushered us to foyer, but Ma stopped before we reached the door. "Tell me the truth. Does tonight have anything to do with me?"

Mr. Ng straightened his spine, as if drawing back the courage the intruder had stolen from him. His expression hardened. The frailty of the last twenty minutes vanished. For the first time, I saw him as the power broker he must have been decades ago, a business man who could afford to buy a property in Deep Water Bay.

He opened the door and glared at Ma. "The world does not revolve around you, Shun Lei. And neither does HKIF."

# Chapter Twenty-Five

Rather than wait for a table at a trendy bayside eatery, Ma had Mr. Tam drive us to the Dairy Road Market at the top of Gung-Gung's street. The name mystified me. Although feral bovine now populated Lantau and the New Territories, cattle and dairy cows had never been imported to this island. Then again, I wouldn't have expected an international school in this secluded hilltop neighborhood, either. Perhaps the Swiss and German expats had named the market as a quaint reminder of their home.

We bought yogurt and fruit to accompany whatever cold leftovers Bao Jeh might have in the fridge and walked across Watford Road to the entrance of my grandparents' complex. When we reached the gold-painted entrance, Ma paused. "You scared me tonight."

"I didn't mean to."

"When you fell off the roof…" Her voice trailed away. She reached for the handle, changed her mind, and leaned her back against the door. "Is this what you do in Los Angeles? Is this why you always look so tired and battered?"

I brushed my shirt and pants. Although the black stretchy fabric looked clean with no signs of wear, I couldn't say the same for my scraped and bandaged arms. "Do you really want to know?"

Although I had confessed the truth to Baba, sharing my ninja escapades with Ma would cause problems. I had enough trouble with Aleisha and Stan monitoring my risks and scrutinizing my health without my mother questioning my every move.

She studied me a moment longer, then opened the door. "It's getting late. We should eat and go to bed, put an end to this horrible day."

I followed her into the townhouse, feeling both relieved and oddly disappointed. Ma thought of me as an aimless bum, a university dropout who had thrown away her life. If I had blurted out the truth of what I did to protect the women and children of our city, would she have considered that respectable work? Too late to find out now. It wouldn't serve either of us to add another burden to this day.

After a quick dinner of cold noodles, tofu, and vegetables, Ma left me in the kitchen with my yogurt and fruit. Not only was I famished, I was too keyed up to sleep. It was ten o'clock at night and seven in the morning in Los Angeles.

I sent Baba a waving puppy sticker and waited for his response. Now that my night had finally calmed, my concern for him rushed in to churn the waters. I sighed with relief when the word "typing" appeared at the top. That one simple word and those three little dots eased my tension.

Baba: *Good morning, Dumpling! How ya doing?*

Me: *Concerned about you. Were you able to sleep?*

Baba: *Like a bear in a cave. Heading for the restaurant in a bit.*

Me: *I thought you were supposed to rest.*

Baba: *I did. How's your mother?*

I hovered my thumbs, unsure what to type. Although I didn't want to worry him, he couldn't comfort Ma if he didn't know what was going on.

Me: *Worried. Tense. Scared.*

Baba: *About the board meeting? How did it go?*

Me: *Not well. Raymond Ng proposed a motion to have Ma replaced.*

Baba: *He's always been her biggest supporter.*

Me: *I know. We went to see him tonight at his home. He wouldn't discuss it.*

I started to describe what had happened with the intruder and stopped. How much should I tell my father? I deleted my text. The typing dots vanished.

Baba: *Spit it out, Dumpling. Unspoken worry rots the gut.*

My belly cramped in agreement. *An intruder climbed onto Raymond Ng's roof and attacked his dog.*

Baba: *What was the dog doing on the roof?*

I laughed. *Good question! Actually, the roof is a deck.*

Baba: *I don't understand. Was this attempted burglary? Was anyone hurt? Are YOU hurt?!*

Me: *I'm fine. Just a few claw marks from the dog when I stopped him from falling off the roof.*

Baba: *Falling?*

Me: *Thrown. I intercepted the dog. The man threw me off the roof instead. An awning slowed my fall. Good landing. Ma freaked.*

Baba: *Oh geez.*

Me: *I'm okay. Promise.*

Baba: *Uh-huh…* Ten seconds later: *Did you catch the intruder?*

Me: *Nope. There's something fishy about this, but I can't wrap my brain around it.*

Baba: *Sleep on it.* (bunny sticker tucked into bed exhaling Zs)

Although adorable, the sticker reminded me of my concern. *How's your head? Did you sleep okay?*

Baba: *Oh, sure. Thick skull. Fragile pride.* (wink emoji) *Off to work. Be safe. Kiss your mama on me.* (hugging bunny sticker)

Downplaying injuries ran in the family. I still remembered the fountain of blood that had spurted from Baba's forearm after he had sliced open a produce box. He drove himself to urgent care, had it stitched, and returned with a gallon of butter pecan ice cream. I'd check in later with DeAndre for a more reliable update.

I signed off with a thumbs up emoji and an adorable green monster blowing kisses.

I took Baba's advice and headed for bed. Once I had changed into a sleeping tee and shorts and walked up the hallway to brush my teeth, I heard noises coming from Ma's bedroom. I pressed my ear to the door then knocked.

"Are you awake?"

She was sitting cross-legged in bed hugging a pillow, cheeks wet with tears.

I crawled onto the bed and sat in front of her, mirrored her posture, and rested my hands on her knees. I didn't ask her what was wrong. I just shared her space.

She shuddered and gasped as grief heaved from her body in gut-wrenching sobs. "I can't lose another daughter. I can't. I'd never survive."

I crawled to her side and wrapped her in my arms as years of unspoken pain flooded from both of us in ugly grunts and moans. Ma hugged me so tight I could hardly breathe. But what good was breath if I couldn't breathe it into Rose?

I sank lower and snuggled my face against my mother's heart, clutching her waist as she rocked me like a child. What childish woes used to bring me to such despair? A broken toy? A stubbed toe? An injured bird? I'd had no idea about the true meaning of pain. Nor had my mother.

"I can't lose you, Lily."

"I know, Ma."

"Whatever it is you do, you can't share it with me. Do you understand? It will break me. A mother can only bear so much."

# Chapter Twenty-Six

I woke to Ma's breath on my face and her arm draped across my shoulders. My temples ached. Cathartic release took a heavy toll. I slid out of her embrace and onto my bruised hip. Slamming into a building hadn't helped. I needed a hot shower and a strong cup of coffee.

Once I'd washed my hair and changed into a tank top and capris, I walked across the street to the Dairy Road Market. The kitchen cupboards of my tea-drinking grandparents offered a dismal selection of instant coffee in jars crusted by moisture and age. Even a thermos of basic brewed coffee would taste better than that. To my delight, the market deli sold coffee milk tea and pineapple buns stuffed with roasted pork. I bought two bolo bao and an extra large cup of yuen yeung. Although not as good as Baba's brew, the caffeine kick cleared the fog from my mind.

I planted myself on a wall outside where I could enjoy my breakfast in the sun. After a second hit of caffeine, Ma's words crashed into me. *I can't lose another daughter. I'd never survive.*

My heart lurched as the emotions from the night encroached on my day. Ma carried her pain as close to the surface as I carried mine. I'd known this intellectually, but I hadn't truly understood. We dealt with our grief so differently I'd forgotten how appearances could deceive. My family had crawled from the rubble of Rose's murder each in our own way: Baba with his restaurant, me with my quest, Ma with her work. Up until last night, I had no idea she had transferred her heartache and fear onto me.

I opened WeChat and sent a message to Baba: *I found Ma crying in her bed last night.*

He answered quickly. *I'm not surprised.*

Me: *She was crying about Rose.*

Baba: *I know.*

I started to type then stopped: I needed more than truncated words for this exchange.

Baba answered my video call from the kitchen with a meat cleaver in his hand. "Hold on a sec."

He perched the phone on the prep counter across from the chopping block and finished segmenting the hind quarter of a roasted duck with practiced precision. He sliced through the leg joint, pounded the back of the cleaver to separate the meat, then hacked the thigh and leg into bite-sized pieces with alarming speed. I cringed with every strike even though I knew he tucked in his fingers and protected them beneath his knuckles. His competency didn't assuage my concern. I'm sure he felt the same way about me.

He slid the cleaver under the pieces, moved them onto a platter, and wiped his hands on the towel hanging from his apron. He smiled into the camera. "Let's take this outside and enjoy the sun. But first…" He turned his phone so Bayani, Ling, Brett, and DeAndre could see me on the screen. "Look who I have all the way from Hong Kong."

Ling and Bayani waved. DeAndre rushed the camera with his mouth wide in a crazy smile. "Hi, Lily. Don't forget my souvenir."

Baba whisked me away before I could reply then walked outside and sat on the alley stoop. "So, you caught your mother crying, did you?"

"Does this happen often?"

"Oh, I don't know, once or twice a week."

"*What?* Why didn't you tell me?"

"Why would I? Your mother's grief is her own to share." He leaned into the camera. "Or not to share. You, of all people, should be able to appreciate that."

I slumped and planted my chin on my palm.

"What have you got there? Are those pineapple buns?"

I picked one up to show him. "Yep. Stuffed with roasted pork."

"Hmm. Maybe I'll add that to the menu."

"You should. It's really good." I held up my cup. "Your yuen yeung is better."

"That's because it's made with love."

I smiled then focused on the gauze bandage wrapped around his head. "You sure you're okay?"

"Shaved a few hairs, sewed a few stitches, no reason to fret. Tell me about your ma. It sounds like the stress is piling up like soybeans in a combine."

"It is. I just didn't expect it to trigger grief for Rose."

"That's not how it works. A mother's grief isn't something that goes away. It's always there, like her love and worry for you."

I stared across the street, imagining Ma still curled under the covers. "What should I do?"

Baba raised one of his bushy brows. "What *can* you do?"

"Find out why Ma's agreement father is trying to oust her from the company and get him to back off."

"Be careful with that."

"Because it might backfire on Ma?"

He shrugged. "Some bulls don't like to lock horns."

"Which kind of bull is Derrick Lau?"

"Your grandfather's seed partner?"

"What's a seed partner?"

"Exactly how it sounds. He contributed the funds to grow HKIF. Aside from Shaozu, Derrick owns the biggest percentage of the company. He's not a bull, he's a hog with tusks. Be careful he doesn't gore you in the mud."

The kitchen door opened behind him, and DeAndre popped into view. "Sony order came in. It's a big one."

Baba looked back at me. "I've got to go. Take care of your mama, and watch out for yourself."

The call ended and our chat history returned, a poor substitute for hugs. I put down my phone and nibbled at the bolo bao.

What was Raymond Ng hiding? And who was that man on his roof? I drank the rest of my coffee milk tea and frowned. Where had I seen the intruder's scorpion tattoo before?

"Holy shit."

I picked up my phone and sent a WeChat message to Lee Chang: *Hey, Uncle. How's Shanghai?*

If my hunch was right, my father's head cook had the answers.

Lee: *On vacation. Don't bother me.*

Me: *Love you too.*

Lee: *Ha! What you want?*

Me: *Where did you get that scorpion tattoo?*

When he didn't respond, I added, *The one on your shoulder.*

Still, no response.

*Me: I saw the same design last night.*

Lee: *Where?*

Me: *At the home of my grandfather's business partner.*

Lee: *No. Where on the body?*

Me: *On the man's shoulder.*

Lee: *Then?*

Me: *He threw me off a roof.*

No response.

The typing sign appeared, stopped, and appeared again.

Lee: *Stupid girl. Stay out of trouble!*

I re-read our exchange and searched for clues in his cantankerous comments. I found more in the pauses in between. Uncle had ignored my question about the tattoo and only responded when I had mentioned seeing it the previous night. He hadn't asked the name of Gung-Gung's business partner or expressed any surprise that the intruder had thrown me off the roof. All that had mattered to him was the location of the tattoo, my stupidity, and warning me to stay out of trouble.

I crumpled the empty pastry bag and stuffed it in my cup.

Lee Chang had secrets.

# Chapter Twenty-Seven

I was brushing my hair when Daniel messaged me the name of a restaurant in Repulse Bay. He wanted to meet out front and stroll around the bayside community before lunch. I had a better idea.

Me: *Are you still at your uncle's place?*

Daniel: *I am.*

Me: *Why don't I meet you there.*

He sent me a thumbs up emoji and the address. *See you soon!*

Sure enough, it was right on the way.

I opened the closet to retrieve the boots Ma had bought for me and discovered a tissue-wrapped surprise: a black shoulder-strap hand-bag. No clunky backpack today. I dangled the rectangular purse just below the sash of the breezy rayon jumper—a perfect match for white peonies on black. With the open Mandarin collar and three-quarter cuffed sleeves, I looked very chic, indeed. Lucky for me, the sleeves covered most of the scratches and the gash, held closed by butterfly tape. Unless we went swimming, no one would see the purple bruise on my hip.

I stuffed a pair of lightweight socks in the boots to put on at the front door and went in search of Ma, who I found sitting at the patio table with Gung-Gung and Po-Po. Exhaustion had relaxed the tension in her face. The puffiness around her eyes from last night's catharsis had smoothed the wrinkles. The effect made her appear younger and calmer than I had expected.

"Thank you for the handbag."

Her gaze held so much love I almost cried.

Po-Po closed her magazine and nudged Gung-Gung in the arm.

"Look at Lei Lei. So pretty. Say something nice."

Gung-Gung nodded with approval, noticed the Sì Xiàng bangle on my wrist, and nodded again. "Are you meeting with Daniel?"

"As a matter of fact."

"Well, it's nice to see you dressed like a girl."

I snorted back a laugh. Po-Po reprimanded him in Cantonese. Ma pressed her lips and tried not to smile.

"Do you need me back at a particular time?"

She shook her head. "We'll be fine. Enjoy yourself."

Her sad eyes dampened her cheery words. I would have stayed to keep her company if I wasn't so eager to snoop around Derrick Lau's house.

"Go," Po-Po said, shooing me with her magazine, then added something in Cantonese that sounded like "Girls don't keep boys waiting."

*Oh, good lord.*

I hurried out of the house before I was tempted to share my thoughts about patriarchal attitudes. When I reached the front door, I stuffed my feet into my luxurious new boots, and sighed. With the sturdy low heels and ankle-fitting buckles, I could have run the five miles to Repulse Bay—if I was willing to sweat, which I was most definitely not.

Mr. Tam greeted me from the car and opened the rear door. "Good morning, Miss Wong. You look very pretty."

"Thanks, Mr. Tam. I'm meeting Daniel for lunch."

"He's a nice young man."

I smiled and hopped in the back seat. I could grow accustomed to nice.

"Should I take you to the address you texted?"

"Yes, please. How's Jing?"

"In school, I hope."

"Well, let me know if she gets into any more trouble."

"This is not your problem. I'm sorry I bothered you."

"Don't be silly. I like her independence. I just don't want to see her swept into danger."

"Me neither."

"Then if either of us hear from her, we'll contact the other. Deal?"

"Deal."

We drove down the winding road and cut across the mid level of the mountain, past high-rise apartment blocks, international schools, and athletic clubs for tennis and cricket built against the rock or cantilevered off of the edge. Every now and again, I'd glimpse the harbor and Kowloon skyline through the trees. Once we traveled through the tunnel to the south side of the island, a small bay appeared.

"See the beach?" Mr. Tam asked, and turned up a street lined with cement retaining walls before I could look. Near the top, he drove down a steep driveway to the base of six skyscrapers, clustered so closely I could hardly see between them.

"These are apartments?"

He chuckled at my skepticism and drove to the last building around the curve. "Want me to wait and give you a ride to the beach?"

"No thanks. We'll find our own way." It wouldn't be the worst thing if we were stuck at Derrick Lau's apartment.

I messaged Daniel. *I'm here.*

Daniel: *Excellent! Last building, nineteenth floor, apartment B.*

I caught my reflection in the polished elevator doors and smoothed the silky fabric of my dress-length jumper. Good thing I had on a sturdy pair of boots to balance this sudden burst of femininity. I wouldn't want Daniel to think I had changed my ways for him. I patted the handbag, dangling at my hip, and smiled. At least, not entirely.

He waved to me from the doorway on the left, one of only two apartments on the floor. "You found it." He kissed me on the cheek. "Love the dress."

"Thanks."

"My uncle went to the store. Do you want to hang here for a bit or head on out?"

"Here, definitely."

The sleek modern living room opened to a sheltered glass-railing balcony furnished with a long white dining table and matching lounge chairs on the side. Beyond that, blue sky and an aquamarine sea.

Daniel gestured from the room to the view. "What do you think?"

"Stunning. And surprisingly stylish." Glass accordion doors had been stacked against the walls to enhance the indoor-outdoor feel with a formal dining area in the back on the way to the kitchen. "Looks more like a bachelor pad than a retiree's home."

Daniel chuckled. "Uncle Derrick is a young seventy-eight."

The ocean breeze cooled the room and played with my hair as I followed Daniel onto the balcony. Lush green hills swooped down to a populated beach and a small tantalizing bay.

"Is that where we're having lunch?"

"It is. I'll drive us down on the motor scooter. Unless Mr. Tam is waiting outside."

"Nope. We have lots of time."

"Want to see the rest of the apartment?"

"Please."

The private wing had a guest bedroom with a hillside view and a primary bedroom and home office facing the bay. Although Mr. Lau's bedroom had the same modern, masculine vibe, the en suite bath showed signs of a woman.

"Does Melanie live here too?"

"At the moment. How do you know about her?"

"I met her at the Ritz the other night."

Daniel nodded. "Your grandfather's banquet. I heard about that."

I bent to examine an intricately carved lavender and green jadeite landscape. "The detail is exquisite."

"Uncle is a serious collector. You should see his emerald jade carving of Pine Tree Mountain."

"Where does he keep that?"

"In his office."

I smiled. "I'd love to see it."

# Chapter Twenty-Eight

Unlike the opulent bedroom, Derrick Lau's office favored clean lines and minimal clutter. Everything in it complimented or drew the eye to the view.

I ran my hand along the low white cabinet that led to his streamlined desk. "Does he still work?"

"A little. He sits on a few boards. Honestly, I don't know what keeps him so busy. Probably managing all his money."

A sky-blue swan chair faced the view. A matching leather chair on the window side of the desk faced the door. The rest of the floor-to-ceiling glass louver windows offered an unobstructed view of land, water, and sky. All were opened to admit the refreshing breeze.

"This is impressive."

"Isn't it? The southern exposure keeps out the sun. His office is always bright and cool."

A leather couch sat against the back wall with a coffee table in front that swept up like a wave. Across it and to the side, an armchair, upholstered in oceanic shades, was swiveled partially toward the view. Another low white cabinet mirrored the first but with display shelves of treasures and a gorgeous seascape painting on the wall. Centered on the shiny surface sat the Pine Tree Mountain, carved in jade on a base of dark polished wood.

"This is beautiful."

"And valuable. This carving could have paid for my car."

I laughed.

"Would you like something to drink? I have iced tea. Or we could pretend it's the weekend, and I could make my famous matcha gin fizz. It begins with a tart, freshly made lemonade, blended at high speed with whole lemons. I barely use an ounce, but fresh lemons makes all the difference."

"It sounds delicious. But time consuming. Are you sure you don't mind?"

"Not at all." He led me out of the office and back to the living area of the apartment.

"Mind if I use the restroom?"

"Make yourself comfortable. I'll meet you on the deck."

As Daniel disappeared into the kitchen, I returned to Mr. Lau's office.

The near cabinet held office supplies, resource books, and a file drawer loaded with household records and receipts. His desk had a laptop and a white jade carving of a mermaid swimming in the surf. I hurried to the other far side of the room and pulled open the first drawer, and the second, third, and fourth. Each one was heavy with files.

I listened for kitchen noises. No blender yet. I still had a little time.

From what I could tell, Derrick Lau's main business had been commercial real estate development, specifically resort properties in Hong Kong, Macau, Lantau Island, and the New Territories. I bypassed the folders from previous decades and shut the first three drawers.

The fourth drawer had folders ranging from 2016 to 2019. Since Derrick was semi-retired, these were lighter with only monthly reports and board meeting notes. A quick perusal showed hard times with a dramatic loss of revenue between 2017 and 2018. This year's reports showed a company hanging on by its teeth.

The rest of the files in the fourth drawer were devoted to personal investments and a few charities and businesses in which Mr. Lau served on the board. The folder for Hong Kong International Finance was the thickest.

The front door of the apartment opened and voices called in greeting. Daniel responded from the kitchen. I was running out of time.

The HKIF folder was segmented into three main territories: Hong Kong, Los Angeles, and London. While the first two only had summaries, the folder for the London office contained records of clients and investments.

The blender whirred and clunked as Daniel grated the lemons. A man's voice grew louder as the newcomers approached my side of the apartment. I shut the drawer with my knee and gazed at the painting on the wall.

"Lily, what are you doing in here?"

I turned around as if startled from my reverie. "Sorry, Mr. Lau. Daniel brought me in to admire your jade, but I wanted to return to examine this seascape more closely."

"Ah, yes. I bought it for one of our hotels then kept it for myself. It's perfect for this room. Don't you agree?"

"I do. You have impeccable taste."

He tipped his head in acknowledgment then chuckled. "I considered interior design when I was younger, but I was already making too much money. It seemed ridiculous to go back to school."

"I can appreciate that. I dropped out after the first year."

"What do you do now?"

"I help small businesses like my father's restaurant with their branding and social media."

"Yes, I heard about that."

"My work?"

"No. Your father's fascination with Hong Kong cuisine."

His emphasis on fascination made Baba sound like a fan boy impersonating a chef. What did he know about Baba's skill or the love and devotion to family that inspired him? A man as vain and self-centered as Derrick Lau probably didn't have the emotional bandwidth to fathom Baba's respect for Hong Kong culture and all that he did to make it part of my daily life. A man like him would never have given up his family name. No matter how much money Derrick Lau had made or how youthful his looks, he would never measure up to Vern Knudsen.

Before I could defend my father's honor, the blender stopped.

Mr. Lau gestured toward the door. "I believe my nephew has almost completed your cocktail. Perhaps, you should join him on the balcony and enjoy the view of an actual bay."

I returned his smirk with my own. "You're right. I always prefer seeing things as they really are."

# Chapter Twenty-Nine

I hugged Daniel's waist and breathed in the alluring scent of his back as he drove the Honda scooter to the beach. Sly old men and business intrigue would have to wait. The rest of the morning was for Daniel and me.

I leaned into his body, chest to back, thigh to thigh, and rested a kiss against his shoulder. The breeze fluttered the fabric of my clothes against my skin like a lover's caress. Or how I imagined a lover's caress might feel. My one and only experience had been so many years ago.

I retrieved my kiss from Daniel's shoulder and shook away the memories of Pete. My college sweetheart had introduced me to love while, elsewhere in Los Angeles, a monster had brutalized my sister. Love and death were forever intertwined. I couldn't stop wondering if her screams had overlapped my moans or if she had expelled her final breath as I exhaled my first release.

I sat up straight as Daniel zipped around the narrow road. I could balance myself just fine without clinging to his back like a koala. I was a ninja, after all. I could even manage without holding onto his hips or pressing my legs against his thighs.

"Are those hotels?" I asked, trying and failing to divert my attention from the feel of Daniel's body and memories of Rose.

"Apartment blocks," he said, and curved under the overpass toward the beach.

We paused at a lookout point to admire the hills, buildings, palm trees, and sand, then dropped into an alley with double-decker buses and a low-rise banquet complex that blocked the view. When the alley opened, Daniel zipped into a beachside lot and parked.

I hopped off the scooter as his feet hit the ground, too anxious to wait for the engine to cut. I needed space around me to think. My skin felt hot and damp. The silky fabric of my jumper clung. I billowed it away from my stomach and thighs. Why hadn't I worn a T-shirt and shorts? This stylish outfit carried expectations of romance I felt ill equipped to fulfill.

"Are you okay?" he asked.

"Yep. Just waiting for you."

He stopped beside me, a couple feet away, as if he knew I needed space. "Want to walk up the strand?"

"Yeah, that would be great."

I slowed my breath and timed it to my gait: four steps to breathe in, four steps to breathe out. The effect was instantaneous. My mind settled and my emotions calmed. By the time we reached The Pulse, a three-story dining and shopping complex that ran along the strand, my outlook had markedly improved.

He pointed to the shops. "Do you want to browse before lunch?"

"Can we stay outside a little longer? I miss the fresh air and space."

Daniel chuckled. "Not like sprawling Los Angeles, is it?"

"More like an elevator. My neck's sore from looking up at all the buildings."

I let my hand swing farther from my hip and smiled when he caught it with his own. We strolled like this for a while, freedom and intimacy occupying the same space.

Daniel squeezed my hand. "Want to visit Gun Yam?"

It took me a moment to recognize the Cantonese word for Quan Yin, Goddess of Mercy and Compassion. When I saw the thirty-foot statue in the front of the temple across from Tin Hau, Goddess of the Sea, I knew for sure.

The artist had sculpted a sweeping sand-colored robe with gold Han characters and traditional brocade over under-layers of sea green and aqua blue. This Quan Yin, like mine at home, held a dharma scroll in her left hand with her right held aloft in the Shuni mudra for patience. The Goddess helped me understand and empathize with the women and children I sought to protect and balanced the violence I was sometimes called to do. She reminded me that my assistance was not about me, it was about *them*.

I fondled my phurba dagger pendant as I thought about this. The Sì Xiàng bracelet dangled on my wrist.

"For an unconventional woman, you seem to appreciate Chinese traditions."

"And for a conventional man, you seem to not mind when I don't."

Daniel laughed. "That's what makes you so interesting. I never know what to expect."

"Ha. You say that now."

"You think it will change?"

I shrugged. "People like predictability. They like to count on things remaining the same."

"And you don't?"

I thought of Rose. I had counted on her to be in my life forever. We were supposed to share everything—our dreams, our goals, console each other in heartbreak. We were supposed to celebrate achievements, marriage, children, graduations…old age. She was my little sister. By the natural order of things, she should have outlived us all. The burden of grief should have fallen to her after each of us had lived a long and happy life. Once again, I had flipped harmless discourse into treacherous waters.

*Breathe and dive, breathe and dive. The waves will ebb, and you can swim to shore.*

Sound advice from Sensei, but little use for me now as Daniel waited expectantly for my reply.

"I used to count on things. Until my sister died."

"I heard about that. I'm so sorry."

"It was a long time ago, but in some ways, it feels like yesterday." I rubbed my finger over the crown of the silver dagger phurba. "Do you know what happened to her?"

He nodded.

130

"It happened the same night that I, uh…" I let go of my necklace and shook out my arms. "I can't believe I'm telling you this."

"You don't have to."

"Yeah, well…I kind of do. If we want to move forward, you need to know some of my past. I was…with someone when Rose texted me that night. I didn't reply."

"You couldn't have known."

"True. But still. I didn't even open her message until my father showed up at my dorm the next morning. Someone had found her in an alley. Baba got the news at his restaurant. He stopped by UCLA to bring me home to Ma. Can you imagine? My mother was all alone when she learned her daughter had been murdered." I clasped my hands and pressed my knuckles into my forehead until it hurt. "Rose reached out to me for help, and I let her die."

Daniel pulled my hands from my face, kissed them gently, and led me to a quiet spot on the pier. We were facing up the coast, away from Repulse Beach, toward the red longevity bridge in front of the temple's pavilion. Children played in the sand beneath its arch while tourists snapped pictures of the temple's colorful statues on the pavilion's plaza—lighthearted scenery for my heavily weighted thoughts.

"You'd have never gotten to her in time," he said.

"Maybe. But maybe I could have talked her out of whatever she had been going to do. I could have told her how to be safe. She was only fifteen. This wouldn't have happened if I'd been looking out for her."

"You went to college."

"I didn't need to live in the dorm. And I sure as heck didn't need to cut Rose out of my new exciting life. I was too busy with freshman events, competing on the Wushu team, and…falling in love."

"Was that who you were with?"

I shrugged. "It was my first time."

"Oh."

"It didn't seem right to try again."

"You mean…"

"Uh-huh."

"Okay…I get it."

"Do you? Because you're the only person I've ever told."

He leaned over and kissed me on the shoulder. "I understand. Thank you for trusting me."

I offered a weak smile and looked away. I felt more naked than if I'd stripped off my clothes. "Want to go in the water?"

"What?"

I pointed to the ceramic walkway that sloped gradually from the base of the longevity bridge into the cove. "As long as we don't fall, we'll be fine."

"You're crazy."

"Come on. I could use some fun."

He chased me up the pier, across the temple plaza, and down to the sand. He slipped off his beach loafers and laughed. "You see? This is exactly what I mean."

I stuffed my socks into my boots. "What?"

"The jungle bar, the dog, the fancy dress…"

I held out a pant leg. "This is a jumper."

"Doesn't matter. The point is, I never know what you're going to say or do. And I absolutely adore it."

"I'll remind you of that if we slip. Come on."

After a couple risky moments, we stood ankle deep at the end of the walkway, surrounded by water.

"No waves out here," I said, thinking back to Sensei's wisdom about breathing and diving until the turbulence had passed. I turned into Daniel's arms. "I think you chased them all away."

He smiled, holding me chastely to avoid an unseemly public display of affection. I moved closer, eyes locked on his, daring him to break from cultural restraints.

"Always a surprise." He gazed into my eyes then pulled me into a kiss.

As water lapped at our ankles and happy tourists laughed on the pier, I gave myself to Daniel with every cell of my being. Freedom *and* intimacy. I wanted more of this. I wanted so much more of him.

# Chapter Thirty

After our epic kiss, Daniel and I strolled back along the shore, kicked at the water and squished wet sand between our toes. The noon-day sun baked our heads, but the breeze and water kept us cool.

"We should come back for a swim." I imagined him shirtless and blushed.

Daniel smiled. "You in a bikini? That would be fun. Unfortunately, I have a meeting this afternoon."

"I thought your week had freed up."

"So did I. But we still have time for lunch…and possibly dinner? What do you say? Can I steal you away from your family twice in one day?"

"Ooh, I don't know. I have other suitors to consider."

He splashed water on my legs. "None so charming as me. Besides, I know exactly what you want."

Heat flushed up my neck.

"Australian big eye tuna."

"Excuse me?"

"For lunch. The best poke tostada you'll ever eat."

Although not exactly what I had in mind, I had to admit Daniel was right. The big eye tuna, charred beef ribs, and jerked coconut corn were out of this world. We stuffed our faces, people-watched from the counter, and sipped ginger beer spiked with grated ginger. The best part of the day was the trip home to The Peak on the back of Daniel's motor scooter. I hugged him close and molded my body to his as every nerve hummed in vibration with the bike. It was a sad moment when we turned onto my grandparents' street, sadder still when Daniel parked.

Once off the bike, he scooped me into his arms. "Did you have a good time?"

"I did."

"Are we on for dinner?"

"If my family hasn't made plans."

"Okay, let me know. In the meantime, I'll find somewhere special."

"Ever the optimist."

"Is there any other way to be?"

I leaned in for another passionate kiss and received a teasing peck on my nose. When I opened my mouth to complain, he stepped back and grinned. "Dinner. Tonight."

He strapped on his helmet and fired up the motor scooter, confident and amused by his ploy to lure me closer by staying just out of reach. I'd tried the same tactic in a training session with Sensei and had landed on my back and out of breath. If Daniel wasn't careful, the same might happen to him.

*It's not a fight: It's a date.*

Was there a difference?

I groaned and headed down the path to my grandparents' townhome, certain of only one thing—everything about dating baffled me. I opened the door to my mother's furious voice.

"Of course I like Daniel," Ma shouted from the kitchen. "But you're using her to gain points with Derrick."

"What's wrong with that? Don't you want him on your side? The board convenes in three days. Every vote counts."

"You think I don't know that?"

"Then why are you arguing with me?"

"Because you're trying to control her the way you controlled me."

"Failed to control. If I had succeeded, you would have married better."

"You pig-headed man. Vern gave them your name. What more do you want?"

"A son!"

I hurried to the kitchen in time to watch my mother reel from the blow. Even Gung-Gung looked surprised by what he had said.

Ma steeled her spine and lowered her voice. "Well…that's not my fault, is it? Last I checked the father's chromosome decides."

"Don't be impudent. You and I had an agreement, and you broke it."

"I fell in love."

"You betrayed my trust."

"Over an unreasonable request."

"I disagree. I paid for your education, bought you a house, and gave you a job."

"A house that's still in your name and a job with no security."

"This is the real world. If you want those things, you have to get them yourself."

They glared at each other so intently that neither of them noticed me.

When Ma spoke again, her voice quaked with emotion. "I followed in your footsteps to make you proud. I thought if I did a good enough job, you would consider me your successor. Clearly, my only value to you was to attract a husband who could do the work *you* educated *me* to do."

I held my breath. Would Gung-Gung's hard exterior crumble? Would he finally tell his only daughter how cherished and important she was?

He cleared his throat as if choking back emotions of his own. Then he took a breath and nodded. "Everyone has filial responsibility. It is my greatest sorrow that you have neglected yours."

Ma turned away then stopped when saw me standing in the doorway. "You're here." Her voice quaked like a child, words loaded with relief and gratitude.

I focused my qì and transmitted the force of my strength into her.

"Yes. I'm here."

Her tension eased. The cords in her neck relaxed. She started to speak, but Gung-Gung beat her to it. "How was your date with Daniel?"

"Great," I said, holding Ma's gaze. "How are things here?"

Gung-Gung answered on her behalf. "Good. Why wouldn't they be?"

Ma closed her eyes and gave her head an almost imperceptible shake. Then she opened her eyes and shrugged. "Do you want tea?"

I smiled. "Sure."

"Where did you go with Daniel?" Gung-Gung asked.

I leaned on the counter and picked at the grapes. "To his uncle's apartment then down to Repulse Bay."

"Oh. That is a very good date."

Ma huffed her displeasure.

"You don't agree, Shun Lei?"

"I'm sure they had a lovely time."

"Do we have any plans tonight?" I asked. "Daniel asked me out to dinner."

Ma nodded. "We're meeting the family for banquet."

"Don't be silly," Gung-Gung said. "You'll see them this weekend. Go out with Daniel. Have fun."

Ma paused, teacups in hand. "Do you really like this man? And not just because we've pressured you into dating him?"

I could still taste Daniel's kiss on my lips. "I do."

"Okay, then. If it's okay with your grandfather to miss the banquet, it's okay with me."

I thought about the London folder in Derrick Lau's office. I wanted to talk about it with Ma, but now wasn't the time. She had Gung-Gung and the entire Wong family to deal with. The London folder could wait.

My purse buzzed against my hip.

Gung-Gung wandered into the family room and turned on the news. Ma scooped tea leaves into a pot. My phone vibrated a second time, paused, then vibrated a third. When I took it out, I saw the notifications. I opened WhatsApp first, expecting to find a message from Daniel and found two images and a message from Jing.

The first image was a screen shot of a news headline: *Pro-democracy Hong Kong lawmaker Roy Kwong hospitalized after attack by three men in Tin Shui Wai car park.* The photo showed a battered man and his girlfriend walking away from reporters. The sub-title said he had been ambushed by three people as he walked to his car.

The second image was a graphic message in a blend of transliterated Cantonese, traditional Chinese characters, and accurately and inaccurately spelled English. There was even a number seven used in place of the letter T for some mystifying reason. Even if I managed to decipher the meaning, it would undoubtedly be layered in protest code.

Me: *Saw the graphic. What does it mean?*

Jing: *We're meeting in front of Central HQ at 3:30. Can you come?*

Me: *Where's that?*

Jing sent a link to the Central Government Complex for HKSAR, located in the Central Business District, a mile from Gung-Gung's offices.

"Is everything okay?" Ma asked, teapot suspended over my cup.

I sent a thumbs up to Jing and messaged Mr. Tam for a ride. "Yep. All good."

Gung-Gung turned up the television in the family room and grumbled about the news.

I sipped my tea. "How about you?"

"Better."

I clasped her hand. "I came on this trip to support you, not to runaway with Daniel. Are you sure you don't want me to attend the banquet?"

She patted my hand and let it go. "No, darling. Follow your heart. No matter what your grandfather believes, marrying your father was the best decision I ever made."

# Chapter Thirty-One

After informing Mr. Tam about his daughter, we drove in silence down the mountain into the traffic-jammed Central District.

"Is traffic always this heavy?"

"Not usually this bad. The demonstrations clog the streets. Back in 2014, the Umbrella Movement occupied this whole area and set up tents on that ramp next to us."

"Isn't that when the first Lennon Wall appeared?"

"It is, on the walkways and wall of the Central Government Complex. The post-it notes went up again in July. The police took them down, but they went up again. Now we have walls all over in MTR stations and plazas. More notes appear every day."

Unlike the original tribute to John Lennon in Prague, the Hong Kong Lennon Walls were covered in notes rather than graffiti and art.

Mr. Tam squeezed between cars and advanced another ten feet.

"How far is the complex?"

"Around the bend, just past the second pedestrian overpass."

I strapped on my backpack and opened the door. "I'll run it from here."

He leaned out the window, face etched with worry. "Find my daughter, please."

"I will."

I ran between the cars to the sidewalk and sprinted the length of two football fields to the bend in the road. The afternoon sun baked the concrete like a pizza oven. Good thing I had changed into running shoes and shorts.

Protesters descended from the elevated walkway onto a corner plaza packed with hundreds of protesters, pumping signs and shouting at drivers as they crept along the eight-lane thoroughfare. No one had blocked the streets. The traffic congestion was caused by curious drivers who had slowed to watch the spectacle, looky-loo gridlock, the kind that happened in Los Angeles every day.

More protesters lined the staircase along the curving Lennon Wall. They added their own notes between the colorful bits of paper while, below the staircase, flyers and protest art blanketed the wall and continued around the bend.

I messaged Jing. *I'm at the wall. Where are you?*

When she didn't reply, I entered the plaza and wove through the crowd. I walked over protest art, taped to the concrete like concert flyers a dozen at a time. Each collection featured a different image and slogan. All were drawn in caricature with bold markers. One set of flyers had a similar style to the dictator art I had seen Jing copying in the retro café.

I looked around for her then called her number. It went to voicemail.

"Hey Jing, it's Lily. I'm here. Where are you? Call me back."

I ran up the curving staircase to the first of three elevated walkways where protesters dangled banners over the edge and chanted slogans. Almost all of the women had long black hair like Jing.

My phone vibrated with a message from Mr. Tam: *Did you find her?*

Me: *Not yet. She's not answering my messages.*

Mr. Tam. *Or mine.*

Me: *Keep trying.*

I crossed the pedestrian bridge to a third walkway and checked every woman close to Jing's height and size. When I heard the police sirens, I sprinted back to the bridge and shoved my way to the railing.

Squad cars swarmed in from all directions, cleared cars from their path with fearsome sirens and bullhorn commands. They parked in the street, flooded from their cars, and assembled in front of the crowd in full riot gear and shields.

Men in black shirts worked their way to the front of the protesters and formed a line of defense.

Officers shouted commands in Cantonese, issued instructions, and threatened arrest as the activists chanted, "There are no rioters, only a tyrannical regime!"

The officers shifted in agitation then pressed forward, shoving those who wouldn't move. When faced with further resistance, they beat them with batons.

The chanting fell apart as citizens scrambled to safety or shouted their defiance. Some fought against law enforcement and were thrown to the ground. The second line of police raised tear gas guns and fired into the crowd. Smoke ballooned up from the sidewalk. People cried and scrambled away. Those with gas masks and gloves rushed in to cover the spreading gas with traffic cones or scooped up the grenades and threw them back at the police.

I searched the crowd for Jing. When I saw a girl who might have been her, I ran for the stairs while the crowd chanted, "Haak ging," black police.

When I reached the plaza, I darted around the Lennon Wall just in time to see an officer rip the sign out of Jing's hand and wrench her arm behind her back.

I had tussled with the cops on numerous occasions back in Los Angeles, but this was Hong Kong. If I interfered with an arrest, not only could I be thrown in jail, I might cause an international incident. That said, I could see what others could not. The officer had broken from his squad to dispatch a bunch of teenagers. When they had rushed in to object, they isolated him further and created a wall between him and his comrades. The officer was panicking. If I didn't find a way to deescalate the situation, things could get out of control.

I held out my phone and pointed it at the cop. "I'm an American reporter from Los Angeles. You're on live video. Why are you arresting this girl? Is the Hong Kong police targeting children now?"

The officer shouted in Cantonese for me to turn off my phone. The teenagers repeated my statement and questions in Cantonese to make sure he understood.

"She's a child," I shouted. "What has she done? Where are her weapons? How could she possibly be a threat to the government or police?"

The teenagers repeated my questions in Cantonese and turned the last one into a chant. Protesters picked it up. Soon, dozens of voices were demanding to know how Jing could possibly be a threat to the government or police.

The officer released Jing and shoved her toward me, backed into the street, and made his escape between the cars.

"Are you okay?"

Jing wrapped her arms around me as the teenagers patted her on the back and voiced encouragements. They raised their fists and shouted with the crowd, "Gayau," add oil.

I led her down the sidewalk, away from the crowd. "Keep walking. I'll call your dad."

"He's here?"

"Check your messages. We've been trying to reach you."

Mr. Tam picked up on the first ring. "Did you find her?"

"I did. We're walking along the government complex."

"That's Tim Mei Avenue. Do you see the traffic circle?"

"Not yet."

"Keep walking. When you see it, go into the street and wait for me on the concrete island. I'm coming now."

# Chapter Thirty-Two

As soon as I shut the car door, Mr. Tam turned to his daughter. "Are you okay?"

"I'm fine."

He caught my eye in the rearview mirror. "What happened?"

I leaned forward in my seat. "You want to tell him, or should I?"

Mr. Tam scolded Jing in Cantonese and demanded that she tell him right away. I let them work it out on their own and checked my messages. Daniel had left a series of them spaced over the last hour and a half.

*I found a restaurant. Two Michelin stars!*

*We have reservations for 7:30pm.* (link to Ta Vie restaurant) *Can you meet me there?*

*PS: I lucked out on the prime time res. They're really popular, even on a Tuesday night.*

*Did you talk to your family? Can you make it?*

Four messages spaced over ten minutes? Daniel was antsy for a reply.

I started to type then messaged Ma instead: *Are you sure about tonight? I don't have to see Daniel.*

She answered quickly. *I'm sure.*

Me: *Are you still fighting with Gung-Gung?*

Ma: *We weren't fighting.*

Me: *If you say so.*

Ma: *He's watching the news.*

Me: *Still?*

Ma: *There's a riot at Central Government. Huge incident. You're not anywhere near there, are you?*

Me: *Nope. All quiet near me.*

Mr. Tam turned left and drove along a familiar stretch that ran parallel to the harbor. The skyscraper with Gung-Gung's offices loomed ahead reminding me of my primary purpose.

Me: *Have you heard anything about the vote?*

Ma: *Not yet. But I spoke with your father. He fell down and cut his head!*

I feigned ignorance so I wouldn't have to explain why I had known about the accident and hadn't told her.

Me: *Is he okay?*

Ma: *Yes. He was just dehydrated. They stitched him up and sent him home. First time he's shut down the restaurant since Rose.*

Me: *I'll give him a call. You sure you're okay?*

Ma: *I'm fine. Have fun.*

Fun didn't seem likely with Mr. Tam and his daughter bickering in the front seat.

I stared at the horizon and considered what I could do to save my mother's job. I'd spent time around Raymond Ng, Derrick Lau, and my grandfather, but not Cecil Chu and Kenneth Hong. Of the two, London Director Chu seemed like an easier bet on short notice. I could return to HKIF tomorrow in a more attractive outfit to wheedle information out of the newly divorced CEO, Kenneth Hong.

I called the offices.

"Hong Kong International Finance, how may I help you?"

"Hi, Katie, it's Lily."

"Oh, hello Lily. How are you?"

"Fine, thanks. Is Cecil Chu still around?"

"Mr. Chu? No. He went back to his hotel an hour ago. Is there anyone else who can help you?"

"That's okay. He recommended a hotel for my friend and I wanted to double check the name—99 Bonham."

"That's right. He always stays there."

"Thanks. You've been very helpful."

I hung up and leaned forward to speak with Mr. Tam. "Do you know where 99 Bonham is?"

"The hotel?"

"Uh-huh. I'm meeting a friend at a shop nearby."

"It's very close. How long will you be?"

"There's no need to wait. Take Jing home. I'll be fine."

"Are you sure?"

"Absolutely."

I leaned back in my seat and sighed. This day had turned out to be surprisingly eventful. In fact, this entire trip had been more exciting than expected.

I opened my messages with Daniel and typed a quick reply: *7:30 is fine. See you there.*

I had two and a half hours to question Cecil Chu, catch a ride-share to my grandparents' place, shower, change, and return to Central to meet Daniel at Ta Vie.

# Chapter Thirty-Three

Mr. Tam dropped me on a crowded, narrow street in historic Sheung Wan. If not for the 99 Bonham emblazoned above the glass entrance, I never would have recognized the slender high-rise building as a four-star hotel, not with the decrepit buildings pressed against it with mere inches of space in between. The bookending neighbors sold tea and electronics on the ground floor of apartments barely fifteen feet wide. The rest were an eclectic mix of sleek skyscrapers and ancient cement-stained tenements.

Red signs with gold characters extended into the one-way street on either side of the road, well above the height of delivery trucks. If I didn't find Cecil Chu, I'd grab a snack in a market or hunt for gifts in the local shops. Unusual treasures could be found in an H.K. pharmacy.

The hotel lobby was clean and sparse with black reflective walls and a frosted-glass reception counter.

A chic concierge greeted me in English from behind the counter. "Hello. Welcome to 99 Bonham. How may I help you?"

"A friend of mine is staying here. I'd like to call his room."

"What's the name?"

I was about to answer when the elevator opened to reveal Cecil Chu.

"Never mind. There he is."

I let my backpack slide off my shoulder and fumbled just long enough to let Mr. Chu go out the door. I had planned to invite him out for tea after supposedly dropping by the hotel to check it out for my friend. Now that he was on foot, I decided to follow and see where he went. That changed when I spotted the men.

Two of them shadowed Mr. Chu from the opposite side of the street. One was stocky. The other was lean. Both carried themselves like dangerous men. The stocky one turned before I had a chance to slow down. We recognized each other immediately. It was the intruder with the scorpion tattoo.

He tapped his friend, and the two of them stopped. Like dogs before a fight, none of us moved. We stared at each other across the street. Cars passed. Delivery trucks unloaded. Mr. Chu entered a ginseng shop farther down the road. The men didn't move. They glared at me between slow-moving vehicles and waited.

Were they warning me to abandon Mr. Chu and walk away? Or had he hired them to watch his back? As I pondered these questions, they headed my way.

Pedestrians flowed around me without a glance. If the men attacked, I doubted any of them would care. With two against one, I didn't want to take the chance.

I backed up the sidewalk as the men wove between the cars. Both wore loose unbuttoned shirts over tanks that could easily have hidden a gun—despite Hong Kong's strict firearm prohibitions—but a knife or pencil shank would be just as deadly. If they worked in tandem, I could easily be stabbed, especially in a public place where I had no justification for a preemptive attack.

First rule of defense: Don't be there.

I turned around and picked up my pace, catching their reflection in storefront windows as they did the same. Within seconds, we were all bolting up the sidewalk. Pedestrians parted as I ran, but not fast enough. In the path I had cleared, the men were gaining.

I turned down a busy side street where I could slip and dodge obstacles, hoping to lose the less agile men. As I swerved around dollies and hurdled over crates, delivery people closed in behind me to block the men's path. A woman swung her parasol, avoiding me but toppling a display of Tempo tissue in my wake. Chatting friends jumped away in surprise and tipped their purchases out of roller shopping baskets. A street sweeper shook his broom at me and knocked over a garbage can. All of this slowed my pursuers, but they still had me in sight.

I darted into an alley and sprinted as fast as I could to the stairway at the end. If I made it before they entered, I could disappear in the crowds. If not, they'd have a clear and straight shot at my back.

A throwing knife clanked off a wall in a puff of stucco and paint.

I charged up the steps, crashed into an old man, and saved him from falling.

"Sorry, Uncle. May I borrow this?"

I took the old man's cane and snapped up the end in a Suso Haneage strike into the jaw of the first pursuer—the man who had terrorized Ma Lik and thrown me off the roof. I struck him again with a thrust to the throat, not into the deadlier windpipe but the pocket beneath, then kicked him down the stairs.

"Get away from us," I shouted in Cantonese. "Leave the old man alone."

Pedestrians stopped to watch the brave young woman defend an elderly man and picked up the cry. "Leave them alone. Police. Police."

The men who had been chasing me ran away down the alley.

I turned back to the old man and offered his cane with two hands and a bow. "Dojeh sai, Uncle."

He stared at me in wonderment and smiled.

# Chapter Thirty-Four

Not wanting to box myself inside the narrow passage a second time, I took a different route to the ginseng shop where I'd last seen Mr. Chu. No sign of him or the men who had been following him, and no way to know if they had been there to protect or do him harm. All I knew was that they were somehow connected to two key players in my grandfather's business, Cecil Chu and Raymond Ng. Was someone also watching Ma?

I took out my phone and called.

"Hey, it's me. How's it going with Gung-Gung?"

"Same as before. We're about to leave. Shouldn't you be here getting dressed for your date with Daniel?"

"Oh, shit."

"What did you say?"

"Nothing."

I'd forgotten all about Daniel. I'd never make it to the restaurant in time if I went home to change.

"I'm, uh, shopping for a dress."

"Really? Well…I must say I'm surprised. Feel free to use my card. I believe you have the number."

"Thanks, but I got this." Did I? I was a hot sweaty mess with only the bare essentials in my backpack.

"Don't be stubborn, Lily. Nice clothes are expensive, and unless you hid a pair of heels in that luggage you insist on carrying about, you'll need a decent pair of shoes to match. Did you take the purse I bought for you?"

"Yep. In my luggage."

Ma sighed through the phone.

"Sorry, Ma. Thanks for the offer. I promise to find something nice."

"Good. Say hello to Daniel for me. I'll probably be asleep when you get home, so I'll see you in the morning."

I opened Google Maps and searched for clothing stores between my location and the restaurant where I was meeting Daniel and found seven bridal shops. If we'd been further along in our relationship, I might have taken it as a sign.

My snorts of laughter drew puzzled stares as I imagined Daniel gaping in panic as I waltzed into Ta Vie in full Disney princess bridal mode. I picked the most likely non-bridal boutique in my half-mile route and took off at a sprint.

I paused in the doorway of the shop and breathed in the cool air. I had forty minutes to calm down, choose an outfit, and make myself presentable. I could absolutely do this. I looked at the collection and blanched. Not a simple black dress in sight. What the hell was I supposed to buy in this stuffy designer shop?

A European sales clerk came to my rescue, draped in a chic calf-length tunic, the kind best suited for women over five foot ten with credit card limits that could buy a car.

"Welcome to Paragon. What are we shopping for today?"

I was definitely in the wrong boutique.

"A cocktail dress. But I don't think I'm going to find one here."

"Don't be silly. You have a perfect figure and a classic face. We will have no trouble at all assembling a spectacular outfit."

Thirty minutes—and dozens of dresses, skirts, blouses, and shoes—later the sales clerk's confidence had waned. "There's a dress here for you. I'm sure of it."

I picked a designer reject from the pile and held it against my chest. I'd need an extra seven inches of height to pull off the layers of black lace and the giant silver bow. But, it was seven fifteen. I was out of time.

"Do you have anything…I don't know…simpler? Short, fitted, no lace, no bows, no animal prints, no couture. Do you have anything like that?"

She looked at me like I was out of my mind.

I slid down the wall when she left, and struggled not to cry. It was only fabric and color. How could shopping be this hard?

*It's not just shopping, and you know it.*

I sat on my butt and pulled the discarded clothes into my arms and hugged them like a giant pillow. Tonight was supposed to be special—a romantic dinner with the man I…

*With the man you what?*

My chest tightened. No wonder I couldn't decide on a dress: I still hadn't decided about Daniel.

*He's caring, insightful, fun, and handsome. What's there to decide?*

I glared at my reflection. "A lot, okay? There's a lot to decide."

Like what to do about those soft lips and seductive eyes—and whether I could lose myself in them without remembering Pete or Rose. Seven years was a long time to hide from love and pain.

*Long enough?*

I dropped my gaze so I wouldn't have to meet my own eyes. My reflection was asking hard questions I didn't want to answer.

*Since when do you run from what's hard?*

After my morning with Daniel, I knew exactly where this evening might go. There was too much chemistry between us and yearning in my heart for us to go home alone. I needed to resolve my issues, sort through my feelings, and enter this encounter with a clarity. That was the only way I would survive the night unscathed.

*A date isn't a fight.*

I wasn't so sure. Sensei said every interaction was a relationship, including—especially—a fight. He described it as a shared reality we created with our adversary that was brief, yet profound. What could be more profound than making love?

That's what I'd felt with Pete before I heard the awful news about

Rose. Then I pushed him away, locked up my heart, and threw away my dreams. I gave up everything I had ever wanted to do with my life to hunt for Rose's murderer. I thought it would give me peace. Instead, it filled me with all-consuming purpose. My life was not my own. It belonged to those who couldn't fight for themselves. What would happen if I carved a piece of that life for me?

I breathed in courage and exhaled strength. Ninja fought from the shadows, but they didn't hide. The time had come for me to step back in the light and honor my own existence, for me and for Rose.

The store clerk knocked on the door frame and held up a dress. "How's this?"

I took in the wide, rounded neck and short capped sleeves, the fitted waist, and knee-length hem. "It's yellow."

"Is that a problem?"

"No. It's just…bright."

She hung it on the rack and took the rejects from my arms. "Try it on with these. It might surprise you." She plopped the thick-heeled sandals in my lap and left me alone. They were wildly stylish, obviously expensive, but surprisingly sturdy. I put them on and crawled to my feet.

My reflection smirked. *Maybe you should go to dinner like that.*

My neck flushed as I thought of Daniel seeing me in nothing but a sports bra, boy shorts briefs, and heels. I flushed even more when I realized the bra wouldn't work with the dress. I took it off and stared at the woman in the mirror until I grew comfortable with what I saw—hard planes, cut muscles, feminine curves, and forged steel. No matter what I wore to dinner, underneath it, I would still be me.

# Chapter Thirty-Five

Daniel waited at a table for two tucked along the wall, like an actor on a movie set. His white Mandarin shirt and silvery-gray jacket blended perfectly with the vertical striped upholstery and matching white and silver linen. The white marble pillars and ebony wood walls made his chiseled features pop. *I should have bought the black lace with the silver bow. At least then I would have blended into the scene. I stood out like a canary in a coal mine.*

Heads turned as I walked, gingerly in the new artsy heels, bolstered by Sensei's past advice. *Commit to the role, Lily-chan, and people will see what they expect to see.*

I straightened my spine and channeled Astrid from *Crazy Rich Asians*. The character had weathered all conditions with grace and elegance. She wouldn't have thought twice about entering a sedate Michelin-star restaurant in a bright yellow dress. Nor would she have faltered with a backpack dangling from her wrist. At least I had Ma's chic black handbag to dispel any vagabond notions.

Daniel rose when he saw me and drew appreciative gazes from the women. "You look stunning."

"Thanks. You don't look so bad yourself." I sat beside him on the sofa and slid my backpack under the table. "Sorry I'm late. I got caught up at the dress shop."

"If this is the outfit you bought, it was worth twice the wait."

I smiled and fanned my flushing neck.

"Would you like ice water?"

"And have them peg me as a tourist? I don't think so. I'll have a frozen daiquiri."

"Regular or coconut lychee?"

"How can you even ask?" Our foodie date was off to a great start.

Daniel nodded to the server and placed our drink orders as she filled our glasses with imported Japanese water.

"Remember the Gruyère-potato beignets at République?" I asked.

"Are you kidding? I dream of them and those fried chocolate croissants."

"And the V.I.P. spot in front of the kitchen? That was bold of you to make a reservation so far in advance."

Daniel shrugged. "When an opportunity presents…"

"Is that what I am, an opportunity?"

"A very special one. When your grandfather asked me to deliver his gift and your mother invited me to family dinner, I took it as a sign. That probably sounds silly to a California girl."

"Not at all. I'm a big believer in signs. Like the fact that you're here in Hong Kong during my first visit in seven years."

He leaned closer. "Are you sure it wasn't eight?"

I leaned closer still. "A luckiest of numbers?"

We stared into one another's eyes, not daring to break decorum with a kiss. The server returned with our daiquiris and released the spell.

"You keep plying me with fancy cocktails. You're not trying to get me drunk are you?"

"On a daiquiri?"

"You're wining and dining a woman who lives on tea and dim sum. Trust me, it wouldn't take much."

"Then I promise to guard your honor."

I studied Daniel's earnest expression. What would it feel like to have someone guarding *me*? "Are you trying to spoil me?"

"That's the idea."

Daniel wasn't kidding. Ta Vie served an eight-course tasting menu that fused French and Japanese cuisines. First up was a sweet corn puffed mousse with Aburi Botan ebi in shrimp broth jelly.

I examined the jellied crustaceans then ventured a taste. "Whoa. That was unexpected."

"I like the unexpected."

"Do you? Because you seem more like a planner."

"All the more reason to shake up my perfectly planned life."

I took another bite. "So, where does Daniel Kwok expect to be ten years from now?"

"Married, family, prestigious work...and gobs of money."

"Ah, the Hongkonger dream."

"Don't forget all those summers I spent with my Aunt. I've had American capitalism fed to me from birth."

"Do you see yourself here or there?"

"Either. Both. I don't limit my dreams."

A server removed our plates as the sommelier came to take our order.

Daniel leaned against my shoulders. "Would you prefer wine or sake?"

"You choose."

"How about an artisan Champagne?"

"Fancy."

"Only the best for the woman in the yellow dress."

I laughed. "Have we entered the rhyming stage of our relationship?"

He shrugged. "We passed the emoji stage. It seemed like a natural progression." He turned to the sommelier, "Laurent-Perrier Grand Siècle No. 24," then looked back at me. "How about you? Where do you see yourself in ten years?"

"Ten years? I hardly think a month ahead."

"Well, what did you want to be when you were a kid?"

"Hmm...it changed all the time, lawyer, reporter, action star, Wushu Olympian."

"They have Wushu in the Olympics?"

"Not yet, but kids dream about all sorts of things." *Except becom-*

*ing a modern-day ninja.*

"What about college?"

"I attended one year as a communications major. Believe it or not, I was quite engaging, a regular social butterfly."

"I knew your somber mystery was a ruse."

"Ha. I'm not that way anymore."

"Maybe you're not hanging around the right people."

Aleisha and Stan popped into my mind, along with all the desperate women, children, and teens. Although my employers were cheerful people and dear friends, our interactions revolved around heartache, danger, and crisis—poor ingredients for lighthearted fun.

The sommelier poured our champagne, and the server returned with a gorgeous pasta in Aonori seaweed sauce, topped with bright orange Bafun uni.

I sipped the champagne and eyed the sea urchin gonads with suspicion. I'd tried them before and wasn't a fan, but this creation was so beautiful, I had to give it another chance. I twirled a fork full of the creamy seaweed pasta, stabbed a hint of the uni, and popped it in my mouth.

"You like it?"

"It's incredible. I'm going to tell Baba about this." I took out my phone and snuck a quick shot of the pasta and the tasting menu description.

Daniel grinned. "Did you know sea urchin contains a chemical neurotransmitter ingredient that causes euphoria?"

"Is this part of your seduction scheme, calling ahead to request aphrodisiac-laced dishes?"

He swirled a bite of his own. "A happy coincidence."

I mopped the last trace of sauce with a crusty hunk of bread then smiled, sheepishly. "I haven't eaten since I last saw you."

"At lunch? That was six hours ago. No wonder you're always hungry, you don't make time to eat."

He had a point.

"Have you thought about going back?" Daniel asked.

"Where?"

"College."

"Are you conspiring with my mother?"

"No, but there were a lot of older students at USC."

"You went to USC? How am I even sitting at a table with you?"

"Because I hid my dirty secret until you were hooked."

"Ha. Typical Trojan."

Our servers returned with petite barbecues for our sherry-glazed Iberico pork suspended over glowing wood surrounded by a ring of dried grape vines. I closed my eyes and inhaled the black truffle-scented smoke.

"Takes char siu to another level, huh?"

"I'll say."

The servers plated our glazed pork, refilled our flutes, and left.

"It's okay if you don't want to finish college, Lily. I just wanted you to know that I'd support that."

"Support?"

"You know what I mean."

"Uh-huh." I didn't know where Daniel was going with the college stuff, but I preferred to concentrate on the food.

"Or you could raise kids."

I sucked in pork, gasped and coughed until my airways cleared, then stared at Daniel, incredulous. "You want me to stay home and raise your kids?"

"No. I mean… I just think you'd make a great mom. That's all."

"Good. Because I'm still working on being an adult." I downed my water so I wouldn't have to talk. This line of conversation was ruining my mood.

The octopus bouillon arrived while Daniel was in the restroom. With no one around to share my astonishment, I snapped a picture of the dead animal coiled in my soup and sent it off to Baba. A moment later, I received a message from Lee Chang.

*What have you done, stupid girl?*

I glanced around the restaurant for Baba's irascible cook, half expecting him to leap from a table and hurl a butter knife my way. Lee Chang prided himself on keeping me on my toes. Whenever I entered his kitchen, cooking chopsticks flew and cleavers swung.

I checked to make sure I hadn't sent Uncle the octopus photo by mistake. I hadn't. He was just being his ornery self.

*Stop bothering me,* I texted, happy to throw his own words back at him.

Lee: Me *bothering you? I'm on vacation, and you won't stay out of trouble.*

Me: *I'm on a date.*

Lee: *You think I care about that? Stay away from the triad!*

I stared at the word. If the scorpion tattoo was a triad symbol, could the men following Cecil Chu and my father's trusted cook be members of the same Chinese gang?

Me: *What does a triad want with HKIF?*

Lee: *Stay out of this.*

Me: *I can't. It's my grandfather's company, and my mother is here. Is she in danger?*

When Lee didn't respond, I tried again. *Uncle! Is she in danger?*

Lee: *Not if you stay out of trouble.*

Daniel slid onto our sofa and gaped at the soup. "Is that a whole octopus?"

I dropped the phone in my lap and covered it with the napkin. "Crazy huh?"

"You should snap a picture and send it to your dad."

"Great idea."

I pulled out my phone, pretended to take his advice, and messaged Uncle instead. *I'll call you tomorrow. I have questions. LOTS of questions.*

I put away the phone and tried to do the same with my concern, but Uncle's warning wouldn't let me go. Only his vague assurance that Ma would be safe if I stayed out of trouble kept me in my seat.

"You don't have to eat it if you don't want to."

"What?"

Daniel nodded toward the soup. "The octopus. You're looking a little wary. We can wait for the next course."

"Yeah. That might be best."

I sipped the champagne and forced a smile. Tonight was for Daniel, not Ma, or Baba, or Uncle. Whatever was going on with HKIF, I'd deal with it in the morning.

By the time we reached the final course, a blueberry-lavender chocolate mousse, my smile had relaxed and I bubbled from more than champagne. Every time Daniel brushed his fingers up my wrist or gazed into my eyes, I forgot how to breathe. How would it feel to have those fingers caress my belly and trace my thighs?

I ordered another daiquiri, non-alcoholic this time, to cool the heat rising up my neck, but the jolt of sugar hurt my head.

"Are you okay?"

"Yep."

"Do you want sparkling water? They'll serve it cold."

"Oh, God, yes."

I rested my chin on my hand and gazed into those dark and dreamy pools. "How have you avoided all the moms trying to snag you for their daughters?"

"The mothers in Hong Kong don't want their daughters to move to Los Angeles, and the moms in Arcadia and Monterey Park don't have the H.K. connections to presume."

"Except mine?"

"Your family's different. We have a long connection through your grandfather and my uncle."

"How are they the same generation? You're only a few years older than me."

"My brothers are ten and twelve years older, and my mother is the youngest of her siblings. Uncle Derrick and your grandfather have been friends since university."

"He must have done well for himself to invest in Gung-Gung's company at such a young age."

"He had a head start. Ah-Gung was quite wealthy."

"Your mother's father?"

"Yes. And Uncle Derrick's. As the only son, my uncle inherited the lion's share of Ah-Gung's estate."

That explained why Daniel's family lived in Kowloon and his uncle lived in Repulse Bay. It *didn't* explain why Derrick Lau had a fat folder in his file drawer for the London branch of HKIF.

"Is your uncle involved in the day-to-day business, or is he just an investor and board member for HKIF?"

"The latter. He was in real estate development, big projects, many of them resorts. He still owns the company, but other people run it for him."

"He seems to be doing well."

"Most definitely. Uncle Derrick is a very rich man."

Was he, though? The monthly reports I saw in his office had shown a company in jeopardy. Was Daniel's uncle investing with Cecil Chu to make back his fortune in European markets? It would explain his interest in the London office. If so, did Gung-Gung know?

"What's wrong? And don't say nothing. I can tell when something is bothering you."

"It's nothing, really. I was just thinking about Ma. She's having a hard time with family."

"Sorry to hear it."

I shrugged. She wasn't the only one. Even Mr. Tam and Jing were struggling. Maybe Ma's trouble with HKIF really stemmed from a squabble between Gung-Gung and Raymond Ng, and the old friends would patch up their differences over shots of baiju.

Daniel frowned. "There you go again."

I raised two fingers like a sword and slashed nine cuts in the air, a ninja technique to cleanse the negative energy we had generated.

"What was that?"

I covered his hand in mine. "Just clearing the air. All I want to think about is you."

Daniel raised my fingers to his lips. "You're the most amazing woman I've ever met."

His mouth touched my skin, lips parted for a tongue I hoped to feel but didn't. I stared into his eyes, barely breathing, at a loss for what to say or do.

"I moved out of Uncle's home."

"You did?"

"Uh-huh."

"Where are you staying now?"

"In this hotel."

My breath escaped in a sigh as I imagined myself in his room, in his arms, on his bed.

He brushed his lips along the back of my fingers, igniting a passion I'd never felt and could hardly contain. This wasn't the nervous excitement of a teenager's first love. This was the gripping demand of a woman.

Surely, Rose would have forgiven me by now for the pleasure I had experienced the night that monster had ravaged her body and ended her life. Surely, I deserved to love again.

"Do you want anything else?" Daniel asked.

"I do. But not from here."

# Chapter Thirty-Six

Daniel rolled toward me and touched his nose to mine, purring like a satisfied cat. "Good morning."

"Hi."

"Did you sleep okay?"

"Uh-huh."

I had no idea how to handle this situation. There was no kata I could have practiced with Sensei for morning-after banter, and I certainly had never discussed such a thing with Ma. Where did other women learn strategies for love—with friends, sisters, romance blogs?

He pulled me closer. "I'm glad you're here."

My limbs wrapped around his of their own accord, some actions didn't require training.

Speaking paused as we explored more intimate means of communication, teasing, tantalizing, direct. I welcomed every new sensation and applied myself to the lessons with acuity and enthusiasm. When our bodies collapsed, I snuggled against his chest and listened to the soothing lullaby of his heart.

"Are you happy?"

I felt as if a filter had been removed from my sight. "I am."

He hugged me close and rocked me to the edge of sleep. My phone rang and jolted me awake. "Relax, Lily, it's just a call."

"Everyone knows I'm in Hong Kong. They should be texting, not calling." I crawled out of Daniel's arms. "Have you seen my bag?"

"The black one or the backpack?"

"Either. Both. Why is everything of yours so orderly?"

He grinned. "You were in a hurry?"

The ringing stopped. "Oh, great. Now I can't follow the sound."

Daniel reached for his phone, set neatly on the night table beside a pack of condoms and a glass of water. "I'll call you."

It rang in the bathroom. I wrapped myself in a towel and checked my messages, a missed call from Ma.

She answered on the first ring. "Lily? Are you okay? Where are you?"

I had forgotten to text. "Hi, Ma."

"Don't 'Hi Ma' me. Your bed hasn't been slept in. Where are you?'

I sat on the tub and buried my face in my hand. I felt like a teenager caught in her room with a boy—as if I would have *ever* done that. "I'm safe. In a hotel room. With Daniel."

Silence.

"I'm sorry if I worried you. I should have texted. Ma, I'm a grown woman, not a child. If I want to stay out all—"

"Stop. When you come back to the house, wear the shirt and shorts you had on before. I'll tell Gung-Gung and Po-Po you hiked to the reservoir this morning. I expect you to say the same."

"You want me to lie?"

"Yes, Lily. That's exactly what I want you to do."

She ended the call, leaving me in shock. Was she so ashamed? After all her matchmaking, she should have been overjoyed about Daniel and me. Was she upset about the pre-marital sex, or that I would shame her in the eyes of her parents?

"Is everything okay?" Daniel called from the other room.

"Yep. Just hopping in the shower," I lied.

He appeared in the doorway, naked and beautiful. "Want company?"

I took in the gorgeous sight and shook my head. "I should go. I have to hike to the Aberdeen Reservoir and back to my grandparents' place in the next hour."

He took my hand from the shower faucet. "What's going on?"

"I've shamed my mother."

"By spending the night with me?"

"Apparently."

"That doesn't make sense, she's been pushing us together. She's surprised and was probably worried, that's all. Besides, you're twenty-five years old."

"Almost twenty-six."

"Really, when? Never mind. The point is you have nothing to be ashamed about." He wrapped a towel around his waist. "Take your shower, go home, talk to your mother. The sooner you work this out, the better you'll feel."

I fell into his arms for a comforting hug. "Thank you." I kissed him chastely on the lips. When a certain part of his anatomy responded, I pushed him away. "I have to go." I grabbed my purse and walked out of the bathroom to retrieve my scattered belongings, then pulled out yesterday's clothes from my backpack.

"What about the shower?"

I pulled on my T-shirt and shorts. "No time. I'll clean up after the hike."

"But why a hike?"

I tied on my running shoes and stuffed my evening clothes into the pack.

"I have never known my mother to lie. I won't let her start now."

# Chapter Thirty-Seven

It took five minutes to connect with the rideshare driver and another ten to arrive at the trailhead at the end of Gung-Gung and Po-Po's road before I jogged down the staircase onto the rain forest slopes. Although I had intended to call Lee Chang first thing this morning, Ma's call had derailed me.

Dried leaves blanketed the ground except for a thin line in the dirt pounded by travelers. I stuck to the path and ran.

The route from my grandparents' street to the Upper Aberdeen Reservoir was less than a mile. I should have been able to run there and back in twenty minutes, but the trail branched in multiple directions, some with signs I couldn't read. I had to double back twice before I reached the steep cement stairs that led to the fitness road and reservoir. Once there, I ran onto the bridge, snapped a selfie of me in front of the water, and sent it to Ma.

*Great hike. Back soon!*

I sprinted to the Watford trailhead and stared at the steps. I hadn't counted them on the way down, but dreaded every one of them for the charge back up. Train to live. Live to train. Sensei's slogan reminded me that every challenge presented an opportunity to grow and improve. My adventures in Hong Kong had already shown me the importance of staying in shape. This three-quarter-mile sprint up a mountain would do me good.

I tightened the straps of my backpack and set my intention—full speed, no stopping until I reached my grandparents' front door.

"Hello. I'm back."

Ma met me in the entryway. "I got your photo. Why did you go to the reservoir?"

"Isn't that where you told them I was?"

"Yes, but—"

"Then, that's where I went."

Ma gaped in surprise as Po-Po walked up the corridor. "You're so messy," she said in Cantonese. "Take a shower before you smell up my house."

"I need water."

"Okay. But don't sit."

Gung-Gung eyed me as I entered the kitchen. "What happened to you?" he asked in English

"I hiked to the reservoir. Decided to run back up."

"Up all those stairs?" Po-Po exclaimed.

"Gotta stay in shape, right, Ma?"

My mother shook her head in amazement. "Lily is a determined woman."

Po-Po scolded me in Cantonese about overheating and handed me a banana.

Gung-Gung poured me a glass of water. "You must have left early this morning."

I chugged the water so I wouldn't have to answer.

Ma came to my rescue. "Go take a shower, Lily. I'll brew you a cup of tea."

I grabbed the banana and bolted. A few minutes later, Ma entered my bedroom.

She watched as I hung up my new yellow dress and put away my designer sandals. "You didn't have to do that."

I removed the handbag Ma had bought for me from my backpack and hung it on the back of a chair. "If it wasn't for my actions, you wouldn't have needed to lie. I'm sorry I shamed you."

"You didn't shame me."

"Really?" I dropped the backpack and turned to confront her. "Then why all of this? I thought you'd be happy about Daniel and me. I thought you'd be relieved that I was finally dating someone. How could you make me feel so…guilty?"

"That wasn't my intention."

I bit my tongue. Strong emotions led to careless words.

She handed me the tea. "I shouldn't have reacted the way I did. You're a grown woman, and Daniel is…well…I can understand the attraction."

"Understand? You've been pushing us together all summer. What did you expect to happen?"

She opened her mouth then shook her head. "Come out when you've showered, okay?" She offered a weak smile. "Po-Po's fixing you a cooling breakfast."

I sank onto the bed when she closed the door and stared at my feet. Trail dust clung to my ankles. Po-Po's cluttered room boxed me in. Ninety minutes ago, I had been with Daniel. This was not where I wanted to be.

# Chapter Thirty-Eight

"Do we have plans today?" I asked, between mouthfuls of Po-Po's broccoli omelet and whole wheat toast.

Ma looked up from the sink. "I'm meeting the relatives of one of my Los Angeles clients. They're sending a car to pick me up."

"Then I'll entertain myself."

When Ma relayed the exchange in Cantonese, Po-Po's eyes lit up. "Oh. Maybe you can visit with Daniel."

"Lily will be fine on her own," Ma said. "I'm sure she has many gifts to buy for her friends back home."

I smiled sweetly. "*So* many gifts."

Despite her apology, Ma was still angry that I had spent the night with Daniel. She had always been stricter with me than with Rose, prohibiting me from dating in high school or even going out at night with friends. Curse of the eldest daughter. Was it any wonder I had jumped at the chance to live on a college campus? Seven years later, Ma still treated me like a child.

"I'll be fine on my own. I don't need anyone to watch over me."

Ma dried her tea cup and set it down with extra force. "As you say. Now, if you'll both excuse me, I have a big day ahead."

Po-Po grabbed my hand with concern. "Are you and your mother fighting?"

"We're fine."

"Okay." She took my plate and cleaned up, happily.

I checked my phone. No messages. I hovered my thumb over the

WhatsApp icon. Was it too soon to text Daniel? Shouldn't *he* be texting *me*? I hit WeChat instead. I hadn't checked in with Baba since our conversation the previous morning.

Me: *How's the head?*

When he didn't answer, I did the math. Eleven in the morning on Wednesday was eight at night on Tuesday for him. Baba would be elbows deep in work.

I sent DeAndre a Facebook message instead. *How's my dad?*

He answered immediately. *Didn't your mama teach you any manners?*

Me: *Hello, DeAndre. How are you?*

DeAndre: *Great, thanks. Sunny day, busy night, enjoying life. How about you?*

Me: *Are we done?*

DeAndre: *Sigh. You used to be fun.*

Me: *No I didn't. How's Baba?*

I waited for the typing notice to appear.

Me: *You still there?*

Nothing.

I went back to WeChat and placed a call.

Metal scraped in the background, amid clanking plates and an industrial fan. "Hello, Dumpling. More noodles, Bayani! It's the dinner rush. Can this wait?"

"Yep."

"Good deal. Talk later."

At least I knew he was alive.

I went back to Messenger and typed angrily to DeAndre: *Don't leave me hanging like that. I had to call my father in the middle of dinner rush to make sure he was OKAY!*

I shook out my nerves.

"Are you good, Lei Lei?" Po-Po asked.

"I'm good."

I opened WhatsApp and stared at Daniel's cheery face. Would it be so bad if I reached out first? I hit a different icon instead. *Hi, Mr.*

*Tam. Can you give me a ride from the house?*

Mr. Tam: *Twenty minutes okay?*

Me: *Perfect.*

"Thanks for breakfast, Po-Po. I'm going to run."

"I thought you already run."

"I meant I'm going out."

"Oh. Hou hou," she said, in a chirping sing-song voice.

Could my grandmother be *any* cuter?

Back in my room, I assessed my wardrobe with a critical eye. For today's mission, I needed something professional yet alluring, feminine yet strong. I settled on charcoal slacks and a crimson short-sleeved blouse. Both were made of lightweight stretchy material so I could move freely in the heat. I left my backpack in the closet in favor of the handbag to complete the look.

Mr. Tam waited for me in the garage. "Where do you want to go?"

With Ma meeting her client's relatives and Gung-Gung at home watching the news, I was free to follow my hunch.

"IFC Mall."

"More shopping to do?"

"Hmm, maybe."

I sent Uncle a text. *Tell me about the scorpion tattoo.*

When he didn't respond, I checked on Jing. Mr. Tam's daughter had sent a link to a pro-democracy message board loaded with personal accounts. "Are there any demonstrations today?"

"I hope not. The police scared her yesterday. Maybe she'll stay away."

I didn't want to worry Mr. Tam, but if the teenagers I had tangled with over the last month were any indication, Jing wouldn't scare off that easily.

I closed the app and put away my phone. "Let me know if she gets into trouble."

"Please do the same with me. And not only about Jing."

"What do you mean?"

He shrugged. "Some trees have deeper roots than others."

"Sorry?"

"You are more than you pretend to be. I don't want to pry, but if you need me, I'm here."

Kansas had said something similar, back home, after picking me up from a particularly gruesome rescue operation. Since then, she had dropped me into and pulled me out of sticky situations with street gangs, sex traffickers, sketchy politicians, and an assassin. If I needed a normal ride about town, I called and paid through the rideshare app. When I needed a warrior's chariot, I called Kansas direct.

Mr. Tam eyed me in the rearview mirror. "Have I overstepped my place?"

"Not at all. You reminded me what it means to have friends."

# Chapter Thirty-Nine

During my last visit to HKIF, I had noticed Kenneth Hong's recently-empty ring finger. I had also noted his hopeful interest in me. Hints about fine restaurants, sightseeing, and coming back to visit him clinched my impression that Kenneth Hong was a lonely, newly divorced man.

A month ago, I had posed as a prostitute to infiltrate a sex trafficker's lair, but I had not—and would never—prostitute myself for a mission. Nor would I take unnecessary advantage of an innocent target like Kenneth Hong. Although the kunoichi of feudal Japan had done whatever was needed to accomplish a mission, Sensei held me to a stricter morality. He stressed compassion and empathy in all things. I reminded myself of those lessons as I entered Kenneth's office.

"Lily. How nice to see you again. Are you here with your mother or grandfather?"

I flashed my brightest smile. "Nope. I was shopping next door and decided to visit."

"Visit *me?*"

"Oh. I thought you had invited me. Please forget I was here, Mr. Hong. I'll leave you to your work."

"No, no, please stay, and call me Kenneth. I did invite you. I was just surprised you would take the time to come." He gestured to one of three armchairs arched around his corner crescent desk and patted his combed-over hair as I sat. "May I offer you something to eat or drink? That is, unless you have plans for lunch."

"No plans. I'm fine for now."

His tiny mouth pressed into a hopeful smile. "We have excellent restaurants nearby. You are wise to preserve your appetite."

"My appetite?"

Embarrassment drove his dimples deep into recessed cheeks. "For lunch. Perhaps, you will allow me to satisfy your hunger."

I bit my lips to keep from laughing and took his words with their intended innocence. Kenneth Hong might be a desperate divorcé, but he was no cad, not with his awkward disposition. This was a case of second language embarrassment, something I suffered often.

He walked behind his desk to the seat of power, swiveled toward the window, and drew my attention to the view.

I sighed as expected. "This must be gorgeous at night."

He swiveled back to me, eyes wide with surprise. "It is. You should come back this evening and see it. The harbor lights are stunning. They will excite you greatly. I mean they will greatly excite you."

I held out my hand. "I know what you mean. How can you work while staring at such an overwhelming view?"

"Discipline. I've had sixteen years of practice."

"Sixteen? Is that how long you've worked for HKIF?"

He nodded. "Your grandfather hired me right after he moved into this building."

"And you handle all the clients in Hong Kong?"

"And throughout Asia." He leaned back in his chair, at ease and empowered, exactly as I wanted him to feel.

"That's very impressive. What about other global clients?"

"Your mother focuses primarily on Los Angeles and San Francisco with additional clients across the United States. Cecil Chu handles European clients from the London office."

I leaned in, confidentially. "Mr. Chu seems a little stressed."

Kenneth chuckled. "He's a formal man, a bit older than your mother and quite a bit older than me. He's worked for HKIF for thirty-five years. He should have retired by now but works harder than ever. He used to have glossy black hair. Now look at him. If he doesn't slow down soon, he'll die of a heart attack. It's important to find balance in life, especially for those of us young enough to enjoy it."

Although closer to Ma's age than mine, Kenneth obviously wanted me to think of him as part of my generation.

"When did you become COO?"

"Eight years ago."

"That's a long time. You must be a major stockholder by now."

He frowned. "One does not always reflect the other." His mouth pinched into a grin as he needlessly repositioned the folders on his desk.

Did resentment brew beneath Kenneth's meek surface? I shook my head in feigned amazement. "And yet, your position in the company is crucial."

"Thank you for understanding."

I leaned in again. "No need for thanks, Kenneth. The situation is very clear. Regardless of stock ownership, a chief operating officer is the captain who runs the ship."

He blushed. "Your grandfather is CEO."

"Yes, but…who *really* runs HKIF?"

He chuckled nervously and glanced out his door to see if anyone had overheard. "Have you enjoyed your visit so far?"

I smiled and answered loud enough to carry. "Hong Kong is a wonderful city. So nice to see where my mother grew up." I wanted to put Kenneth at ease. It also couldn't hurt to remind his associates that Ma was one of their own.

Kenneth sighed in relief. "Perhaps you'd like to see more of this building? The Hong Kong Monetary Authority has an exhibition and library on the fifty-fifth floor. It will excite you—"

"Greatly?" I offered, with a mischievous grin.

He laughed nervously. "My English is not good. Please forgive me."

I rose from the chair. "Not at all. Your English is perfect." So was his suggestion to leave the office. I needed Kenneth to speak freely, and he wouldn't do that within earshot of his colleagues.

# Chapter Forty

As Kenneth escorted me to the elevators, he nodded at every employee to make sure each of them noticed him with me. A young, single woman? Or Gung-Gung's heir-apparent grandchild? Which quality was more important to Kenneth Hong?

"Your world intrigues me," I said, as he pressed the elevator button.

"How so?"

"Finance, stocks, board of directors...these things mystify me, and yet, I should probably learn. For example, I always thought board members were selected by stockholders to oversee a company and elect the CEO."

Kenneth nodded. "That is true for all publicly-traded companies and many privately-traded companies. However, your grandfather set up the charter when he formed Hong Kong International Finance so he would always remain in control of the family business."

"Very wise."

"HKIF is a limited partnership with your grandfather as the sole general partner and majority shareholder. Raymond Ng and Derrick Lau are silent investment partners with the second and third largest shares and full voting rights. Neither of them have anything to do with the day-to-day business. Both have successful companies of their own."

We entered the double-decker elevator and headed down to the fifty-fifth floor.

"Are there other stock holders?"

Kenneth nodded. "All of the directors—me, your mother, and Cecil Chu—have two percent shares."

"So you own *and* run HKIF." I flashed a flirtatious smile. "Impressive."

This time, he accepted my grandiose praise without objection.

"Do you also have voting rights?"

"I do. Only your grandfather, the silent partners, and we three directors can vote."

"Equally?"

He tensed. "Not equally. Our votes are weighted according to our shares."

I hurried to build him back up. "But you're still an owner."

He nodded in appreciation. "I am."

We exited the elevator into the lobby of a spacious exhibit and proceeded to the service counter.

"Hello, Mr. Hong." The attendant greeted him in Cantonese with a slight bow. "Your secretary called to inform me you were coming. Is this your guest?"

Kenneth nodded. "Lily Wong is the granddaughter of Shaozu Wong visiting from Los Angeles."

She switched to English. "Please enjoy your visit."

Kenneth's introduction of me as Shaozu Wong's granddaughter and not his friend told me he was hedging his bets. For all he knew, I could one day be his boss.

Kenneth led me into the exhibition area and gestured grandly at the numerous displays. "Where would you like to begin? The policy section explains the work of the Monetary Authority, the timeline traces the history of our banking systems, and the currency section shows design, security features, and fun facts about our notes and coins." His eyes twinkled as if he were introducing me to Disneyland.

I didn't want to burst Kenneth's bubble, but I didn't have time—nor the inclination—to learn the historical nuances of banking. "Perhaps, we could just stroll through the exhibit and enjoy each other's company."

He beamed, happy to comply.

As we ambled through the currency section, I paused to admire the metallic thread and shimmering security patterns in the bank notes.

"Your profession is as beautiful as it is fascinating. But it's also complicated. For example, I still don't quite understand how these board meetings work. Katie said there were three members of an advisory board in attendance, specialists from outside the company. If they can't vote, why did they attend the meeting?"

"That is an insightful question. Mr. Wen, Mr. Lee, and Mr. Zhao offer guidance in banking, information technology, and international business trends. In larger companies the advisory board is bigger and meets on their own. Your grandfather prefers we all meet together so we can to share knowledge. However, they will not attend the vote on Friday."

"But you will."

He offered a humble nod.

As we continued our tour, I considered what I had learned. Although Gung-Gung had elevated Kenneth to COO, he had done so without awarding him additional stock or voting power. Kenneth's resentment was obvious, but did he have the will and means to act? If so, how would ousting Ma from her position improve his own? Raymond Ng and Derrick Lau were silent investment partners. Why were they meddling in HKIF business? And why was Cecil Chu working himself to death when he should already have retired?

Kenneth stopped in front of a hanging mosaic of Victoria Harbour comprised entirely of coins. "Students created this using coins of all age and value."

"Sounds like HKIF."

"How so?"

"All of you are important, but some of you provide more value than the weight of your vote."

Kenneth considered this a moment. "I suppose that's true. Your grandfather's vote is the only one that counts, but the board meetings give all of us a chance to raise questions and offer better practices. I have never seen the majority of us vote in one direction and your grandfather in another. He takes our counsel seriously."

"As well he should. Your opinions as chief operations officer are important."

He peered at me through his lenses, as though seeing me anew. "You're right. I should speak up more often. Thank you for these words. They give me new perspective."

Sensei would be pleased. When dealing with an innocent, he had taught me to always give something in return. Not only had I acquired important information, I was building trust, gaining an ally, and empowering my target—morality for the win.

As we wandered out of currency section and into the policy exhibit, Kenneth gestured to the colorful displays and rambled about financial stability and the management of the Monetary Authority's Exchange Fund. I listened for anything that could steer us back to what I wanted to know.

"Are you saying that cities and countries manage their investments the same way HKIF does for its clients?"

Kenneth shrugged. "On a larger scale."

"Do they also have shareholders and transparency? For example, if Gung-Gung were to sell enough of his shares to drop below fifty-one percent, would the rest of the shareholders be informed?"

Kenneth shook his head. "He would never do that."

"But what if he did?"

"The charter he created allows us to sell our shares without restriction. Since we could all, theoretically, sell our stock to the same entity, it would be dangerous for him to drop below fifty-one percent."

"Not if my mother voted with him."

"True. If he could count on her vote, he would only need to control forty-nine percent."

"Would you know if this happened?"

Kenneth shrugged. "Not until the mid or end-of-year statement.

But aside from giving each of his directors two percent, no one has sold a share of HKIF in forty-six years."

If HKIF's mid-year statement came out in June, that would leave three months for shares to have changed hands undetected. Could a shift in voting power have something to do with Raymond Ng's motion to remove Ma from her position as Los Angeles director? Mr. Ng had watched over Ma since the day she was born. Why would he turn against her now?

"I'm sorry," I said. "Did you say something about a crash?" Kenneth had paused in front of a digital wall display of Hong Kong's monetary timeline.

"I did. It happened in 1987 with runs on multiple banks in 1991. This was followed by the Asian Financial Crisis of 1997 and the Global Financial Crisis of 2008."

"Did it harm you financially?"

"Not me, personally. I invest my money carefully, but it was a challenging time for HKIF. Fortunately, we are not a publicly-traded company."

"Why does that make a difference?"

"Private equity firms like ours are protected from wild swings in stock market prices. And since we don't seek outside investors, we are not obligated to assess our value. Private trading also provides confidentiality, the right of non-disclosure, and other tax and liability advantages."

"With all these advantages, why would a company *want* to be traded publicly?"

"To raise capital by selling stock or bonds through the financial markets."

"What does Gung-Gung do to raise capital?"

"In the beginning, he went to Raymond Ng and Derrick Lau."

"What would he do now?"

"Apply for a loan, invest his own money to raise capital, or—"

"Sell his stock?"

Kenneth shrugged. "If there was no other way." He studied me closely. "You are an unusual woman, Lily Wong."

"Thank you."

"Would you join me for lunch? The Four Seasons Hotel is attached to the International Finance Center and has impeccable restaurants, two awarded with three Michelin stars. I would be honored to take you."

My stomach growled. Although I would love nothing better than to dine on fancy food, I wouldn't take advantage of Kenneth any more than I already had. Prying for information was one thing, an expensive lunch and toying with his emotions was another.

"That's very gracious of you, but I must be going."

He sagged with disappointment. "I didn't mean to impose."

"Not at all. You're a thoughtful and impressive man, Kenneth, with so much to offer. Any woman would be honored by your attention. I hope you realize that."

He looked at me with surprise then straightened with newfound confidence. "Thank you for your visit. You have given me much to think about."

# Chapter Forty-One

The midday heat singed my face and sucked in my blouse like cling wrap to a pear. I needed the waterfront breeze to loosen its grip and give me space to consider what I'd learned.

I headed across the avenues to a covered footpath with glass railings and bright blue zigzagging steel beams. The harbor breeze circulated above the protective glass and cooled me as I walked.

Hong Kong accommodated its dense pedestrian traffic with an intricate network of tunnels, bridges, escalators, and passages that connected certain buildings and malls. Depending on the route, a person could walk all day and never set foot on actual ground. Those who couldn't avoid it hurried across the hot pavement, breathed in exhaust, and wove toward their destination along the confusing web of roads and highways. Two men glanced up from below, as if wishing they had chosen my shadier route, then lowered their gaze and powered up the sidewalk.

It was peaceful up here, away from the exhaust and the noise. Peaceful enough to think.

Between what I'd learned about HKIF's share-holding and voting structure and Gung-Gung's carefully constructed charter, my grandfather should have complete control of his company. If he supported Ma and kept his promise to take care of things, Raymond Ng's campaign would fail. If Gung-Gung had sold stock since the mid-year report and lost his majority vote, Ma was doomed.

I thought back to Gung-Gung's evasive comments in his office two days earlier when Ma had asked if he was going to vote against her. He had said the situation was not as simple as she believed. What had he meant by that? And why had he redirected their conversation to Ma's unhappy childhood? Gung-Gung clung to his bitterness like a dragon to treasure. Family and legacy were his favorite jewels. Would he really hurt his own daughter out of spite?

I looked across the avenues to the harbor skyline on the right and wondered about the truth, where to find it and who to believe, when my phone vibrated with a call from Daniel. Now that we had made love, I had no idea how I was supposed to answer. "What's up?" wouldn't cut it, and "Hello, lover," made me want to gag. Better to keep it simple and safe. From there, I could assess the situation, feed off Daniel's response, and guide the interaction to the best possible outcome.

"Hey."

"Hey, yourself."

I stifled a groan. Apparently, post-sex phone calls were more nuanced than a fight.

Daniel chuckled. "How did it go with your mom?"

Between the hectic hike and wheedling information out of Kenneth, I had forgotten about my abrupt departure from the hotel room. "It went okay."

"You didn't shame her? Because I can't believe that you did. She might be from another generation, but your mother is a sophisticated, modern woman."

"If you say so. My hike calmed the waters."

"Why hike at all?"

"It was the lie she told my grandparents."

"And now it's not a lie?"

"Nope. I even sent her pictures to prove it."

Daniel laughed. "You're a good daughter."

"Ha. Don't push it. It's only a temporary truce."

I smiled in the silence as I remembered the warmth of Daniel's chest against my face. If Ma hadn't called, would we still be in his hotel room, snuggling in bed, making love, feeding each other strawberries and cream?

*Strawberries and cream?*

"You didn't answer," he said, sounding a little worried.

"Sorry, what?"

"I asked if you had any regrets."

"About last night? No. Do you?"

"Not at all. But you ran out so quickly, I didn't get a chance to ask."

I exhaled with relief. "We're great. It's everyone else I'm worried about."

"What's going on?"

"Nothing. Just the typical Wong family drama that's already stolen too much of my attention from you."

"Hmm. I like the sound of that."

"Yeah? Well, I'd like to make amends."

"I admire a woman with ethics."

"And I admire a man who holds me to them."

He laughed. "Who are you, and what have you done with my inscrutable girlfriend?"

I laughed. "Is that what I am?"

"Which, inscrutable or girlfriend?"

"Either."

"Yes."

I smiled. Intimacy *and* mystery? Maybe I could actually make this relationship work.

"What are you doing now?" he asked.

"Walking to the waterfront."

"In Central?"

"Yep."

"Damn. I'm in Kowloon."

"Guess we'll have to wait."

"Not too long, I hope."

My neck flushed as I imagined his lean, tanned body draped in silky white sheets.

"You still there?"

"Yep."

"Will I see you soon?"

"Um…"

"Inscrutable Lily has returned."

"Very funny. I'll call you later, okay? Once I figure out what's what."

"Promise?"

"You betcha."

I ended the call with a smile. Maybe conversations with Daniel didn't require ninja strategies. Maybe we only needed to *talk*.

I skipped down the stairs to the Star Ferry Pier, feeling lighter than I had since Ma's wakeup call. Even on a weekday, the waterfront bustled with visitors. Some commuted to and from Kowloon while others ambled through the shops or strolled along the promenade. Such a normal thing to do. Why not give it a try?

I bought a skewer of deep fried curry fish balls from a food cart peddler and strolled along the water and thought of Baba, which happened whenever I used one of his North Dakota idioms. *You betcha.* As soon as I said that to Daniel, my father's sweet face popped into my mind.

I leaned against the railing and sent him a message. *You still awake?*

His trip to the E.R. had me nervous. When he didn't answer, I imagined the worst. If the fall had given him a concussion, he could be in trouble. Why had we left him alone in Los Angeles? I tossed my trash and pulled myself together. To begin with, we hadn't *left* Baba anywhere. He had stayed behind because Uncle had gone to Shanghai and the restaurant needed at least one of them to function. And second, Vern Knudsen was tougher than a Dakota winter.

Even so, I messaged DeAndre. *Hey, D. How's it going?*

The typing ellipsis started, stopped, and started again. When it stopped a second time, I gave up waiting and continued down the promenade. I had reached the observation wheel at Vitality Park when DeAndre's message finally appeared. *How are you holding up?*

I started to type then hit the call button instead. "What do you mean, how am I holding up. Did something happen to Baba? What's going on? Is he okay? Why didn't you call?"

"Whoa, girl. Slow your ass down."

"My ass is fine, thank you very much, but yours is gonna get kicked to the curb if you don't tell me what's going on."

"Nothing. I was just being solicitous."

"Solicitous?"

"Well, yeah. You've been a little edgy lately."

Edgy? I'd show him edgy…with the business end of Uncle's cleaver. I took a breath. "So, nothing's wrong?"

"Nah. Kinda dull without you and Lee around."

"And my father's okay?"

"You mean like, did he fall down again?"

"Yes, DeAndre, that's exactly what I mean."

"Nah, he's fine. Just a little edgy is all. Maybe it runs in the family."

"Or maybe you bring it out in us. Ever think of that?"

"Not possible. Everybody loves DeAndre."

"Oh, good lord. I gotta go. But let me know if anything happens."

"Relax. Your dad's fine, okay. Have fun and buy me something nice."

"Like what?"

"How should I know? I've never been out of L.A."

I ended the call and took a breath. If DeAndre gave me another scare like this, he'd get stinky tofu and duck tongues.

# Chapter Forty-Two

I left the waterfront and headed across small lawns and plazas toward Tamar Park, the location of this Saturday's protest. Jing's friends had asked her to design political art flyers for the park's amphitheater. It was still days away, but it couldn't hurt to check out the area in advance.

Dozens of flyers already decorated the plaza with more stuck to the low walkway walls. As I crossed over a garden-like pedestrian bridge, I saw more protest art fluttering from other walls, plazas, and buildings. By Saturday, Tamar Park would be plastered in flyers.

When I'd gained more elevation, I turned around to admire the Kowloon skyline across the harbor. That's when I saw the men who had chased me the day before. They froze in surprise, but I continued the sweep of my gaze as if I hadn't seen them. I paused a moment to enjoy the view then turned around and continued on my way.

Had they been following me since I left the IFC tower? Since the elevated footpath had been a straight shot, I should have noticed them behind me—unless they had been following from below. I thought back to the men I'd seen looking up from the street. Had that been them?

I called Mr. Tam. "It's Lily. Can you meet me in Central?"

"Where and when?"

"I'm in Tamar Park, but I'm on the move."

"Is everything okay?"

"I'm being followed."

"Hold on." A screech of tires and a series of honks filled the pause. "Okay. I'm on my way. Where do you want to meet?"

"What's around here?"

"The Central Government Complex, the People's Liberation Army Garrison, the Admiralty Shopping Center—"

"A mall? Where's that?"

"At the end of the park. Do you see two rectangular buildings connected at the top?"

"Like giant glass building blocks?"

"Exactly. Go through the gap to the other side. It leads to an overpass above a highway. You can enter the mall from there or take the escalator and enter from the street."

"Where's the most logical place to meet you?"

"Drake Street, on the McDonald's side of the center. There's a taxi stand and bus stop. I'll look for you there."

I picked up my pace, as if eager to reach the mall on the other side of the overpass, and resisted the urge to check behind me. In place of railings or security fence, the open passage was bordered by cement planters with hedges and shrubs. Two strong men could hurl me over the edge.

When I reached the other side, I hurried down the escalator and entered the mall through KFC into a food court with seating in the center. I bolted to the other side. Once there, I paused in front of a display and waited for the men to enter the mall. I glanced in their direction, pretended to see them for the first time, then bolted through McDonald's. Once outside, I sprinted for the taxi stand.

I hopped in the first car but kept the door open so he wouldn't drive. "Central Pier. Pick up my friend. She'll pay you more." I tossed $200 HKD onto the driver's seat, made sure I was spotted, then ducked out of the cab. "Drive," I said, and shut the door.

As the men dodged across the street, I crouched low and ran up the line of taxis, but my driver didn't move. Had my offering—the equivalent of $25 US—been too little to motivate him? Although the distance was short, I had promised a longer and more lucrative fare.

I hid behind a pillar and searched for Gung-Gung's black Mercedes. I spotted it in a loading area ten yards away in clear view of the men hurrying across the road. Soon, they would peer into my empty taxi and know they'd been fooled. Just as I prepared to run, the taxi driver I had paid drove away. The men commandeered the second taxi in line.

I sprinted to Mr. Tam and hopped in the front seat. "Follow them."

He pulled into traffic before I had even shut the door. "What's going on, Lily? Who are those men?"

"I'm not sure, but they chased me in Sheung Wan yesterday. One of them attacked me the night before at Raymond Ng's house."

"*Attacked* you?"

"Close enough. He attacked Mr. Ng's dog. I got in the way, and he threw me off the roof."

Mr. Tam accelerated in anger.

"Hold back. I know where they're going, at least for now."

When we exited the roundabout along the waterfront, the two taxis we were following, the one I had paid and the other with the scorpion men, pulled in front of the Central Ferry Pier complex behind a double decker touring bus. Mr. Tam parked across the road behind a line of cars.

Neither taxi moved.

When the driver I had paid cut off his engine, the leaner of my two pursuers got out and went to check. When he didn't find me, he turned back to his partner and threw up his hands in dismay. The stockier man with the scorpion tattoo stepped out of the taxi. They yelled at each other in Cantonese, got back in their taxi and drove away.

Mr. Tam eased onto the road a couple cars behind. "Where to now?"

I glared at the taxi. "Let's find out."

# Chapter Forty-Three

We followed the taxi up the ramp to the Wong Nai Chung Gap Flyover, a highway that ran above the streets toward the mountains. Hong Kong had many of these, usually walled in by high-rise buildings. What would it be like to grow up in one of these apartments, breathe in the exhaust, watch an endless stream of vehicles fly past my window? I was so fortunate to have been raised in spacious Arcadia, in my parents'—or rather my grandfather's—million-dollar home.

The high-rise buildings fell away from the highway, offering moments of space as we flew over streets and structures. The hillier terrain added lush hillsides to the mix, and the Jockey Club's racecourse and football field gave breath to the skyline, until an apartment block closed in and the Aberdeen Tunnel swallowed us whole.

"How far does this go?"

"About two kilometers. We're traveling into the mountain."

"Beneath all those apartment blocks on The Peak?"

"Different mountain. Different blocks."

We emerged on the south side of the island to denser trees and shorter, less frequent structures.

"Where are we we now?"

"This is Shousan Hill. If they continue on this road, it leads to Deep Water Bay."

"Is that near Repulse Bay?"

"Repulse is the inlet to the southeast. But even if they were going to the most southern point of the island, they would also take this route."

The bay and hillside views had seemed more peaceful when I had seen them from the back of Daniel's scooter.

"Why are these men bothering you and your family?" Mr. Tam asked, as we descended toward the white-sand beach.

"I'm not sure, but I think it has something to do with HKIF."

"Have you told your grandfather?"

I shook my head. "I need more information. Besides, he's been… distracted."

Mr. Tam nodded as if comparing this to his own observations. "What do you do for work, Miss Wong?"

"I wondered when you'd ask."

"I didn't want to pry."

"And now?"

"We are following dangerous men. Now, it is my business to know."

He had a point. And yet, he was in Gung-Gung's employ. "What are you obligated to tell my grandfather?"

"Nothing."

"What if he asks a direct question? I'm not asking you to lie, but are you willing to evade?"

He considered this thoughtfully. "I have watched you save your mother and my daughter from dangerous situations. I will keep your secrets."

"Okay. I work for a women's shelter in Los Angeles, extracting and protecting women and children from violent situations. To do this work, I rely on extensive martial arts training and the ninja arts."

"Ninja? You mean the Japanese assassins?"

"Not quite. Modern ninja training focuses on more altruistic objectives. The techniques, concepts, and strategies I study have been handed down over centuries through nine lineages to one grandmaster in Japan and to another after him. Students became teachers, and those teachers spread across the globe. There are thousands of dedicated students studying ninja martial arts through many systems and under many names. Some practitioners, like me, strive to become Tatsujin."

"What is Tatsujin?"

"A fully self-actualized human being. I know. Sounds pretty lofty. But it's actually the core of my studies. Every lesson, no matter how physical, furthers me along this esoteric path. One might call it a profound pursuit of an unattainable goal."

Mr. Tam nodded. "Those are often the most important."

I thought about the wisdom and lessons Sensei had shared with me over the years. Every bit of our physical training had an emotional, spiritual, and moral component, and all of it guided me along a higher path toward enlightenment. The unattainable goals were always the most important of all.

When we climbed up the hillside road and into the next bay, I recognized the area. "Isn't this the route we took to Derrick Lau's apartment?"

"Yes. The road from The Peak intersected behind us."

"I have a bad feeling about this."

"You think these men are connected to Derrick Lau?"

"Possibly. Or maybe they mean him harm. They've harassed Raymond Ng and followed Cecil Chu. Why not Derrick Lau?"

When the taxi turned up Mr. Lau's road, I pointed to the corner. "Hang back a little. I don't want to get caught following them up that narrow road."

"How long do you want to wait?"

"Until they're out of sight. We know where they're going. I just have to figure out how to get inside."

Derrick Lau lived on the nineteenth floor of a high-security building. If I had been in Los Angeles, I might have slipped past the guard, broken onto the roof, and repelled the two floors down to Mr. Lau's sheltered balcony, but that would have required gear and planning. A ninja made use of whatever she had at her disposal, which, in this case, was a classy outfit and a plausible excuse.

I messaged Daniel. *Are you still in Kowloon?*

He answered quickly. *Back on the island. Why? Have time to meet?*

Me. *Depends. Where are you?"*

Daniel: *Pottinger. Come by. Gradini Ristorante serves an old school afternoon tea.*

"What's so funny?" asked Mr. Tam.

"Daniel. He's always plying me with food."

"Is that so bad?"

"Not at all, just unnecessary. He's amazing."

Mr. Tam's brows raised with interest. I shrugged and went back to typing. *Sounds yummy, but I'm on the south side of the island.*

Daniel: *Near Repulse.*

Me: *Could be.*

Daniel: *Want me to come to you?*

Me: *Nope. Just wondered if you were nearby. I'll call you later after I check in with Ma.*

Daniel signed off with a thumbs up emoji as Mr. Tam drove along the hillside to Derrick Lau's apartment block. The taxi was parked in the shade with only the driver inside.

# Chapter Forty-Four

"Lily. How nice to see you," Mr. Lau said, when he opened the front door. "But I'm sorry to say Daniel isn't here."

"He's not?" I asked, with a show of equal surprise.

Mr. Lau shook his head. "He moved to the Pottinger House in Central."

"Oh, right. I thought that was temporary."

"No, he'll be staying there for the duration. I'd invite you in, but I'm leaving soon."

"Of course. Sorry to trouble you, Mr. Lau."

"It's no trouble, but I do have to hurry. Have a good day."

I turned as if to leave then reached behind me and slipped a credit card in the door to block the bolt. I waited a moment in case he opened it again and relaxed when he didn't. Even if he had invited me inside, I would have politely declined. I didn't know whether the scorpion men were friends of his but I new for certain they were enemies of mine. I was here to spy, not fight. If I discovered Mr. Lau was in danger, that would change.

I waited a bit, then cracked open the door and peeked inside. All was quiet and the dining and living areas empty. I checked the balcony to the right, the kitchen to the left, then entered, closing the door quietly behind me. Muffled voices carried from the office. I hurried into the hallway and crouched beside the doorway. Using my phone as a mirror, I inched it past the wall, and angled it so I could see. The leaner scorpion man stood with his back to Mr. Lau's seascape painting and nodded toward the sitting area on the other side of my wall. I extended my phone farther into the room, but my view of the sitting area was blocked by the side of the long blue couch. I snapped a picture of the standing man, returned my phone to my purse, and listened.

"What was Shaozu's granddaughter doing at HKIF?" Mr. Lau spoke in Cantonese, so close he must have been sitting on the couch around the corner.

A harsh voice answered. "I don't know. We didn't go inside."

A younger voice—the leaner man standing in front of the painting? —said something about me walking and eating like a tourist.

"Don't be foolish. She spoke with Raymond and followed Cecil. Did she meet with Kenneth Hong?"

The harsh man grunted a negative and added something about it not being his job.

"Your job is what I say it is," Mr. Lau said.

"You don't run us. We run you."

"Your boss would disagree."

The man laughed. "You want to ask him?"

Mr. Lau shifted on the couch and made it creak. "Nothing can interfere with Friday's vote."

"Again, not our problem. We sent your message to Raymond Ng. The rest is up to you."

"What helps me, helps you. What hurts me, hurts you."

The chair scraped on the wooden floor as if someone shoved it back as they stood. "Be careful, Mr. Lau. Your life is not as precious as you believe."

I jumped to my feet and ran to the kitchen before the men exited the office. Once there, I hid in the pantry and peeked around the corner.

The scorpion men marched to the entryway and opened the door. The man with the harsh voice—the stocky man who had thrown me off the roof—turned to confront Mr. Lau. "Saan Zyu won't wait. You have until Friday. Assurances are expected. Put your man in Los Angeles or find another way to fulfill your promises."

Once the men had gone, Mr. Lau locked the door and sagged with relief. No longer a young seventy-eight, his youthful radiance had faded into the pallor of an ancestral ghost.

He walked into the kitchen, turned on the electric kettle, and hung his head, muttering in Cantonese about a fool in a hurry who drinks tea with a fork.

Whatever deal he had made with Saan Zyu had obviously backfired. But what did it have to do with Los Angeles? And who was this man Mr. Lau wanted as the L.A. director in place of Ma?

When he crossed to the cupboard for tea, I crawled behind the kitchen island and dashed out the doorway to the dining area. When I heard the clicking of porcelain, I hurried to the front door. Although in clear view of the kitchen, Mr. Lau was too miserable and focused on his tea to notice as I unlocked the bolt—then changed my mind.

I might never get another chance inside his apartment. I needed another look at those files.

# Chapter Forty-Five

I found the HKIF folders exactly where I'd seen them before, in the low cabinet beneath the seascape painting. I pulled out the ones for London and Los Angeles and set them on the floor behind the far end of the couch. Los Angeles was thinner, with biannual summaries for this year and last. I snapped photos, then focused on the fatter London folder, packed with detailed client information and investment summaries. I didn't know much about the finance business, but anomalies had a way of standing out.

I scanned the documents in the same way I scanned an area for danger, with a soft focus and non-specific view. If I predetermined the results, I'd only notice the details that supported my assumptions. The rest of the truth would remain hidden. Like most of Sensei's lessons, this strategy offered wisdom far beyond ninja craft.

When I reached the final document, I fanned all of them on the floor at the end of the couch so I could see them as a whole while still hidden from view. The clients mostly resided in Western Europe with outliers in Canada and India. Although Cecil Chu had more clients than Ma, their investments seemed more conservative.

I snapped shots of the documents together and in smaller groups. When footsteps approached, I scooped them together and huddled on the floor against the armrest of the couch.

Mr. Lau entered and set a tray with tea and cookies on his desk then, thankfully, took a seat in the guest chair facing the view. I squeezed closer to the wall and assessed my options: escape unnoticed without replacing the folders, or wait and hope Mr. Lau wouldn't catch me in his office.

I didn't like my odds. At some point, the man would get out of his seat. It was too much to hope that he'd turn away from me and simply leave the room. More likely, he would walk to the window, retrieve something from his cabinet, or sit behind his desk. Any of these actions would expose my hiding spot.

I pulled my blouse out of my slacks and stuffed the folders inside the waistband against my back. Since I couldn't return them to the cabinet, I'd take them with me. With luck, Mr. Lau would blame the scorpion men for the theft. All I had to do was sneak behind his back and leave. Except Mr. Lau was so nervous he kept swiveling in his chair to take a sip of tea, gaze at the painting, eat a bite of cookie, stare at the bay. The man would not hold still. Any moment he would surely get up and walk around.

I army-crawled between the front of the couch and the wave-like coffee table and froze when I heard the swan chair creak. I pressed my cheek to the floor and watched as Mr. Lau rose and walked away from his chair. When his toes pointed toward the window, I escaped.

I found Mr. Tam in the complex parking lot, pacing around the cars.

"Are you okay? You were in there for such a long time."

"Did you see the men leaving the building, one lean and the other stocky?"

"I did. They got into the taxi and left. I expected you to follow them out. Where have you been?"

I got in the car and pulled the folders from behind my back. "I didn't plan to actually take them, but it couldn't be helped."

"What's in them?"

"Client information and investment reports."

"Aiya, that's confidential. You're not supposed to have those."

"Derrick Lau is working with someone to replace my mother. Raymond Ng is part of it, and those men you saw are the muscle. If the answers are in these files, I couldn't care less about exposing HKIF secrets."

Mr. Tam drove in silence, clearly uncomfortable with this revelation. When I didn't give a destination, he headed up the winding tropical road toward The Peak and the north side of the island. Soon, I'd have to decide where to go: return to Gung-Gung's home and inform him and Ma what I had learned or continue the investigation on my own.

"I'm sorry I compromised you, Mr. Tam. I won't do it again."

He shook his head. "I'm the one who must apologize. I meant what I said this morning. You helped Jing. Whatever you need, I will help you."

"Are you sure? I don't want to get you in trouble."

"If someone is trying to hurt Mr. Wong's business, trouble has already arrived."

Mr. Tam was right. I just hoped Gung-Gung wasn't part of the problem.

I straightened the documents and closed the folders. "Could you drive me home? I'd like to put these in my room."

"Leave them with me."

I shook my head. "If my grandfather finds these in the car, he'll accuse you of stealing and fire you. He might even report you to the police."

"He won't see them."

"Still. I'd rather not take that chance."

"Okay. And then? Where do we go next?"

"Not a clue."

I unmuted my phone and checked for messages, one each from Baba and Ma.

I checked Baba's first and found a recorded clip in place of text.

"Hello, my Dumpling. Sorry I missed you last night. I was full worn out when I got home. Fell asleep straight away and woke with the roosters. What's with the octopus?"

I pressed the record button to answer. "Hey, Baba. You still there? I had dinner with Daniel. It was…"

I released record, which automatically sent the unfinished clip. How could I describe the most magical evening of my life? And how much of it did I want to disclose to my father?

*Stick with the food.*

I pressed record. "It was really special. He took me to a two Michelin-star restaurant. The octopus was in my soup. Did you get the photo of the Bafun uni with seaweed sauce pasta? First time I've ever enjoyed sea urchin."

Satisfied with my deflection, I recorded a final clip.

"Ma's holding up, but something's not right. Derrick Lau's involved, and he has muscle. I don't know what's going on, but I'm going to find out."

I considered mentioning the scorpion men but didn't want to alarm him any more than I already had. Those men had the same tattoo as Uncle. Until I found out why, I'd keep this to myself.

"Mr. Tam, do you know a man named Saan Zyu?"

"Saan Zyu isn't a name, it's a title. It means Mountain Master. Triads call their leaders this or sometimes Dragon Head or simply Boss. I don't know if it's still this way or how active they are. Some say the police have hired triads to beat up protesters. Others say the PRC have sent over black society members to cause trouble."

"Black societies?"

"Triads are in Hong Kong, Macau, Taiwan, Singapore, like that. The criminal organizations in mainland China are called black societies."

I thought of Uncle's scorpion tattoo. He was from Shanghai, not Hong Kong.

"Do triads and black societies work together as part of the same brotherhood?"

"I don't know. The police cracked down on triads years ago. It's worse on mainland than here."

I filed away this information and checked WeChat for my mother's message.

Ma: *My client's family has invited me to dinner, so I won't be home until nine-thirty or ten. If you go out with Daniel, please don't stay the night.*

I hadn't thought of that possibility, but now that she put it in my head, my body responded in embarrassing ways.

Me: *Will do. Have fun.*

I closed the app and adjusted the air-conditioning vent.

"You okay?" Mr. Tam asked.

"Yep. Just feeling a little warm."

I switched apps and sent a message to Daniel. *Ma has plans for dinner. I'm on my way home to change. Still want to meet?*

He responded as we turned onto Peak Road. *Definitely! Want to take the Star Ferry to Kowloon and catch the Symphony of Lights?*

Me: *Perfect.*

The Symphony of Lights was the worlds largest nightly laser light and music show. It lasted fifteen minutes and engaged forty-two buildings on both sides of the harbor. We could have watched from Golden Bauhinia Square on the island side, but I liked Daniel's idea better. Not only was the Avenue of the Stars promenade longer, it wasn't located in Central. Between HKIF and the scorpion men, I needed a break from the island.

Daniel: *Meet at Central Pier 5:45 for a sunset ride?*

I glanced up from my phone and caught Mr. Tam watching me. "What?"

"You're smiling like a kid at Spring Festival. What's going on?"

"Another date with Daniel."

"I like him. He's a good man."

"Yeah. I like him, too. After we stop at my grandparents', can you take me to Central Pier?"

"I can do that. I'll check on Jing afterward."

I texted Daniel. *Okay. See you then!*

When Mr. Tam pulled into the garage, I stuffed the folders back into my pants and covered them with my blouse. "I won't be long."

He turned off the engine and scrolled through his phone. "Take your time."

Gung-Gung and Po-Po were asleep in front of the television, him snoring with his head back in a chair and her nodding over her needlepoint. I crept into my bedroom and hid the folders under my bed. I had fifteen minutes to shower, change, and fix my face. No thugs to dodge or conspiracy to solve, just an average girl prepping for a dreamy date.

# Chapter Forty-Six

We boarded the Star Ferry as a warm reddish light bathed the skylines on both side of the harbor. Daniel had arrived early to hold a place in line, impressing me again with his thoughtful attention.

He took my hand as the electronic gates swung open and led me quickly to the section in the center of the top level, where our view would be unobstructed by windows. "Sit on the right, all the way on the end."

I hurried down the aisle, taking a seat by the railing, and flipped the backrest so I could face the proper direction. Daniel grinned his approval—only tourists rode backward on the ferry.

"Do you plan everything?"

"Only what's important."

I squeezed his hand then gazed past him across the aisle of boarding passengers toward the setting sun. Although lovely, once we pulled away from the pier, our east-side view of the skylines would be vastly superior.

Daniel caressed the back of my hand with his thumb. "It's good to see you smile. You were upset when you left the hotel this morning and a little tense when you arrived at the pier."

"Sorry about that."

"Is everything okay?"

I paused before answering and considered how much to say. "Things are a little rough."

"How so?"

"Ma's under fire."

Daniel nodded. "That happens. Corporate structures change, new practices are employed. If businesses don't grow, they lose their relevancy and their clients."

I bristled. "Ma stays relevant and her clients are overjoyed. Besides, she isn't the oldest director in the company. If the board members want to infuse HKIF with young blood, they should replace stuffy old Cecil Chu."

"The London director?"

"Ma is way more youthful and forward thinking than him."

"I didn't mean to offend you. Your mother is a smart woman. Everything will work out for the best."

"I wish I had your confidence."

"Borrow as much as you want. When it comes to you and your family, I have plenty in reserve."

I folded my arms on the railing as the ferry pulled away from the dock. Daniel rested his chin on my shoulder. Together we watched the skyline appear, steel and glass ablaze in reflected gold and red. The breeze off the water nipped at my face and made me glad to have worn my light leather jacket. I leaned into his chest. Daniel's assurances had lightened my mood. Would I feel the same if I shared more secrets with him?

"Remember when you asked about my work and thought it would be more physical? I do martial arts."

"You're a teacher?"

"Mmm, I'm more of a..."

Modern-day ninja? Protector and rescuer of women and children? How could I adequately describe what I did or the passion that motivated me?

"Practitioner?" he offered.

I laughed. I didn't practice martial arts, I executed them. But I couldn't very well call myself a martial arts executioner. Protector was closer to the truth. Daniel's way was simpler.

"Yep. Been practicing the martial arts since I was a four."

"No wonder you're so fit."

"And lethal."

Daniel took it as a joke. If he and I were to have a future, I'd need to come clean and tell him about the blood I had shed and the lives I had ended. For now, I preferred to bask in his adoration and enjoy the view.

The Convention and Exhibition Centre jutted off the island like a giant manta ray riding atop a glowing wave. Mirrored skyscrapers dragged in its wake. Another double-decker ferry, green on the bottom and white on top, passed us on its way to the pier. Barges, cruise liners, and festive red-sail junks cruised across the sun-streaked water, beyond which, the Kowloon skyline had just begun to ignite.

I leaned farther into Daniel's warm embrace. "This is so relaxing."

"The busier we get, the more we need to slow down."

I looked over my shoulder and smiled. "You remind me of my teacher."

"College or martial arts?"

I started to answer, but the word ninja wouldn't pass my lips. Daniel wasn't like Mr. Tam or my father who had accepted a portion of the truth. He was more like Ma, with set ideas about propriety and safety. He had worried when I crawled down the cliff to save the little dog. How would he deal with me in actual danger?

I pointed across the harbor. "What's that huge building with the curving roofline?"

"The Cultural Centre. When it gets darker, the whole thing shines bright white and the clock tower in front lights up like a golden statue."

"Ooh. What do you want to do until then?"

"Stroll, eat, whatever you want."

*Slow kisses? Seeking tongues?*

"Whoa, Lily, are you okay? You're radiating a lot of heat."

"Huh?"

"Your forehead's sweating. Do you feel feverish?"

I fanned my face and turned back toward the water. "Nope. Just being close to you, I guess."

"Well, in that case…" He brushed his lips against my neck.

I closed my eyes and struggled for control. "Um, I thought Hong-kongers avoided public displays of affection."

"No PDAs here, just enjoying the view."

"Uh-huh."

"Besides, I was born in L.A."

His breath tickled my neck and clenched my thighs. If I felt like this ten minutes into our date, I'd never survive.

"There's a shop at the end of the promenade that serves rose gelato and vitality bubble tea."

I sighed with relief. An iced dessert and drink sounded perfect.

# Chapter Forty-Seven

Once at the Tsim Sha Tsui Pier, we ambled to the tea shop at the end of the waterfront promenade, where I chose a longan bubble tea to calm my mind and strengthen my heart. When I shared my reasoning with Daniel, he laughed.

"What's so funny?" I asked, sucking up the tapioca pearl from the bottom of the drink.

"Longan has a lesser-known benefit as a sex tonic for women."

I choked down the boba. "I did not know that, honest."

"Uh-huh."

"I didn't. You set me up."

He shrugged. "I recommended vitality. You insisted on the other."

"I did not insist."

Daniel grinned, eyes glinting with mischief. "I don't know, Lily. You sounded pretty forceful about it." He held it together a moment longer then burst out laughing. "Definitely intimidated the tea vendor."

I smacked his arm. "Oh, my god, you made that up."

"I'm not. That's what's so funny."

I switched my drink with his and took a long pull on his straw, which made him laugh even harder. "Don't say it." I hid my mouth behind a hand.

"What?" he asked, innocently.

"*Anything.*" Where had this trickster come from and what had he done with my sweet, mild-mannered boyfriend?

An unwelcome face popped into my mind—disturbingly sexy with a single raised and pointed brow. J Tran would have mocked me in this way, smirked with hard, full lips, and bored into my soul with his cruel, dark eyes. His fascination with me had disturbed me almost as much as my obsession with him. I had thought my therapy sessions with Aleisha's PTSD specialist had banished the assassin from my thoughts. Apparently, I was wrong. Every silhouette up ahead reminded me of him, especially the one on the deck staring across the water like the captain of a ship. That's how Tran had stood, perfectly balanced and in control.

I sipped Daniel's tea and shook the assassin from my mind. Tran had helped me save lives in the past, but he had no business in my future, and I certainly didn't want him mucking up the present.

"I was only teasing," Daniel said, nudging me with his shoulder as we walked.

"I know. Want your drink back?"

He held my longan boba possessively to his chest. "I don't know. This one's pretty tasty." He smiled and held it out to exchange.

I felt pretty silly about the whole affair but didn't want to compound my embarrassment by discussing it. Instead, I sipped my "women's sex tonic," which was annoyingly delicious, and enjoyed our stroll.

We stopped in front of the Cultural Centre, where Daniel claimed the view would be best. It didn't matter to me. All I cared about was spending time with my charming, light-hearted man. I wouldn't have chosen him in a million years, but we balanced each other perfectly. Ma knew me better than I thought.

We squeezed into a spot at the railing. Daniel's arm felt warm against mine, a promise of more intimate contact to come. Then, my phone chimed with a message and spoiled the mood.

Lee: *Meet me tonight.*

Me: *I'm on a date.*

Lee: *9 p.m.*

Me: Wait…*you're here?*

Lee: *Obviously.*

Me: *Why?*

Lee: *Stupid question.*

I clenched my teeth. Only something important could have motivated Uncle to leave his family and spend time and money to fly all the way to Hong Kong.

Lee: *Chicken Lips Bar, Mong Kok. Soy Street, alley entrance. Don't be late.*

Daniel nudged my shoulder. "Everything okay?"

I pocketed my phone. "Yep. When does the light show begin?"

"Eight o'clock."

I snuggled closer. "Excellent."

# Chapter Forty-Eight

Every fiber in my being screamed to stay with Daniel and ignore Lee Chang, but no matter how much I hated to leave, my primary objective superseded all. Ma was in trouble. Uncle was the key.

"Are you sure you have to go?"

The golden light of the Peninsula Hotel framed Daniel like a Disney prince. If Uncle's information didn't pay out, he better duck the next time we passed each other in Baba's kitchen. My father's head cook wasn't the only one who could *accidentally* hurl woks, cleavers, and blades.

"Unfortunately, yes. But I'll make it up to you, okay?"

I sealed the promise with a kiss and boarded the bus to Mong Kok. Ten minutes later, I disembarked at Cheung Sha Wan and walked cautiously through the seedy neighborhood to the Soy Street address. Although Hong Kong had a stellar reputation for being one of the safest cities in the world, predators took advantage where they could. Most of the street-level shops in grungy old tenements were locked down behind metal roller doors for the night. The few that stayed open flashed brightly-lit signs.

I paused in front of a gap between buildings where the Chicken Lips Bar should have been. The alley was no more than seven feet across with a dingy awning draped over the entrance from the tiny corner shop. More awnings slanted from one side or the other. Light from unknown sources seeped into the darkness. Could this be Uncle's alley?

Glad to be dressed in black with quiet leather boots, I ventured to find out. The buildings I passed were too narrow to reach the actual streets and opened into this ugly passage beside trash bags, garbage bins, and bare metal tables chained to chairs. The awnings I had seen from the alley's entrance hung over locked-down shops and slum housing doorways. A man and woman emerged from one of the apartment buildings, said a cursory goodbye, and went their separate directions, him wobbling into the dark toward the street at the other end of the passage and her into the bar beneath bright pink lights and a neon yellow chicken with pursed red lips.

I had found Uncle's Chicken Lips Bar.

As the sex worker and client vanished, other men appeared, one from deep in the alley, one from the street behind me, and a third standing in bar's entrance. All were young and tough and mean.

The bouncer called to me in English. "Eh, drink-along girl, why you not dressed for work?"

I angled my stance so I could see all three. "I am. Just not the work you mean."

"Oh, yeah? Then why come here? No other business for a little miss like you."

I nodded to the sign. "Is this the Chicken Lips Bar?"

He grinned as if my question had proven him right.

"Don't get your hopes up. I'm meeting someone, but not for that."

His eyes narrowed, and the two men advanced.

I held out my hands. "Wait a minute, guys. I don't want any trouble, and neither do you."

Instead of calming emotions, my words inflamed them.

The man from the alley reached me first. As he grabbed for my jacket lapel, I redirected his hand and guided him past me into the street-side man who, inadvertently, slapped him across the face. The bouncer in the doorway laughed to see one of his men bitch-slap the other.

The alley guy shoved away the other man and came at me again, fists up and ready to box. Instead of waiting for the inevitable jab, cross, or hook, I lunged forward with a finger strike to his eyes. When his head flung back, I snapped the toe of my boot into his groin, then followed up with an Ura Shuto knife-hand strike to the throat. He scrambled backward and fell against the wall.

The bouncer flicked open a switchblade and grinned.

I shrugged off my jacket and let the slippery leather fall off my arms and turn inside out behind me. Having caught the cuffs, I tossed the jacket over my head onto the bouncer's arm as he attacked. When he pulled back the knife and swiped at my belly, I looped my jacket around his wrist and yanked him off balance, buckled his leg with my knee, and drove him to the ground.

The man was larger, stronger, and meaner than me. I didn't expect my advantage to last.

When he continued the fight, I followed his motion, looped a sleeve over his head, and choked him from behind. Two forceful knees to his spine, and he dropped the knife.

The other two men looked from the blade to me.

Since my choke wouldn't hold the bouncer for long, I swept the knife back with my boot, picked it up, yanked my jacket off his throat, and stomp-kicked the base of his neck. He planted on the pavement between me and his friends.

As they advanced around him, a new man called from the bar, "This one's not for you." He spoke in Mandarin, but I recognized the voice.

Uncle stepped in front of the men with a metal pipe in his hand. Although older and slighter, Lee Chang radiated menace. No longer the crotchety cook in my father's kitchen, but a seasoned fighter ready to kill.

The street-side man, who had come at me first, flicked out a knife and attacked. Uncle stepped aside and cracked the pipe onto his wrist. Bone snapped. The man howled in pain. The alley guy yanked his friend out of the way, grabbed a trash can lid, and charged.

Metal clanked on metal as Uncle and the alley guy fought, like gladiators armed with shield and sword. Chicken Lips patrons watched from the doorway. The bouncer lay unconscious on the ground. The man with the broken wrist held it to his chest and picked up his knife. As he came at Uncle for a second attempt, I swept my jacket across his eyes and knocked the knife away. He leapt back with a yelp and stumbled over the bouncer, who had just begun to stir. After a moment of confusion, both men crawled into the shadows.

I dodged to the right to avoid the swinging trash can lid as the alley guy sliced it down onto Lee Chang's face. Uncle shifted inside the strike and buckled the man's arm—exactly as I would have done—then back-elbowed him in the nose. Cartilage crunched.

The man stepped away, bloodied but far from done. He had extra forty pounds of muscle and put it behind every kick and strike. Uncle managed, but how long could his sixty-four-year-old body last?

As the alley guy wound up for another swing, Uncle faked high with his pipe then struck the side of the man's knee. The patrons of the bar cheered as the alley guy fell to the side and dragged himself to safety.

Uncle stood where he was—tired, not spent—and turned his head toward me. We stared at one another in a way we had never done before—ninja to triad. Nothing between us would ever be the same.

# Chapter Forty-Nine

The inside of the bar was as seedy as I had expected, with private corners, colored lights, and groping hands. Unlike a strip club, the women in this establishment didn't spiral around poles or grind their naked behinds into horny men's laps. They enticed the clientele with strategic glimpses up their micro-mini skirts and frank descriptions of services offered.

Prostitution was legal in Hong Kong as long as the women worked for themselves. That said, I'd bet the bank that the owners of this bar also ran the apartments above and parceled out cage homes for the sex workers to use as one-woman brothels. The women could ply their trade legally inside the bar with a constant stream of potential customers and unofficial protection, then take their clients off premise to consummate the deal. A shady and clever way to bend the law.

Uncle led me to a dark corner and gestured for two customers to vacate the table. They complied without hesitation.

Who was this man my father had taken into his life and business?

Baba had discovered him roasting ducks and sizzling shrimp in a second-rate eatery in Shanghai and offered him a position as lead cook in Wong's Hong Kong Inn. I was nine months old at the time and had always thought of the irascible man as family. When I moved into the apartment above Baba's restaurant, Uncle's sharp tongue lashed with stinging barbs. His eyes watched and judged. Yet he always left special treats for me to find—a plate of the crispiest duck, the sweetest steamed crab, the juiciest soup dumplings. With these obvious signs of caring, I attributed his ill temper to a prickly nature and advancing age. Now, I wasn't so sure.

"How long have you known?" I asked.

"About you?" He snorted. "Since the day you moved into the restaurant."

"I hadn't done anything."

"You would. I could see it in your walk, hear it in the bitter tone of your voice. Your sister's murderer also killed you. The girl who moved in was not the same as the girl I had known."

"Then why were you so cruel?"

"To save your life." He shook his head and scanned the room. "These are the people you would meet, desperate, dangerous, devoid of the decency you grew up with in your safe and fancy home. You were too blinded by anger and grief to understand your foolishness. Same for your parents. Nobody saw it but me."

"I had a teacher."

"So what? We all have teachers. Is he with you now? Did he follow you into the night back in Los Angeles? Did he mop up the blood from the wounds you acquired?" Uncle raised his brows in challenge. "You think I didn't notice? I know a knife wound when I see it."

I chuckled at the irony. Aside from that one particularly nasty incident, Uncle's blades were the more frequent threat. "Is that why you're always throwing things at me?"

"It isn't a game, stupid girl. Once you set foot on the path, no one and nowhere is safe."

I studied the crowd and considered his words. "Why here?"

"I already told you."

"Not the whole of it. Those men gave up this table without a moment's hesitation. Why?"

Uncle shrugged. "We have friends in common."

"Friends or affiliations?"

"I told you to stay away from the triads."

"You didn't tell me you belonged to one."

"Not your business."

"The thug who threw me off the roof had a scorpion tattoo exactly like yours." I nodded to the sleeveless men at the bar. "Their tattoos are different, but they look like gang symbols to me. Why meet me here if you didn't want me mingling with the triads?"

"You think I'm proud to be part of this?"

"What exactly is *this*?"

Uncle planted his elbow on the table and folded his hands to cover his mouth. "Chicken Lips is run by a sub group of the 14K. You know who they are?"

I nodded. The 14K was the second largest international triad, begun in Hong Kong as an anti-Communist action group by fourteen members of the Kuomintang. They had a relatively small presence in Los Angeles, overshadowed by the more powerful sub groups of Wah Ching, Wo Hop, United Bamboo, and a sub group from the number one international triad, Sun Yee On. These cells operated independently from the parent triad and frequently worked with other ethnic criminal groups in other countries to conduct narcotic and migrant trafficking, money laundering, credit card fraud, and intellectual property piracy. Some dealt in prostitution. So far, none of the women I had rescued had been persecuted by them.

Uncle glanced at his arm, drawing my attention to his tattoo. "The Scorpions are another sub group of 14K."

"I thought you were from Shanghai."

"We emigrated from Hong Kong when I was one year old, two months after the Double Ten riots in 1956. A Shanghai benevolent society offered my family assistance, loans, and protection. The tong also introduced my father to the Scorpion Black Society, a triad cell of the 14K. My father joined. When I grew of age, so did I."

The bouncer I had fought outside eyed us from the door while the other two men, whose wrist and knee Uncle had broken with his pipe, sat in a booth icing their injuries until someone, presumably, would drive them to a hospital.

"And your connection to those men?"

"Professional courtesy."

"I'm not sure they'd agree."

He lowered his hands and shrugged. "They disregarded my warning."

"The locals won't retaliate?"

"It was a fair fight."

Three young men against one sixty-four-year-old cook didn't seem too fair to me. But then, Lee Chang wasn't who he had purported himself to be.

"Does Baba know you're triad?"

"Does he know you're ninja?"

"As a matter of fact."

Uncle's surprise came and passed too quickly for me to gloat.

"Why am I here? You could have called or texted me your information about Ma."

He scoffed. "Your mother can take care of herself. Plenty of women content themselves with book clubs and mahjong. What do I care if she works or not?'

"And yet, you came all the way to Hong Kong."

He pressed his lips shut against the words he did not want to say.

"You came here for me?"

"Why else?" Anger blasted through his clenched teeth and flooded over me. "Have I not been your uncle from before you could walk? Have I not picked you up when you scraped your knees? And when you began training with that old Japanese ninja in Los Feliz, poking your nose into other people's business, tracking down your sister's killer...that's right, I know all about *that*. If I had known you would do something so foolhardy, I would have beaten sense into you and locked you in your apartment."

"But how did you—"

"Find out? You're not the only one who can watch and follow. As for the killer, when I saw the state you were in the next day, I knew something bad had happened. I found your clothes in the laundry basket, wet from soaking yet stained with blood. A crumpled paper was in the trash with the names of bars, crossed out except for one—a bar you were seen flirting with a man who matched the killer's description."

My gut clenched. I hadn't felt this exposed since I tangled with Tran.

Uncle shook off his fury and clasped his hands at his mouth. "It tore out my heart wondering what had happened to you."

Images of that night flashed through my mind: the twirling olive, the seductive smile, the spiked martini. The monster in the car. "He didn't…"

"Good." Uncle sagged with relief. "*Good*."

"But I—"

He held up a hand. "I know what you did. I saw it in your eyes."

"And do you know if it was ever found?"

"The body?"

I nodded. Nothing was ever reported in the news, nor could I find a stabbing victim that matched his description in any of the L.A. hospitals. It was as if that horrid night had never happened.

Uncle shrugged. "Even stupid girls get lucky."

# Chapter Fifty

We sipped our Tsingtao beers in silence and adjusted to our new relationship. This man I had thought indifferent to my daily struggles had been observing every detail of my life with an eagle eye. He didn't just care, he cared deeply.

"Uncle, why are you here?"

"This business with your mother is not good. You need to leave. Forget about HKIF and go home."

"We can't do that. L.A. Director isn't just a position, it's the stepping stone to CEO. If the partners vote her out, Ma won't only lose her job, she'll lose her chance at inheriting Gung-Gung's company."

"Better than losing her life."

I lowered his bottle. "You told me she wasn't in danger."

"Circumstances have changed."

"In what way?"

Uncle freed his beer and took a fortifying gulp. "The Scorpions are laundering money through the London office of your grandfather's company. They want to do the same with Los Angeles."

"What? Ma would never do that."

"Of course she wouldn't. Which is why she has to go."

"And you knew? How could you betray my family after everything Baba's done for you?"

"I didn't know until you asked about my tattoo."

"And now?"

"I will help, of course. But there's only so much I can do."

"Because you're more loyal to a triad than to us."

"No. Because they'll kill us all."

I shoved aside my beer and took a cleansing breath. Indignation would not protect my mother or save my grandfather's company. I needed a clear head and a calm mind.

"Start from the beginning and tell me how this happened."

"Back in 2008, your grandfather's partner Derrick Lau ran into financial trouble and borrowed money from the Scorpions—short term, high interest. When he couldn't pay it back, the mountain master ordered him to launder Scorpion money or die."

"Why would Mr. Lau go all the way to Shanghai to borrow money?"

"He didn't. He borrowed from the H.K. Scorpions not the Shanghai Society. The two gangs, including the Scorpions in Guangdong, work independently but also together on some business."

"Such as?"

"Money laundering."

"So you *did* know."

Uncle shook his head. "I broke contact with the Scorpions when I moved to Los Angeles."

"And when I asked about the tattoo?"

"I renewed my interest."

Part of me worried that I had put Uncle in a dangerous situation. The other part didn't care. Ma's life and livelihood was at stake. Lee Chang could fend for himself.

Poor Daniel. This news would crush him if he knew.

"How long has Derrick Lau been laundering money through the London office?"

"Nine years."

"Nine *years*? Does Cecil Chu know?"

Uncle snorted. "He makes it happen."

"No wonder he looks so stressed." I thought of the Scorpion thugs following him on the street. "Is the triad threatening him?"

"Probably. He has a family to protect."

"What about Gung-Gung?"

"He doesn't know. Or anyone else, except maybe Raymond Ng."

"Ma's kai ba is in on this? But he's family."

"I don't think he knows everything, but Derrick Lau pressured him to vote against your mother. The Scorpions are there to enforce."

"The intruder at Mr. Ng's home—if I hadn't been there to stop him, would he have thrown poor Ma Lik off the roof?"

"If he was there to send a message."

I glared in challenge. "Is that what you would have done?"

He stared back, unflinching. "Yes."

I turned away so he wouldn't see my disdain. "What now?"

"You take your mother and go home."

"Not gonna happen. I broke into Derrick Lau's apartment and stole the London folder from his file cabinet. I haven't had a chance to examine the files, but I'm pretty sure there will be something to nail his ass to the wall."

"Stupid girl. Who will you put in danger next, your grandfather, your grandmother, your *father*? Don't you understand how this works? A triad has targeted Shaozu's company. There's nothing to do but roll over and pay."

"What about the police?"

"They won't help. Even before the protests, the police have relied on triads to keep the peace and inform them about criminal activity. Sometimes, they even hire triad members to intimidate or harass. With the protests, many triads would do this for free."

"To stir up trouble?"

"To support China. Triads are patriots. They believe pro-democracy protesters are trying to overthrow the Chinese government that has worked hard to recruit them into the communist camp. Once mainland China began to prosper, the triads rushed to set up operations across the Hong Kong-China border. They seek favor with the pro-Beijing political elite in Hong Kong because this group has the power to make or break fortunes. Do you understand what this means? The police work for the Hong Kong government that is influenced by the pro-Beijing elite who the triads want to please. Right now, the goals of the triads and the police are the same. They will not risk this cooperation over such a small corporate affair on the suspicions of an American girl."

I thought about the brutal attack in July when more than a hundred triad gangsters in white T-shirts had rushed a train full of people returning from a protest. They terrorized families and beat the men and women with steel bars and wooden sticks. By the time they were done, nearly fifty people were injured and the floors splattered with blood. Emergency calls were made, but hardly any police responded. The ones who did scanned the scene and faded away. A few were even caught on camera chatting with the attackers. When a handful were finally arrested, they turned out to be members of two of the world's most notorious triad societies, including 14K.

The more I learned, the more overwhelmed I felt, as if I were climbing from a muddy ditch as it caved in on me. I dropped my head and squeezed my temples until the pain seared through the sludge, then released my grip and glared at Uncle. "I won't quit, and neither will Ma. Derrick Lau has a man ready to replace her. If we can take him out of play, we can stop or postpone this takeover."

"It won't matter. Your mother will be voted out, and Lau will find another pawn."

"Gung-Gung won't vote against family."

"He no longer has the majority stock."

The news hit me like a slap in the face. "How do you know?"

"If he did, the Scorpions would be targeting him."

"Maybe they are. You said Ma and I were in danger."

"That's different. You're causing trouble. She's in the way. The mountain master is losing patience. There is talk of killing you and your mother before the vote."

"Your triad put a hit on us?"

"The H.K. Scorpion Group is not my triad. I have no say in what they do."

I grabbed my beer and slammed it on the table, no closer to a solution than before. If we got rid of Ma's replacement, Derrick Lau would find another. If we convinced Raymond Ng to vote for Ma, the Scorpions would hurt his family. If we gave the evidence to the police—providing the files I had stolen even *contained* evidence—they'd disregard it.

"What *can* we do?"

Uncle smirked. "We convince the Scorpions that the firefly they would eat is an owl swooping in for the kill.

"You mean…".

He nodded. "We convince the triad Derrick Lau is stealing from them."

# Chapter Fifty-One

Fragments of ideas swirled through my sleepy brain as I woke but refused to coalesce. If only I had a plan. And more than twenty-six hours. And a way to keep the triad from killing me and Ma.

I checked my messages and found a voicemail from Baba left while I had been asleep. The time difference was killing our communication.

"Hello, Dumpling dear. Glad to hear your mother is okay. Try not to worry too much, she's stronger than you think. As for this business with Derrick Lau…what do you mean by muscle? Please respond soon. Your words have dug into my thoughts like a tick."

Baba was responding to a message I had left after stealing the files from Derrick Lau's apartment and before meeting with Uncle. At that time, I had only suspected the Scorpion thugs of belonging to a triad. Now, I knew the whole ugly truth.

I stared at my phone. How much of it should I share?

He answered on the fourth ring. "I've been waiting for your call."

"I just woke up. Can you talk?"

"Hold on a sec."

The clatter of metal. Rushing water. The hiss of steam. Voices in the kitchen. "Bayani, sauté the black bean cod, would ya?"

"Sure thing, Vern."

The bustle of the kitchen dwindled as Baba walked outside and closed the alley door. "I only have a few minutes. What's going on?"

"Derrick Lau is laundering money for a triad."

"He *what?*"

"He borrowed money and couldn't pay it back. They've been forcing him to work for them ever since."

"Does your mother know?"

"Not yet. I don't want her in any more danger than she already is."

He heaved a sigh. "I don't like this one guldarn bit."

"I'm containing it."

"Oh, for the love of Pete, you think that calms my gut?"

After a moment of silence, he tried again more calmly. "Look… you don't have the support in Hong Kong that you have here, you speak marginal Cantonese, and from what I'm reading in the news, you can't expect to receive any help from the police. I gotta say, Dumpling, I don't think much of this at all. What if someone gets hurt."

"No one's been hurt."

"Yet."

I held my tongue. I had already fudged a bit on my definition of hurt, I didn't want to make promises I couldn't keep.

He breathed into the phone like a bull after a charge.

"Baba?"

"Nope. You've said your piece, and I've said mine."

"But—"

"The woks are waiting. I have to go. Take care of your mother. Be safe."

He ended the call before I could say goodbye.

Ma knocked on the door. "Breakfast is ready. Are you coming out?"

"Be right there."

I was fairly certain he wouldn't tell Ma and a hundred percent certain I shouldn't have told *him.* Neither of which had any effect on my growling stomach. I'd been in such a rush yesterday that I hadn't eaten anything except Po-Po's omelet, curry fish balls, and the tapioca pearls in my *sex tonic* bubble tea.

Daniel's teasing expression popped into my mind. By the time I entered the dining room I felt almost chipper.

"Good morning, Po-Po." I kissed her cheek then moved onto the Gung-Gung and Ma.

"You want jook?" she asked.

"I do." I took my seat and ladled rice porridge from the communal bowl and turned the lazy Susan to reach the condiments Bao Jeh had provided—pork floss, Chinese pickles, dried shrimp, salted duck egg, and fried peanuts. She had even deep-fried yau ja gwai.

*Dip or slice?*

When Rose and I were kids, Ma would bring the deep-fried devil sticks home from Sam Woo B.B.Q., crispy on the outside and puffy on the inside, in a paper sack stained with oil. From the intoxicating smell coming from the kitchen, Bao Jeh had fried her yau ja gwai fresh this morning.

I picked up one of the savory sticks, bit through the crunch, then set it on a plate and added two more.

*Definitely dip.*

Po-Po grinned as I added more of the shredded pork. "You like yuk sung?"

"I do."

Ma shrugged. "What doesn't she like?"

She rolled her eyes at my over-stuffed bowl of porridge. I didn't care. Although I loved Baba's homemade jook, he rarely served it with yuk sung or suen gua. The dried candied meat was tedious to prepare and whenever he took the time to pickle the Japanese cucumbers with licorice root, soy, and sugar, Uncle and I ate the blossom-shaped slices right out of the jar.

If I was in heaven, Ma was in hell. Tension wrinkled her unmade face and dulled her eyes in a worried gaze. The lustrous hair, usually styled, hung limp over her slumped shoulders. My ferocious mother had given up the fight.

I nudged her foot with mine. When her mouth twitched toward a smile, I left it there as I ate, reminding her she wasn't alone. On my way home from the bar, I had debated whether or not to show Ma the folders I had stolen, but the probable risk of what she might do outweighed the possible reward of what I might learn.

"What's on the agenda for today?" I asked.

Gung-Gung looked up from *The Economic Times*. "It's a work day. I'm going to the office."

Po-Po patted his hand. "To do what? Stay here and visit with Violet."

"Or I can come with you," Ma asked.

I cringed to see the hope and need on her face. Since when did my mother beg to tag along?

Gung-Gung swiped his tablet to another page. "It's not father-daughter day at work. Go shopping with your mother. You can help her pick out rug yarn for her next project."

"Rug yarn?" Ma clenched her fork.

I pressed on her foot and willed her not to stab him with it.

"You could join me and the ladies for Tai Chi," Po-Po suggested.

Ma set down her fork. "I suppose. What about you, Lily? Care to join us? Or is Tai Chi too mild for your hyper-athleticism?"

Although tempted to surprise her with my daily meditations and occasional Tai Chi practices, it was more convenient to let her think otherwise. "Enjoy your mother-daughter time. I have a date with Daniel." I didn't yet, but I expected to at some point in the day, even if only for a kiss.

I gobbled the last bites of jook. "In fact, I better get going." I rose and stacked my cup and bowl on the plate.

Po-Po waved her hand. "Leave it, Lei Lei. Bao Jeh with take care of it it when we're all done."

"You sure?"

"Go."

I walked over and kissed her cheek. "Have fun with Ma. Don't work too hard, Gung-Gung."

"Mm-hmm," he said, with barely a glance.

I walked behind Ma and gave her a hug. "Call if you decide to go into town, okay?"

She patted my hand. "I'll be fine."

"What if I want to come along?"

"Okay, I'll call. But only if that's what you really want. One of us should be enjoying this trip."

With Ma's promise and plans established, I hurried to my room, pulled out Derrick Lau's files, and fanned them on the bed.

I recognized many of Ma's clients, especially those from Arcadia like Rudy Leong who had passed out at her birthday party after exchanging shots of baijiu with Gung-Gung. Mr. Leong had invested millions earlier in the year, bumping Ma's biannual numbers higher than the entire previous year. A gain like this should have earned her a bonus not a fight.

Cecil Chu also had notable gains.

In addition to a solid and active European clientele, Mr. Chu had acquired a big-ticket U.K. client called Whitman and White Ltd. that had purchased a ten-million-dollar townhouse in Hamstead, U.K. and invested four million in the Tiemann Group Investment Fund. Could Whitman and White be a front for the Scorpion group? Possibly. But on paper, everything looked legit.

I straightened the files and hid the folders between the mattresses—deep, in case Bao Jeh decided to change the sheets—then I made a call.

"Hi, Kenneth. It's Lily Wong."

"Lily. How nice to hear from you."

"I wanted to thank you again for yesterday's tour and conversation. I really enjoyed it."

"So did I. I'm only sorry you couldn't join me for lunch. I would have enjoyed feeding you."

I stifled a giggle as I imagined Kenneth attempting to do this and me tossing him, spoon in hand, over my head in a Tomoe Nage sacrifice throw. "Maybe we could try for coffee. This morning, perhaps? If you have a favorite place, I could meet you there."

"The Four Seasons Lounge serves breakfast if you're hungry."

My stomach distended with a double serving of jook. "Coffee's fine."

"Then we can sit by the pool."

"Perfect. See you in an hour."

I had no idea how Uncle and I could cast suspicion on Derrick Lau. Perhaps a conversation with Kenneth Hong would show me a way.

# Chapter Fifty-Two

After all the fights, dashes, and dog rescues I'd encountered in this supposedly safe city, I decided to dress more for action than attraction. Although, from the appraising gleam in Kenneth's eyes, my turquoise muscle tee and black stretch jeans served both functions equally well.

He led me to a poolside umbrella table overlooking Victoria Harbour. "Is this okay?"

"Perfect." I shrugged off my backpack. "Do you come here often?"

"Almost never."

"Ha. You're too busy investing in stocks, buildings, and mutual funds."

His brows raised in surprise. "You know so much. Do you invest?"

"Not yet, but I'm considering it. What makes the most money?"

He chuckled. "That depends on the risks you're willing to take and the funds you have to invest."

"That would be few and inadequate."

He grinned. "In that case, a piggy bank would be best." He waved to the waitress and ordered cappuccinos and scones.

"Have you heard of the Tiemann Group Investment Fund?"

"No, but new funds are always seeking investors."

"Does that make them a good deal?"

"It makes them less particular. New funds tend to have lax CDD: customer due diligence."

"What about real estate, does that also have a lax CDD?"

"Almost none. You just need to prove you have the funds and a legitimate way to transfer them."

I nibbled on a scone. If Whitman and White Ltd. was actually a Scorpion front, Mr. Chu had chosen wisely. "Is it more advantageous to invest as an individual or as a limited company?"

"That depends. U.S. or U.K.? Ltd. has a different meaning in each country. The U.K. private limited companies are similar to your LCCs and are very easy to establish—some might say, too easy. But, no, you don't need to be a company." He raised his cappuccino. "You can invest your pennies as you wish."

Although he said this with a smile, I could see the annoyance in his eyes. If I continued on this course, I'd loose him for sure. "Enough business? Tell me about *you*."

"Me? What do you want to know?"

I leaned forward in rapt attention. "Everything."

The most challenging part of the next ninety minutes was staying alert and engaged. Somewhere in this litany of banal interests and personal history lay the key to casting suspicion on Derrick Lau. Or so I hoped.

"Wait, *who*?"

"What?"

"Who did you say works for the OCTB?"

"My cousin. The one who grew up across the street and took photography with me in junior secondary school."

"Oh, right. Your mother's cousin's youngest son."

Kenneth shrugged. "Who would have thought such a skinny kid would join the Organized Crime and Triad Bureau?"

*Bingo.*

I checked my phone and gasped. "Oh my, I've kept you from your work for nearly two hours."

"Really? It seemed so short."

*Not to me.*

"Thanks the conversation and this lovely poolside view. I hate to leave, but my uncle's waiting for me, and I'm sure you have lots of work to do."

His brows furrowed at the mention of work. "This is true. Your grandfather is coming into the office today. He'll want a report."

I touched Kenneth's arm as we rose. "Not about our coffee date?"

"No, no, of course not. This is only between us."

"That's good. I'm not sure he'd approve."

"Oh. Perhaps not."

"I won't tell if you don't."

Kenneth nodded. "That would be best."

As we strolled through the hotel lobby, I thanked him again for the coffee and conversation. "I enjoyed hearing about your family. They're all so interesting. And that cousin of yours in the OCTB, what was his name?"

"Kevin. Kevin Ching."

"Ah, he favors his English name, just like you."

"Many Hongkongers do, especially those who are young like us."

I nodded in agreement even though Kenneth was closer to Ma's age than mine.

When we reached the street, he extended his hand in a business-like way. "Enjoy the rest of your visit."

I nodded with equal detachment. "Gung-Gung is fortunate to have you as his COO."

Neither of us offered to meet again. As we parted ways, I pulled out my phone to text Uncle about what I had learned and received a call instead.

"Hey, Mr. Tam. Is everything okay?"

"I just spoke with Jing. She's cutting out of school early today to attend the community dialogue with Chief Executive Carrie Lam at Queen Elizabeth Stadium."

"She admitted to cutting school?"

"She's proud of it. Four of our ministers will be joining Carrie Lam to answer questions from the public. The audience has already been selected, but she's going to demonstrate outside."

"It sounds like a controlled event. Are you worried about her safety or cutting out of school?"

"Both."

"What time is the event?"

"Six o'clock. I would look out for her, but your grandfather wants me on hand into early evening. The stadium is in Wan Chai, down the hill from the Jockey Club."

"I'm headed across the harbor to meet a friend. I'll make it back in time."

"I just dropped your grandfather at the office. Want me to give you a ride."

"Not necessary, but I'll reach out to Jing later today if she doesn't message me first." I didn't want Mr. Tam driving me anywhere near Uncle or his associates.

"Okay. I'll let you know if I hear from her again. And, Lily…"

"Yes?"

"Whatever you're doing today, be careful."

He hung up before I could offer meaningless assurances and messaged Uncle instead.

Me: *I have an idea.*

Lee: *So do I. Meet me at Mong Kok Station, 45 minutes.*

# Chapter Fifty-Three

With time to spare, I walked to MTR Central and caught the Tsuen Wan Line to Mong Kok Station. In Los Angeles, I rode mass transit to tune in to the pulse of the city. Today, I felt that pulse in the rumbling heartbeat of steel wheels on rails sparked by fear, frustration, and rage. Even the clean, fast, efficiency of Hong Kong's MTR couldn't cut through the crackle and ache of a people in revolt. Transit workers could wash off the blood and graffiti and repair the broken and burned station kiosks and displays, but the truth of the city's discontent remained.

I wrapped my arms around a pole, opened the app on my phone, and sent Daniel a smiley face surrounded by hearts. Was that a mistake? Although we clearly had strong feelings for each other, neither of us had said the word. And yet, I could feel his love radiating from his smile, tingling my skin, burrowing into my bones.

Had I fallen in love?

I rolled the question in my mind like a candy on my tongue, tasted the sweetness and confirmed its solidity. After last night's hasty departure, Daniel's feelings for me might have soured, but mine promised a future almost too delicious to bear. I sighed with relief when Daniel sent a matching smiley face with hearts.

Me: *Miss me yet?*

Daniel: *As soon as you stepped on the bus.*

Me: *Sorry about that. I had a weirdly unexpected emergency.*

Daniel: *Is everything okay?*

Me: *Yep. Just family drama.*

Daniel: *Want to talk?*

Me: *I'm on a train.*

Daniel: *To where?*

Me: *Errands.*

Daniel: *For your mother?*

I paused. Did plotting with a gangster to convince other gangsters to stay out of my grandfather's business and not kill my mother count as an errand?

Me: *Yep.*

I tapped my forehead on the pole. Our romantic emojis had devolved into an exchange of quips and veiled truths.

Daniel: *Want to meet later.*

As much as I yearned to spend time with Daniel, I had more urgent demands.

Me: *I would, but I'm not sure I'll have time. Call you later?*

How many times could I put this man on hold before he wandered into more attentive company?

I stared at his thumbs up response and willed the typing indicator to appear. Was he waiting for an affectionate tag from me or a sticker with a panda hugging a heart? Or had he shut me out and moved on with his day? Never had a simple emoji caused me such angst.

Daniel: *Sorry about that…business call came in. Message me when you know your plans. We never did try Gradini's afternoon tea.* (wink emoji)

Gradini's Ristorante was located in Daniel's hotel. This time, his meaning came through loud and clear.

I responded with an excited smiley face and stepped off the train into a river of people. No one disrupted the flow with questions about schedules or stops. Information was clearly conveyed in symbols, and the trains arrived with only a few minutes in between.

I tucked my phone in the zippered pocket of my backpack and hurried to the street to find Uncle.

"You're late."

"I'm early."

"We don't have time to argue about your tardiness," he said. "We have a meeting with Saan Zyu in forty minutes."

"The mountain master? Of the *Scorpions?*"

Uncle smirked. "I told you I had a plan."

"You said you had an idea, not a way to get us killed."

"We could die crossing this street. Better to face our enemy and fight."

I would have trusted the advice more if it had come from Sensei.

We power walked down Nathan Road, passed the big-brand stores and tourist busses, then turned onto a one-way street. When Uncle darted into a pedestrian alley, narrower than the spread of his arms, I stopped.

"What's the matter?"

"Every time I've gone down one of these alleys, I've been attacked by gangsters."

"Don't be so dramatic. Everyone walks down alleys. The next street is Ladies Market, wall to wall people. Not good."

Caught between lousy options, I followed Uncle past back door exits strewn with cigarette butts and overturned buckets for seats. Pink rubber gloves dried on wires like pop art hooked onto doorways and pipes. Clothing and linen fluttered from windows above. As the walls of the buildings funneled us down the shoot like cattle to slaughter, I focused on the thin strip of sky overhead.

A familiar tightness constricted my chest as memories of snuff-film dens and traumatized girls invaded my mind. Most had survived. The one who haunted me was the woman Tran had shot that I could not, *did not*, save. I thought I'd made peace with this ghost, with the help of Aleisha's PTSD therapist friend. Why had the woman chosen this moment to return?

I walked faster and pushed Uncle out of the alley with the force of my need.

"Stop it," he said, as I burst past him onto the busy sidewalk.

He smacked my arm. "What are you doing?"

"Stopping. Isn't that what you told me to do?"

"Not on the sidewalk, stupid girl." He pointed across the street to a cha chaan teng where a couple was leaving a wooden booth by the window. "Over there. We can eat while you pull yourself together."

I started to complain, but Uncle had bolted across the one-way street to claim the table in front of a hungry pair of men. I shook off the remnants of my triggered anxiety and anchored myself in this time and place—no Tran, no teens, no dead woman.

The waitress arrived as I slipped into the cramped wooden booth. Uncle ordered macaroni soup with ham, peanut butter-stuffed French toast with condensed milk, and tea. "Tell her what you want."

"I just sat down."

He shook his head. "Give her—"

"Salty beef sandwich and hot lemon tea," I said, in Cantonese before Uncle could order me a double dose of sugar and carbs. Our food would arrive faster than a horse to trough. I didn't have much time.

"What's your plan, Uncle? What have you learned?"

"You first."

"All right. The London director is investing in an upstart investment fund and high-end real estate for a company called Whitman and White Ltd. I met with Gung-Gung's COO this morning, and he told me these types of investments have had a lax due diligence."

Uncle nodded. "Whitman and White is a new shell company for the Scorpion Group." He gestured to my backpack. "Did you bring the files?"

"No. But I have photos." I handed him my phone and continued in haste before the waitress arrived. "I also found out that Kenneth Hong's second cousin is an investigator for the OCTB. What if we make it seem as though they're watching HKIF and maybe even Derrick Lau? Would that concern the mountain master enough to stop laundering money through Gung-Gung's company?"

Uncle grunted in response.

"Did you hear me?"

He looked up from a photo. "The London director is doing more than easy investments. I learned about two of the companies in these reports. One is linked to a local bank account in London. The other, Crowded Corner, has an international account through Lloyds Bank. Both of these shell companies were registered this year. The Scorpion Group is using HKIF to run Cuckoo Smurfing scams."

Smurfing was banking jargon for structuring financial transactions to avoid the scrutiny of regulators and law enforcement. It could occur at any of the three stages of money laundering: placement, layering, or integration. *Cuckoo* Smurfing was new to me.

"Explain."

"A legitimate client wants to buy or invest. The Scorpions want to clean. They also need layers of protection. They use money shops and trusted smurfs to place cash into banks then deposit this money into many shell company accounts. A financial advisor, like Cecil Chu, would help them open shell companies in the U.K. He would use the money from one U.K. account to buy or invest for the legitimate client and deposit the legitimate client's money into the other U.K. account. When the Scorpions want to collect, they transfer their money to the international account and withdraw it from the Hong Kong branch. This provides layers of protection for the triad."

"And if the authorities check?"

"The legitimate client and Mr. Chu will be blamed."

The waitress set down our plates and cups with noisy efficiency and left. Uncle returned my phone and dug into his meal while I considered the ramifications of what I had learned. If Uncle's guess was correct, Cecil Chu had compromised himself beyond repair.

I lifted the lid of my sandwich, toasted white bread with the crusts cut off, and retrieved a fork from the utensil drawer in the table. After dipping it in a washing teacup, I picked at the layers of scrambled eggs and salty corned beef. After the jook and scone, I didn't need bread, but I hadn't wanted to complicate my rushed order.

Uncle eyed me as he slurped his macaroni soup. "Why you order if you're not going to eat?"

"You haven't told me your plan."

He cut the peanut butter French toast with his fork, swirled it in condensed milk, and stuffed it into his mouth. "We convince Saan Zyu that HKIF is no good."

"You said that last night."

"So what? It's still a good plan." He gobbled another bite and pointed his fork at my food. "You going to eat that?"

"Help yourself." I slid over the plate and sipped my tea. If that was the sum total of Uncle's plan, I'd need a clear head and an empty belly to fight.

# Chapter Fifty-Four

The entrance to the Scorpion den was down the block between a dispensary and dessert shop on the left and a competing dessert shop and money exchange on the right. All of the shops occupied the street-level floor of a shabby, gray-stucco mid-rise with the ubiquitous air-conditioning units and protruding laundry poles and racks. The security gate stood open to a metal staircase so cramped, Baba's shoulders would have brushed the walls.

"What floor are they on?"

"Fifth. But there's no fourth."

"Of course there isn't." Even triads didn't tempt bad luck.

When we reached the fourth/fifth landing, a scowling guard with buzz-cut hair barred our way.

Uncle addressed him in Cantonese. "We have business here."

The guard leered at me and replied with something I didn't understand.

"Not her," Uncle said. "Information."

"What kind of information?"

Uncle crossed his arms and angled to show the scorpion inked into his shoulder. "The kind too important for 49ers like you."

The guard tensed, but Uncle remained relaxed and confident. After a few moments, the guard nodded. "Wait here."

When he disappeared into the apartment on the right, I leaned toward Uncle. "What's a 49er?"

"A soldier. Bottom rank."

"Will our meeting be in Cantonese?"

"Probably. Unless he wants to keep it private."

I checked the stairway in both directions. If things went badly, we'd have to fight the triad, one-by-one on steel steps. As long as Uncle and I fought back to back, we could guard our rear as we forged down to the exit—pretty straightforward if not for machetes and other weapons the gangsters would undoubtedly use. Although glad I had brought a first aid kit in my backpack, what I really wanted was my knife.

The guard returned and motioned us toward the apartment he had vacated.

"Do they have the entire floor?" I whispered.

"Yes."

"We'll be cornered in all directions."

Uncle shrugged. "We were corned the moment we entered the building."

He pushed open the door and entered. Yellowed paint peeled from walls, uncomfortably close, and funneled us toward ratted couches and random plastic and metal chairs. Equally mismatched tables of varying heights were shoved into corners or centered in the room, the surfaces crowded with dirty dishes, cups, wrappers, containers, and money in both U.S. and H.K. bills.

Two muscled men stood, one near the door as we entered and the other beside the table stacked with money. A third man, older than Baba and younger than Uncle, sat on a couch with his arms stretched over the back. He couldn't have weighed much more than me, but his bare arms were sinewy with strength. The real story was in his eyes, amused, intelligent, and cruel. When he greeted Uncle in English I glanced at the men. Neither gave any signs of understanding.

"Lee Chang. I heard you were in town."

Uncle inclined his head. "And I heard you were Saan Zyu."

The mountain master chuckled. "How times have changed, eh? You and me, we could have ruled together, Shanghai and Hong Kong."

Uncle shook his head. "Red Pole is not Dragon Head."

"You could have risen. Instead, you ran."

Uncle smirked. "I prefer to die in bed."

"In America?"

"They have very comfortable beds."

The mountain master laughed. "Come," he said, rising from the couch. "Since you've grown accustomed to soft living, you will be more comfortable in my quarters."

He walked through a door to an adjoining apartment while his men herded us like sheep. We crossed the threshold into an opulent sitting room more suited for an emperor's dalliances than a mob boss' lair.

Uncle glanced from one antique to the next and settled his gaze on the intricately carved opium daybed. "You hide your riches."

"I show our neighbors what they expect to see, but like you, I enjoy a comfortable bed."

He reclined on the velvet cushions and gestured to the carved wooden chairs across the pearl-inlaid tea table. Uncle sat. I stood, serving as sentry to him as the 49ers did for their boss. The mountain master nodded then turned his attention to Uncle.

"So, what do you want from me?"

"Not from. For."

"Eh?"

"Your operation is in jeopardy. We have information."

The mountain master nodded at me. "From the troublemaker?"

"She is Shaozu Wong's granddaughter."

"I know who she is, and so do my men. Fu, in particular, has eagerness to meet her again."

I inclined my head as if receiving a compliment.

The mountain master smirked and returned his attention to Uncle. "What is this girl to you?"

"Family."

"Really? I was not aware that your familial pool had diluted."

Lee bristled at the insult then shrugged. "A monsoon hits and streams appear. Who can predict where a river will flow?"

I kept my face passive through the exchange, neither offended nor proud.

The mountain master's eyes squinted with amusement. "So, Red Pole Chang, what information do you have to sell?"

"Not sell. Give. The Triad Bureau is investigating Hong Kong International Finance."

"Huh. Is that so?"

Uncle nodded. "They are very interested in the recent transactions of certain shell companies in the U.K."

"Which companies?"

"Whitman and White, and Crowded Corner." Uncle chuckled. "It was risky to name one of your companies after Mong Kok. And to connect it to such a big bank." When the triad leader didn't react, Uncle added, "5209."

"What's that?"

"The last four digits of your Lloyd's international bank account."

The triad leader tensed. "You are not as separated from the black societies as you pretend to be."

Uncle shrugged.

"Which transactions are they watching?"

"Real estate, mutual funds." Uncle waited for him to relax then added, "And a suspicious exchange between you and another client of Cecil Chu."

"Where are you getting this information?"

Uncle tipped his head toward me. "She stole it from Derrick Lau."

All pretense of friendliness left as the mountain master barked an order in Cantonese.

One man yanked the backpack off my shoulders. The other frisked my waistband, pockets, and legs. The man with my backpack tossed my phone to his boss and dropped the pack at my feet.

"Did you think she was stupid enough to bring the documents?" Uncle asked.

The triad leader held out my phone. "Unlock it."

I braced for a fight. "No." My phone had contact information on everyone closest to me, many of whom were in Hong Kong. I would not willingly put them in danger.

"The proof is not in the phone," Uncle said, turning Saan Zyu's attention onto himself. "It's in safe hands, ready for delivery."

"To me?"

"No."

"You have lost your trust."

"I never had any."

"Ha! No. Neither did I." The triad leader leaned back on the cushions. "Derrick Lau is part owner of the company. So what if he has bank account numbers and investment statements? None of this shows proof of scrutiny from the Triad Bureau."

Uncle glanced at me. "Tell him."

Back at the cha chaan teng, after devouring my salty beef sandwich, Uncle had told me what to say and assured me that the triad would not go after Kenneth Hong or his cousin.

*"Why not,"* I had asked.

*"Because we will lay the blame on Derrick Lau."*

I narrowed my eyes at Uncle to remind him of his promise. If anything happened to Kenneth Hong, he and I were done.

The triad leader issued his own silent promise: lie to me and die.

I took a breath. "HKIF's Chief Operating Officer Kenneth Hong is second cousin to OCTB Investigator Kevin Ching. Kenneth told me, in confidence, that the bureau was investigating my grandfather's company for money laundering. He also said his cousin had an inside man."

"Derrick Lau?"

I shrugged.

"You see?" Uncle said. "Your bird has found an opening to escape its cage. Soon, you will be left with husks and shit."

The leader and Uncle locked wills like Judo players in a match, shifted and countered too subtlety to be seen. The triad soldiers edged forward.

"I thought you were old friends," I said, breaking the tension.

The leader kept his eyes on Uncle. "Memories fade."

"Not all," Uncle said.

The leader scowled. "No. Not all." He broke eye contact and stood. "I will check your information and get back to you…one way or another." The cruelty in his eyes left no doubt as to what that *other* way might be. He snapped a command in Cantonese, and a soldier closed in on Uncle.

Lee stopped him with a glare.

I positioned my back against his and waited.

Saan Zyu tossed me my phone. "Take your things and leave."

I kept my eye on the soldier in front of me, picked up my backpack, and zipped the flaps. Once I had strapped it securely into place, Uncle and I left through the ratty front apartment. The guard waited for us at the top of the stairs. No one barred our way. We left without a fight and vanished into the crowd.

Four blocks later, I finally relaxed. "You didn't mention being pals with the Scorpion's leader."

"That was another life."

"Really? He called you Red Pole, said you could have become Dragon Head. Care to explain?"

"Red Pole is chief enforcer. Dragon Head is like Mountain Master, another term for boss."

I replayed the highlights from Uncle's highly skilled kitchen assaults. "A triad enforcer posing as a cook. Guess you've cleaved more than ducks."

"You should talk, pretending to be an innocent daughter. So transparent."

"Not to DeAndre."

"DeAndre is a child. How long did it take for your father to figure it out?"

Baba and I had that conversation two months earlier, when he had lured me into his office under the pretense of a friendly visit. I had spilled the beans between bites of stir-fried broccoli and stoic North Dakota silence. I admitted to rescuing and protecting women in need, and Baba admitted that he and Ma had always known about my secret ninja teacher in the park.

"What now?" I asked.

"Saan Zyu will make his decision before tomorrow morning's vote. In the meantime, protect your mother, and stay out of trouble."

I grinned. "But I'm the Troublemaker."

"Stupid girl. You think it's a *good* thing that a triad gives you a name? Better to be nobody than a hornet in their nest."

Uncle was right. I was masking nervous energy with humor.

"I know you don't like it," he said. "But we have to wait. And for God's sake, stay away from Daniel Kwok."

# Chapter Fifty-Five

"*Why?* What's Daniel got to do with this?" I said, as I threaded through the crowd to catch Uncle.

"I didn't tell you?"

"Tell me what?"

"Daniel Kwok is the man Derrick Lau has chosen to replace your mother. He wants a director in Los Angles he can trust and control."

"That's not possible. Daniel would never betray my family. He would never betray *me*."

Uncle scoffed. "No one knows what a person will and will not do."

"*I* know."

He stopped on the sidewalk, eliciting grumbles in Cantonese. "You think love conquers all? Family. Duty. Respect for ancestors. This is the Chinese way."

"Daniel was born in Los Angeles. He's American."

"Even worse. He betrays you for himself."

I grabbed his arm as he tried to leave. "Will you please stop."

"What for? You don't listen. You don't believe. I might as well go home."

"To Shanghai?" My voice cracked with worry. How would I protect Ma without Uncle's connections and intervention? I had to get my emotions under control. I couldn't afford to offend Red Pole Chang.

Uncle shrugged off my grip. "Not Shanghai, to my relatives in Junk Bay. You're not the only one with family obligations. I have a banquet to attend. Go home. Stay with your mother. Forget about

Daniel Kwok. I'll contact you when I hear from Saan Zyu."

I let him go and leaned against the graffitied wall as he descended the stairs to the subway. Relief that Uncle would stay in Hong Kong washed over me like surf foam on a beach then receded as I thought about Daniel. Even a well-connected person like Lee Chang could be mistaken. He could have heard about Derrick Lau's plans and assumed that Daniel had known. Or perhaps Lau had offered his nephew the position, and Daniel had turned him down. There was no way Daniel could know his uncle was laundering money for a triad. He spoke about him like a playboy, not a shark.

I unlocked my phone and studied Daniel's smiling face.

*What have you done?*

Suspicion forced through the cracks of my resolve like weeds through cement. I needed solid counsel or my future with Daniel was doomed. I opened WeChat and hovered my thumb over Baba's strong face. After this morning's argument, would he answer my call?

"Hello, Dumpling."

"Hi, Baba. Did I wake you?"

"I'm settling in, is all." He paused. "Are you safe?"

I sniffed at the sudden rush of tears.

"Hey now, what's in the way?"

I sniffed harder, swallowing emotions I didn't have time to feel. "I need your advice."

"About?"

"Daniel."

Baba's tone hardened. "What did he do?"

"Nothing. I mean…I don't know. That's the problem. I was told something that I haven't yet confirmed."

*Where should I begin? How much should I say?*

"Spit it out, why dontcha."

I took a breath. "Derrick Lau is behind the vote to have Ma fired from her position. My contact claims Daniel Kwok is Lau's choice to replace her."

"I don't understand. Why would he want Daniel?"

"Daniel is his nephew."

"I didn't know that, did you?"

"Yes, but Daniel's supposed to be in Hong Kong for his own business. He never said anything about taking Ma's job."

Baba huffed and hummed in thought. "How well do you trust your contact?"

The time had come. Should I tell Baba about Lee Chang's history or not?

Uncle had walked away from his violent life to begin a new one in Baba's kitchen. In all those years, he had never done anything to put anyone in danger—except me, but now I understood why. I didn't condone his past as a black society enforcer, but I couldn't hold it against him, not after I had teamed up with Tran to rescue Kateryna and Ilya. If an assassin could work for good, couldn't a former red pole enforcer do the same?

"My contact is reliable." I took a breath. I knew what Baba was going to say: Don't borrow trouble.

"Daniel is ambitious."

"Wait, *what*?"

"Don't get me wrong, I like him fine, but ambitious men can make selfish decisions."

"So you believe it's true?"

"I believe you need to tread carefully. You haven't dated anyone since that Pete fella back in college. I don't want to see you rushing in like a horse to stable only to find the trough empty and the hay net bare."

I leaned my head against the wall and watched the pedestrians pass by. This wasn't the advice I had expected to receive.

"Dumpling?"

"I'm here."

"I just want you to protect yourself, is all. Daniel seems like a fine young man, but the only one I care about is you."

I nodded, as if he could see me.

"Holler if you need me, don't matter the time."

"I will. I love you, Baba."

"And I love *you*."

He left me feeling comforted yet even more concerned. Should I confront Daniel or avoid him as Uncle had suggested? Either way, Baba's advice to tread carefully seemed wise.

I opened WhatsApp to study Daniel's face and found two messages waiting for me from Jing. She had sent an article about tonight's community dialogue with Executive Carrie Lam, Queen Elizabeth Stadium from seven to nine. One hundred thirty residents had been chosen by lottery from twenty thousand applicants to voice their concerns. A crowd was expected to gather outside.

Jing: *Join us in front at 5:30. Info in link.*

It was almost two.

I sent a thumbs up emoji and returned to Daniel. I had enough time to meet him for afternoon tea, ask my hard questions, then, if all went well, smooth the waters with make-up sex. Who was I kidding? I couldn't have this conversation over tea sandwiches and cake. I needed a clear head and an easy escape. I wouldn't have either in a restaurant inside Daniel's hotel.

As I deliberated over what to type, a call came in from Ma.

"Hey. How's your day with Po-Po?"

"Not even a hello?"

"Hello, Ma. How's your day with Po-Po?"

"Very amusing. I made my escape. I'm shopping for a watch at 1881 Heritage."

"Wait, you're there now? I thought you were going to let me know if you left the neighborhood."

"For goodness sake, Lily, I'm more than capable of entertaining myself. I'm only calling because there are several stores and shopping malls on Canton Road that might appeal to you. I'm sure we could find you another outfit."

The instant Ma had mentioned her escape, I had pulled up Google Maps, found my route, and was sprinting down Nathan Road to the Soy Street bus stop to catch the N21. If I made it in time, I could reach her in twenty minutes.

"Did you hear me, Lily?"

"Yeah, Ma."

"Why are you panting?"

"I'm running for a bus. I'll be there soon. What store are you in?"

"Schaffhausen, but I'm heading to Chopard."

"Okay. See you in twenty." I ended the call, ran onto the bus, and swiped my Octopus card to pay for the fare.

Uncle and I had only left Saan Zyu a few minutes ago. There hadn't been time for him to check our information. Would the triad leader have informed his soldiers to leave Ma alone, or would he have left his commands in place until he had confirmed our information? What had he commanded his soldiers to do?

Worry ate at my stomach. Until my mother was safe, Daniel and Jing would have to wait.

# Chapter Fifty-Six

I found Ma as promised, in Chopard trying on a sophisticated-yet-sporty ruby-studded watch.

"What do you think, Lily, too casual for me?"

She turned her wrist to show off the red alligator band and winked. The price tag was a cool fifty-three thousand U.S. dollars, not Hong Kong.

"Way too casual. Try the white gold with diamonds."

"Good point. The rose gold dresses it down."

I bit my lip to keep from smiling. Diamond-inlaid buckles and ruby and diamond dials were *so* everyday.

Ma extended her wrist for the salesman to unbuckle the band. "I've had enough watch-shopping for one day. Perhaps I'll have better luck with a handbag and scarf."

"Hermès is down the road," I suggested.

"My thought, exactly."

We giggled like school girls as we left the shop.

"Do you really want a handbag?"

"Of course not. But I had tortured that man long enough. Imagine, spending fifty thousand U.S. on a watch when I could buy a perfectly nice car—for you."

"I don't want a car."

"I know. How about an outfit?"

I laughed. "Sure, Ma." I would have been happier in a taxi on our way up The Peak, but the fastest way to accomplish that goal was to find an outfit I could pretend to love. "Were you serious about buying me a car?"

She raised a brow. "Were you serious about not wanting one?"

I imagined zipping around Los Angeles in a sporty BMW, music blaring, wind blowing in my face. A car could be nice. Travel where and when I pleased. No need to call for a ride, borrow Baba's delivery car, or cycle to the nearest Metro station. I could use the time I saved to practice ninjutsu, rock climbing, or Parkour. But in reality, the traffic and parking would sap my energy and sour my mood. Even a free car would be a literal pain in my ass and an unnecessary expense. I'd take an hour of hard cycling over an hour of sitting on my butt in a hot leather seat, any day of the week. I might arrive a sweaty mess, but my muscles would be warmed up and ready for action.

"Thanks for the offer, but I'm happy with my bike."

I squeezed Ma's hand then scanned the shopping plaza for suspicious characters and easy escape routes. The former marine police compound resembled a British palace courtyard, surrounded with stone. It had two major openings: the entrance I had used on Salisbury Road that led to the Star Ferry and an egress onto Canton Road that ran north along the wharf. A grand staircase led to a higher level with more shops, fine dining, and a hotel.

"Do any of these shops sell clothes?"

"Only watches. Unless you'd like something to eat?"

"No thanks." My stomach growled, but I didn't want to stay in Kowloon any longer than necessary.

"Harbour City is down the block. I'm sure we could find something there for you."

Although I preferred the fortress walls and security guards of 1881 Heritage, triad soldiers would be just as easy to spot and evade in a mall. I glanced at Ma's flat, ankle-strap sandals. If the need arose, she'd be able to run. I buckled the waist strap of my cycling pack and cinched it tight.

"Lead the way."

We exited via Canton Road and walked up the brick-paved sidewalk past storefronts for Cartier and Montblanc. The one-way traffic flowed toward us with no shoulder on our side for cars to slow or park. I glanced behind us for triad soldiers and relaxed. In the Beverly Hills of Hong Kong, this avenue might be the safest one to walk.

Ma locked her right arm in my left and ambled up the sidewalk. If she hadn't looked so content, I would have switched sides and walked along the street. "You seem in better spirits."

She shrugged. "Nothing I can do."

"Is Gung-Gung rallying support?"

"So he says."

"Do you believe him."

"Honestly, Lily, I don't know what to believe anymore."

I thought of Uncle's accusation about Daniel. "I know what you mean." I glanced into a window and admired a sparkly Piaget watch. "Is that casual enough for you?"

Ma yanked my arm and screamed.

A man in an oncoming car was pulling her into the backseat.

I caught the door's handle, ran alongside, and jumped onto the floorboard into a crouch. Ma kicked her legs as the triad soldier dragged her across the seat. The sole of her flat, strappy sandal smacked me in the face. I trapped her legs and climbed over her body to free her from his choke, but her frantic hands clawed the air. Deflecting her nails, I drove my palm into triad soldier's nose.

"Go," I yelled, and continued my assault.

As Ma squirmed toward the open door, the triad soldier shoved me against the front seats and grabbed for her leg. I hammered his face with my elbow, hooked my foot behind her back, and shoved her out the door.

With his target out of reach, the triad soldier turned on me.

Ma shouted from the street. The traffic was slow. I could still escape.

I deflected his strikes and slammed my forehead into his face. His crushed nose splattered blood on my chin. Before he recovered, I drove my elbow into his gut and raked the driver's eyes with my nails.

The car swerved into the curb, hit an obstacle, and slammed the car door shut.

With so little room to maneuver, I was losing the fight.

As I struggled to break free, the soldier punched me in the jaw and knocked me across the seat, climbed onto my body, and bludgeoned me with his fists. I turtled into my arms as he continued his assault and protected my face and ribs from his blows. The car accelerated. Soon we would leave the slow-moving traffic and bolt onto a flyover highway.

I reached behind me for the handle of the door, yanked it open, and tumbled into the street.

# Chapter Fifty-Seven

Ma threw her arms around my neck from the pedestrian side of the railing. "Are you okay? Climb over here before you're hit by a bus."

I leaned my head on her arm. "You have to let go of me first."

"Okay," she whispered, and hugged me tighter.

A car zoomed by within a foot of grazing my legs.

"Ma?"

"Sorry."

She let go and I climbed over the railing. The moment I landed, she folded me in her arms. This time I hugged her back.

"I almost lost you," she whispered.

"I almost lost *you*."

She released the hug and looked into my eyes. "Who were those men?"

"Not here." I led her down the ramp toward the subway station, out of sight from the street. After walking through tunnels to a terminal as vast and sleek as L.A.'s Union Station, I found a bench and sat.

"Now will you tell me what's going on?"

I unbuckled my backpack and took out my phone. "One sec."

Hong Kong's MTR system was fully equipped with 4G LTE coverage. Now that we were safe, I needed a moment to type.

Me: *The Scorpions tried to abduct Ma. What's going on?*

Lee: *When?*

Me: *Just now.*

Lee: *Where are you?*

Me: *Underground in the East Tsim Sha Tsui Station.*

Lee: *I'll check with Saan Zyu. Stay there.*

"Who was that?" Ma asked, as I put down my phone.

"A friend. He's helping me protect you."

"Protect me from whom?"

"A triad."

"That's ridiculous. What would a triad want with me?"

"I was going to wait until we were back at Gung-Gung and Po-Po's."

"Tell me now."

"I am, but it's going to be a lot to handle."

"Gangsters just attacked us in broad daylight. I can handle whatever you have to say."

I took a breath. "Derrick Lau is in debt to a triad group called the Scorpions. They're forcing him to launder their money through the London offices of HKIF. Cecil Chu has also been coerced into the scheme. I stole files from Derrick Lau's apartment and have seen the evidence."

"My God."

"Derrick Lau wants to replace you with someone else so he can launder triad money in the U.S."

"What about Raymond? If Derrick wants me out, why didn't he raise the motion to have me fired himself?"

"He didn't want to draw suspicion."

Ma shook her head. "I don't understand. The vote is tomorrow. Why attack us if everything's going as planned?"

"The triad boss lost confidence in Lau and has become annoyed with me."

"Why you?"

"Because I stopped his man from hurting Mr. Ng's dog and caught the same man and another gangster following Mr. Chu. We got into a fight when they chased me down an alley."

"They *what*?"

"Please, Ma, I'm trying to explain."

She clenched her jaw and nodded for me to continue.

"The triad leader decided not to wait for the vote. He felt everything would move more smoothly if you and I were out of the way. When my friend heard that the triad was going to kill us, he took me to meet with the leader. That's where I was before I met with you. We told him HKIF was being investigated by OCTB and that it was no longer safe for money laundering. He was supposed to have called off his men while he checked on our information. My friend is calling him now to see what happened."

I paused.

"Do I get to speak now?"

"Yes."

She heaved a great sigh. "If I hadn't just seen you thrown out of a car—"

"I jumped."

"What?"

"I jumped from the car. I wasn't thrown out of it."

The look she gave me could have blasted through a glacier.

"Sorry. Go ahead."

"As I was saying…if I hadn't just watched you *jump out of a moving car*, I would say this whole story of yours was preposterous."

"And now?"

"I'm frightened. Who else is in danger? Is my father a part of this?"

"I don't think so. I'm not even sure your kai ba knows exactly what's going on. He seemed remorseful when we were at his home and terrified when the gangster snuck onto his property to terrorize Ma Lik."

She scoffed. "Well, that's something at least. What now?"

"We get you home." I unlocked my phone and placed a call. "Mr. Tam? It's Lily. I'm at the East Tsim Sha Tsui Station with Ma. I know you're on call for Gung-Gung, but is there anyway you can pick her up and take her home?"

"What about you?" Ma asked.

I turned away from her so I could listen to Mr. Tam's instructions. "Sure. That would be great. See you there." I turned back to Ma. "He'll meet us outside Central. Are you okay with taking the subway?"

"I grew up here, Lily. I've ridden more trains and buses in my youth than you have in your entire lifetime. Now be quick. It's a long walk to catch the Tsuen Wan train."

I marveled at my mother, marching through the tunnel in her designer sandals and spotless dress. Even pulled into and shoved out of a car, she managed to look like a queen.

Me? Not so much.

My cheek and jaw throbbed from the soldier's fist, and my head ached from slamming against the door. The force of his punch had nearly knocked me unconscious. If things had gone differently, I could have been sinking to the bottom of Victoria Harbour, leaving my mother undefended and bereaved.

I cradled my sore rib and picked up my pace. Once our subway course had been decided, Ma navigated through the commuters with efficiency and speed. Never in my life, had I seen her move this fast. Once on board, I leaned against the back door to rest.

"Are you okay?"

I nodded, then wished I hadn't. Fighting close quarters with a larger, stronger opponent had taken its toll. Without room to dodge, slip, and evade, the triad soldier had pummeled me like one of Baba's mallet-beaten steaks. "Do you have an ibuprofen or something?"

"Panadol."

"That'll do."

The H.K. equivalent of Tylenol was made from the chemical twin of acetaminophen. I had stronger stuff in the first aid pouch of my backpack, but just the prospect of shrugging off the shoulder straps hurt. Besides, I couldn't afford to cloud my mind or dull my senses, not with the Scorpions still on the hunt.

I chewed the caplets and grimaced. "Don't worry, Ma. I'm hurt, not injured."

"Is there a difference?"

I chuckled then winced. "Yes."

"Well, your nose is bleeding."

I wiped it with back of my hand. "Actually, I think this one came from you."

Her eyes widened in shock.

"You put up a good fight, Ma. I'm proud of you."

She shook her head in disbelief. "I've put my daughter in danger and she's *proud* of me. This isn't right. We need to leave Hong Kong, immediately."

"No. You need to stay in the townhouse while my friend and I dig the Scorpions out of HKIF."

"How do you plan to do that?"

"We're working on it. Which reminds me…" I pulled out my phone and texted as the train stopped at Admiralty Station. The response came before the train started up again.

Lee: *I told you to stay where you were!*

Me: *I'm protecting my mother. What about Saan Zyu?*

Lee: *Nothing yet. Keep your head down.*

Me: *Doing my best.*

Ma leaned over my shoulder to look. "Well?"

I shut the app and smiled. "It should be fine."

"You're a horrible liar. Come back to the house, and I'll clean you up."

"Not yet. I have somewhere else to go." I wouldn't be able to rest until I had met with Daniel and asked the hard questions, face to face.

We exited the train and followed the crowd upstairs.

"Where are we meeting Mr. Tam?"

"Charter Road between Pedder and Ice House. There's a loading lane in front of Bvlgari."

She checked the signs and led the way through the complicated concourse.

Mr. Tam hurried out of the car to greet us. "Lily, your face. What happened to you?"

"Does it look that bad?"

Ma huffed. "I've been trying to tell you."

Mr. Tam grimaced. "The side is all swollen and purple."

"Oh, great. Soon I'll look like Violet Beauregarde."

"Who?"

"Willy Wonka's gum-chewing brat? Never mind. I have things to do in town, but I need Ma safe at home. Can you take her?"

"Of course. Should I drop you somewhere first?"

I checked the area: food carts across the street, Mandarin Oriental down the block.

"This is fine."

All I needed was a bite of food to settle my stomach, a lounge to wash up, and a bag of ice for my swelling cheek. And the courage to find out if the man I had given myself to was betraying us all.

# Chapter Fifty-Eight

I laid my backpack across one sofa and sat on the other, saving the conversation nook like a kid saves prime lunch-table seats at school. Although Pottinger House was only a few blocks away, I had asked Daniel to meet me on neutral ground. The lobby lounge of the Mandarin Oriental was public enough to avoid a scene, private enough to avoid being overheard, and—most important of all—not within an elevator ride of the hotel room where Daniel and I had made love.

As he approached, I pulled my backpack off the adjoining sofa and set it beside me. His brows furrowed for a moment, then he took the seat I had left. I leaned back to discourage a kiss and kept my face angled to hide the purpling bruise on my cheek. Daniel's wounded expression hurt my heart, but until I learned the truth, I would remain strong.

"This is an elegant hotel," he said, in a light-hearted tone. "Maybe I should move in here."

I shrugged. The longer I had sat with Uncle's accusation, the more suspicious I had become. Speaking with Baba hadn't helped nor had getting pummeled in the back seat of a car by triad thugs. My agitation level was high. Any benefit of the doubt I might have had was slipping through my fingers like sand.

"Is something wrong? You seem…distant."

"I need to ask you a question, and I need you to be truthful with me."

Daniel's face drooped like a scolded puppy. "I'd never lie to you."

"Good. Because this is important." I took a breath. "Why are you really here in Hong Kong?"

Daniel shrugged. "My uncle asked me to come."

"Your uncle Derrick Lau?"

"Yes."

"Why?"

Daniel paused.

"You promised to tell me the truth."

"Okay. He said there might be a position opening up in HKIF that would be perfect for me."

"What position is that?"

"Your mother's." The words came out casually, as if commenting on a plant.

I reined in my anger. "You came here to take my mother's job?"

"Not exactly. But if she was going to lose it, why not to me?"

Words birthed and died on my tongue as I struggled for a coherent response.

*Why not to me?*

"Look, I know this is awkward," he said. "But wouldn't it be better if your mother was replaced by someone in the family?"

"You're not *in* my family."

"I could be." He reached for my hand, but I pulled it away. "Don't be like that. You know how I feel about you. I'm pretty sure you feel the same way about me. Just think of it. If we were to marry, our son or daughter could inherit the company. Isn't that how a family business works?"

"My mother will inherit HKIF."

He shook his head. "No, Lily, she won't. But even in the unlikely chance that the board voted to keep her, who would she pass it to? You told me yourself that you don't care about finance and business. You're not even ambitious."

"That doesn't matter."

"But it does." He leaned forward again, this time, like a teacher about to explain a difficult concept to a particularly dense student.

"If I join the company as a director, I can earn their respect. If I enter as an underling, everyone will see it as nepotism. I'll never have a chance to rise to my full potential. And when the time comes for your grandfather to pass the reins, and it will, very soon, no one will think of your mother or me as the next CEO of HKIF. The opportunity for our unborn child will be lost forever."

"Unborn child?" I blinked in disbelief. There were so many things wrong with his argument, I didn't know where to begin: Ma wouldn't be losing her job if Daniel's crooked uncle wasn't trying to force her out of the company; no one, not even Gung-Gung, would choose the next CEO based on a *viable heir*; and Daniel hadn't even told me he loved me let alone asked if I wanted to bear his children.

"I'm sorry I upset you, but you asked for the truth. I didn't tell you about Uncle Derrick's offer because you're not interested in business."

"This isn't business. It's corruption. Do you have any idea what your uncle has done?"

"Will you please lower your voice?"

"Answer the question."

Daniel held out his hands as if it were self evident. "He's shared his views with Raymond Ng, and they both agreed. You may not like it, but this is how business works. Once your mother is voted out, Uncle Derrick will recommend me, and Raymond will vote accordingly."

I couldn't believe what I was hearing. Not only had Daniel planned the future of our *unborn child* without the least concern for me, he was actively participating in a coup to destroy my mother's career.

"You are so stupid," I said.

"Excuse me?"

"First off, Gung-Gung has the majority stock. Your uncle and Mr. Ng won't have enough votes to pull off this scheme. Secondly..." I leaned forward and spoke through gritted teeth. "Your uncle is laundering money for a *triad*."

"Don't be ridiculous."

"Me? You're the one selling out my mother and treating me like an obedient trophy wife." I held up a hand to forestall whatever nonsense was about to spew from his mouth. "You don't have the slightest idea who I am. You don't know what's important to me, and you cannot begin to fathom what I am willing and capable of doing to stop injustice and protect the people I love."

"Injustice? It's business."

"No, Daniel, this is about so much more. And the fact that you don't realize it is crushing."

I stood and swung the backpack across my aching shoulders.

"Where are you going?"

"It doesn't concern you. In fact, I don't see anything in my future that will *ever* concern you."

# Chapter Fifty-Nine

I crossed the street into Statue Square and disappeared into the maze of pathways. I'd had enough of Daniel's infuriating appeasements and didn't want to be followed. I needed time alone to calm my emotions and reset my intentions. I also needed to check on Ma.

Me: *Are you back at the house?*

Ma: *Yes. And you?*

Me: *Checking out some things. Please stay home.* (praying hands emoji)

The news about Daniel should be delivered in person where I could see her expression and she could hug me if I broke down and cried.

I shook away the thought. *Nope. Not going to happen.*

We exchanged thumbs up emojis and left it at that.

I put away my phone and meandered through the park along pathways, lawns, and plazas with swimming pool-sized fountains where Hongkongers gathered to relax. It looked lovely, but I needed something deeper to calm my mind. Since Sensei had trained me to maintain outward awareness, I was able to meditate safely in public places. I could sense when people or animals focused their attention on me. The energy they gave off felt like pricking needles pushing me away. Because of this, I could meditate in the wilderness or beside strangers and still be on alert. I could even meditate on my feet with my eyes open. But right now, I needed a semblance of solitude. I found it in a shady spot beneath a majestic tree.

I folded my legs in Fudoza no Kamae, the immovable seat posture with one leg in front and the other foot tucked under my seat. As with

Shizen no Kamae, the kneeling posture I habitually used for meditation, I could launch into action from this position. I didn't expect to be attacked in a public park, but with the way things had been going, I'd meditate more peacefully if I was prepared.

I rested my hands on my knees, palms up, thumbs and middle fingers touching in the Shuni Mudra seal of patience. I breathed deeply and focused on the flow of energy between the divine nature represented by my thumbs and the courage, duty, and responsibility represented by my fingers. With this connection made in body and mind, I traveled to my imaginary dojo.

The journey always began in a shadowy forest with me on a trail lined with ancient trees. If I continued far enough, I would meet my inner teacher in a Japanese cottage made of delicate shoji walls. Other times, I learned what I needed to know along the trail. I breathed deeply and journeyed to see what I would discover today.

As I entered my forest, I looked behind me and saw Daniel wave his hand then turn away. I continued up the trail, unperturbed. In a clearing up ahead, Mr. Tam helped Ma into Gung-Gung's car. She gazed out the window at me and blew me a kiss. My heart swelled with love and relief as he drove her to safety. When the car vanished into the forest, I continued up the trail where Uncle waited for me, arms crossed, leaning against a tree. Rather than speak or hurry me along, he nodded farther up the path where a crowd of protesters gathered around a platform. On it, stood Jing. Before I could determine her emotional state, the crowd swallowed her from view.

I pondered the meaning of these visions as I walked and breathed, but the forest pressed into my trail and forced me to stop. There would be no shoji wall dojo today. I had already received the message from my inner teacher: Daniel was gone. Ma was safe. Uncle would wait. Jing could not.

I returned my awareness to the ground beneath my seat, the scent of grass and earth, and the murmur of passing conversation. When I had anchored myself in present time and space, I opened my eyes. The sun had set, and the plaza lights cut through the dusk.

I stood gingerly and stretched my legs and back. Once loosened, I set off at a brisk pace. Queen Elizabeth Stadium was a mile and a half away. The jog would do me good. I chose a route down Queens Road East and saw protesters forming a human link through an outdoor shopping mall.

"Is this where Carrie Lam is speaking?" I asked a cameraman in English.

He shook his head. "Another nine hundred meters at the stadium."

"Are these people protesting against it?"

"Not against the community dialogue, against Carrie Lam and her refusal to fulfill the five demands."

"What time does the dialogue begin?"

"Seven o'clock. The audience was chosen by lottery, but the demonstration outside has already begun."

"Thanks."

I checked my phone for updates from Jing and saw one from Uncle instead. *Call me.*

He answered on the first ring. "What took you so long?"

"I was running and didn't hear my phone ping. What's going on?"

"I spoke with Saan Zyu. He called off his men. They may still be watching, but no one will touch your mother without his okay. Same goes for you."

"Did the mountain master buy our story?"

"He's concerned about the secrets we know, but he wants proof that we learned them from the files you stole from Derrick Lau."

"How else could we have learned the names of his shell companies and bank accounts?"

"Through other sources who may not be trustworthy enough for officials to believe. If I tortured a criminal for this information, Saan Zyu wouldn't care. He needs proof that Derrick Lau was collecting evidence against him and that you had that evidence in your possession."

"Had?"

"I told him the files were in safe hands, ready for delivery, remember?"

I did. Uncle's bluff was our safeguard against premature death.

"What kind of proof does he want? You mean like pictures of me in Derrick Lau's office snooping through file cabinets? Why would I do that? I was risking my life in that apartment. I wasn't there on a sightseeing tour."

"You took photos of the reports."

"So I could examine them later. I didn't plan to steal them. I just couldn't put them back."

"Check the background for anything in those photos that would place you at Lau's."

I scrolled through shots of individual documents and groups of statements fanned on the floor. "I can see the color and pattern of his office rug, a bit of hard wood flooring, and the base of his antique cabinet. There's also a blurred shot of his coffee table and chair that I must have snapped by accident. Will that do?"

"Send them to me."

"What about the Bureau? Does the mountain master need proof the OCTB is investigating HKIF?"

"No. Kenneth Hong's family connection is enough. Saan Zyu would expect loyalty from family."

I sent Uncle the photos. "Now what?"

"We wait."

"For word?"

"Or an attack."

"You said we were safe."

"I said he called off his men."

"You're not comforting me."

"Children need comfort. Warriors deserve the truth."

I frowned at the phone. This warrior wouldn't mind a bit of both.

"So that's it? There's nothing more we can do?"

"Sleep with a blade in your hand, and pray you wake in time to use it."

# Chapter Sixty

Hundreds of protesters crowded the road in front of Queen Elizabeth Stadium, chanting slogans and waving signs.

"Independent inquiry."

"Police are twisting the truth."

"Free Hong Kong."

"Carrie Lam must go."

A small group of people wearing white tees shouted from across the road. Unlike the pro-democracy protesters, the signs held by the pro-government protesters were exclusively in Chinese. I couldn't read them, but I knew from listening to Gung-Gung what they supported: maintaining order, stopping the riots, and working with Beijing.

With the crowd packed tight, I couldn't see beyond more than a handful people in any direction, so I headed toward the stadium's brightly lit wall of glass where pro-democracy protesters chanted demands, pumped signs, and aimed their laser pointers at the building. The crowd cheered every time the green streaks of light appeared. I shoved my way through the chanting people to quieter groups talking amongst themselves and checking their phones for updates on the protests happening across the city. From what I spied on their screens, the demonstrations seemed peaceful with human chains, similar to the ones I had already passed.

I climbed onto a street lamp pedestal for a better view. Police officers guarded the front of the stadium in case anyone tried to enter.

News reporters in neon yellow vests roamed the crowd, capturing footage with professional grade cameras and microphones. No sign of Jing.

So many people. How would I ever find one petite girl?

Activists spoke to clusters of people on the blocked off street and along the front of the stadium. Two young men caught my attention. They stood a couple feet higher than the crowd, as if standing on blocks, voices amplified by bullhorns. One was short, the other tall, both wore black-rimmed glasses and button-down shirts. They were Matthew and Kris, Jing's activist friends from the retro café.

I slid down the lamppost and squeezed between bodies toward the far side of the stadium's entrance. As I grew closer, I heard Matthew shouting in Cantonese about Carrie Lam and the Five Demands. I couldn't understand it all, but I caught the words police, abuse, democracy, and freedom.

Kris, the taller of the two, shouted in between Matthew and translated the most important messages in English.

"The police are abusing their power and attacking the public. This must stop. Carrie Lam and government officials are twisting the facts. The people demand the truth. We must accept nothing less than all five demands."

Yellow-vested reporters shouted questions in Cantonese about Agnes Chow. I recognized the name from news reports and videos. The girl was a prominent teenage activist along with Joshua Wong and Nathan Law.

The reporters wanted to know if the girl with Matthew and Kris was her.

"We want Agnes Chow."

"Let her speak."

I squeezed toward the front in time to see Nate—Jing's other activist friend—help her onto the plastic crates. She was dressed in the same type of blouse and slacks I had seen Agnes Chow wear in a recent interview. Jing even wore her long black hair parted to the side in a similar way. When she raised her hand and smiled at the cameras,

Matthew and Kris did the same. They bore a striking resemblance to the famous young heroes.

"This is Jing Tan," Matthew shouted to the media in English. "An up-and-coming activist from Kowloon. She is only seventeen yet fights for our democracy. She reminds us all how important our freedoms are and why we must protest to make our demands heard."

A reporter raised a microphone to catch Jing's words.

"My name is Jing Tan. I am seventeen. I protest on behalf of democracy and freedom. It's not enough that Chief Executive Carrie Lam has withdrawn the extradition bill, she must meet all of the five demands—stop characterizing protests as riots, provide amnesty for arrested protesters, begin an independent inquiry into police brutality, and implement universal suffrage for Hong Kong citizens."

The crowd cheered. They didn't care that Jing had parroted what they already knew. They cheered to hear the demands spoken from a girl who looked like the famous young activist they had all heard about but probably never seen in person.

Matthew clasped Jing's hand and raised it high, then held the pose so the audience would have time to snap photos and video. Within minutes, Jing Tan's face would be known in the city and shared around the world.

Now that the main attraction had been presented to the press and said what she'd obviously been coached to say, the audience moved on to hear other activists speak. I moved forward with the influx of new ears and tapped Jing on the shoulder.

"Lily. I'm so happy you made it. Did you see me on the platform? Matthew says I'll be on the news. Isn't that exciting? With all these people, the reporters interviewed *me*."

"I saw. But didn't your friends think you were older that seventeen?"

"They did. But when I couldn't recruit any college students, I had to tell them the truth. Instead of being angry, Matthew was pleased."

"I'm sure he was."

Nate joined us, dressed as distinctly as before in a billowing red blouse and skinny jeans. "Did you see Jing on the stage. Wasn't she fabulous? You should capture her on video the next time and share it with your American friends."

"Next time?"

Nate swept his arm to indicate a new surge of people. "They're coming to meet the newest voice in student activism."

I looked at Jing. "Is that what you are? I thought you were more interested in art than politics?"

Matthew interrupted. "Her art supports her politics, isn't that right Jing?"

"Um, yeah…of course."

"See? Now, if you don't mind, we have things to discuss before she speaks again."

*Things to discuss? Or new words to feed her?*

As Jing's friends closed rank around her, I fell back and called Mr. Tam.

"Lily," he answered with relief. "Have you found her yet? Is she safe?"

"I have, and she is."

"Is she at the community dialogue?"

"She's outside, speaking to protesters and reporters."

"She's only a kid Why would anyone care what she has to say?"

"Her friends have dressed her up like Agnes Chow and are feeding her propaganda to inspire the crowd and draw publicity to themselves."

"I don't like this. Chow, Wong, and Law have attracted good *and* bad attention. Beijing and the H.K. government tolerate them for now, but what if that changes? We may have two systems, but we are still one country. I don't want my daughter drawing notoriety here or in China."

Mr. Tam had a point. A Communist regime had the power to outlaw inflammatory speech or political dissidence. If Chinese government officials viewed Jing as a threat to the interests of the People's Republic, they could arrest her without recourse. Although she was currently protected by the freedoms of Hong Kong law, there was no guarantee this would last.

"Try not to worry, Mr. Tam. From what I've seen, Jing doesn't have the ideological zeal or political dedication to last. Once that becomes apparent, she'll fade into the background. That said, you need to brace yourself for the videos and photographs that are going to be shared across messaging platforms and social media."

"Can you stop this?"

"She's already been filmed and photographed. If I dragged her off the stage, her friends and even the crowd might fight against me. We could attract the police and create an incident in an otherwise peaceful demonstration. She'd make headline news for sure. I think we have to let this play out. Fortunately, she hasn't said anything that hasn't already been heard a thousand times. But you might want to have a heart-to-heart with her later tonight."

"Heart-to-heart?"

"A serious conversation. Jing is craving attention and purpose. Her activist friends are providing both."

Mr. Tam sighed into the phone. "This is my fault. Jing has been sad and lonely ever since her mother and I separated. We used to have so much fun. Now, all I do is worry and criticize. Have my actions driven her into bad hands?"

"Not bad, ambitious. I can talk to her about this when they're not around, but I can't give her the love she's craving. Maybe set up some family time? And ask about her art. That's where her real passion lies. If you take an interest and support her dreams, I think she'll turn away from Matthew and the others."

Mr. Tam sighed again. "We've made so many mistakes. When Jing asked us about art classes, her mother and I told her focus on her studies. Maybe if we—"

"Don't go there." I thought about Rose and remembered all that I did and did not do. So many regrets. So much guilt.

"Trust me on this, Mr. Tam, nothing good ever comes from obsessing about what might have been."

# Chapter Sixty-One

After several futile attempts to separate Jing from her keepers, I encouraged Mr. Tam to message his daughter and arrange to give her a ride home when the community dialogue inside the stadium had finished. Jing had agreed, and Mr. Tam had used the wait time to drive me back to Gung-Gung and Po-Po's.

"Text me when she's home," I said, as I got out of the car.

"I will. Thank you for looking out for her. This isn't your problem"

"Teens in trouble are everyone's problem. But for what it's worth, I think she'll be okay."

He nodded, but didn't agree.

"Tell her I was sorry I couldn't stay, and ask her to let me know about the next event."

As I watched him leave, I thought about Josie, Brianna, and all the other teenagers I had struggled with in the last month. Earning their trust had taken time, so had my understanding. Every new detail I had learned about them had shifted my perspective and increased my empathy. Not all of those girls had made it. The ones I had lost would haunt me forever.

I entered the complex and closed the gate on the past, then proceeded to my grandparents' townhouse to check on my family.

"Lei Lei's home," Po-Po called out in Cantonese the moment she heard me shut the front door.

"Is that you, Lily?" Ma said. "Dinner's on the table. Wash up and come eat."

"Be right there."

I left my shoes at the door, stored my pack, and joined them in the dining room where I'd eaten my last and only decent meal of the day, Po-Po's hearty jook. If I had known I'd only have time to consume a scone with Kenneth and a bag of boiled peanuts before meeting with Daniel, I never would have given Uncle my scrambled egg and corned beef sandwich.

Ma studied me nervously. "Are you hungry?"

"Famished."

Gung-Gung frowned as I took my seat. "What's wrong with your face?"

I touched my swollen cheek and winced. In all the commotion, I'd forgotten about the fight. Now that I remembered, the soreness returned, not just in my jaw but around my ribs, shoulders, and back. After dinner, I'd need a long hot shower and several packs of ice.

"Small bruise. Nothing to worry about. Are those oysters?"

Po-Po smiled and spun the lazy Susan until they stopped in front of me, lightly battered and stir-fried crisp. I spooned out a portion and moved on to the steamed chicken with scallions and ginger.

Po-Po smiled as I chose several hunks of pork belly, roasted crisp and sweet with fat. She sat on my left and hadn't noticed the bruise. "You like siu yuk?"

"So good." I added a fourth piece and a hefty helping of snow peas and bok choy.

Gung-Gung watched in amazement as I filled my bowl with steamed rice. "How do you stay so thin when you eat like a man?"

"Leave her alone, Shaozu. The fat is good for her skin," Po-Po said in Cantonese. "See how it shines?"

I bit into the crispy siu yuk and sighed. After two days of missed meals, Bao Jeh's cooking tasted like Heaven. I cleaned my plate and added more, stuffing my belly in case I didn't get another chance to eat. With the way this trip was going, I'd grab my food and sleep when I could.

Ma sipped her tea and watched. Either she'd eaten before I arrived or worry had stolen her appetite. Having me in her sights seemed to calm her nerves. Hearing the news I had to tell would not.

Once the food had been eaten and the table cleared, I retrieved Derrick Lau's folders from my bedroom and joined Ma and Gung-Gung in the den.

"I've learned things you should know about HKIF."

Gung-Gung frowned. "My business is not your concern. Please stay out of it."

"I can't. The situation has escalated and put us all in danger."

"What nonsense is this?"

"Hear her out," Ma said. "Lily and I were attacked on the street today. We could have been killed. That swollen bruise you see on her face is not the only injury she suffered."

"Attacked? Why didn't you tell me about this before?"

"I didn't want to say anything until Lily was here to explain. The situation is confusing, and I'm still learning the facts."

Gung-Gung looked at me in exasperation. "Well? What is this about?"

There was so much to say, I hardly knew where to begin. I needed to ease him into the new reality, step by logical step, so he wouldn't raise his defenses and shut me out.

"I'm not sure if Ma told you, but an intruder entered Raymond Ng's property a few nights ago while Ma and I were visiting. The man terrorized Mr. Ng's dog. When I tried to save Ma Lik, the intruder threw me off the roof."

"What?"

"Let her speak, Ba."

I nodded my thanks to Ma and continued. "The intruder had a tattoo of a scorpion that I recognized from…" I paused. If I told anyone about Uncle's membership in the Shanghai Scorpion Black Society, it would have to be Baba first.

"Well?" Gung-Gung prompted.

"I recognized the tattoo from an article I'd read about triads. The next day, I saw the intruder with the scorpion tattoo and another man following Mr. Chu in the street."

"Cecil Chu?" Gung-Gung's eyes narrowed with suspicion. "What were you doing near him?"

"I was leaving IFC Tower after picking up something I had left in your office. Mr. Chu was walking down the street. When I spotted the intruder who had attacked me walking behind him, I followed. The men spotted me and chased me into an alley and attacked me with knives."

"This is preposterous. Shun Lei, your daughter is living in a fantasy world."

Anger radiated from Ma. "And what about me? Do you think my abduction was all in my head? This isn't a fantasy, Ba. Men dragged me into a car on *Canton Road*."

I held out my hands. "Please. Let me continue."

Gung-Gung and Ma crossed their arms in mirrored agitation. I nodded at their tacit agreement and pressed on, putting the events in order and rewriting the truth to protect the secrets I didn't want to disclose.

"The triad's interest in Mr. Ng and Mr. Chu made me wonder about Mr. Lau. So when I visited Daniel at his uncle's apartment, I did a little snooping."

"Snooping into what?" Gung-Gung asked.

"His files."

"This is unforgivable. What kind of delinquent daughter have you raised?"

"She was concerned about your company," Ma snapped, then turned to me. "What did you find?"

"He keeps folders on all of the offices and has extensive documents, statements, and ledgers concerning Mr. Chu's clients in London."

Gung-Gung's surprise about Mr. Lau tempered his disgust with me. "Derrick is an investor. He shouldn't be watching the day-to-day business."

"That's what I thought. When I went back to his apartment, I took a closer look."

"You went *back*?" Ma asked, in alarm.

"I did. This time, he had visitors—the same triad men who had attacked me in the alley."

Ma gasped. "Oh, my God."

Gung-Gung shook his head in disbelief.

"I know this is hard to believe, but hear me out. When the men told

Mr. Lau I had been following Mr. Chu near the HKIF offices, Mr. Lau was very concerned that I might have met with Kenneth Hong. When he demanded answers, the men told him they didn't work for him and that their boss would be angry. That's when Mr. Lau brought up tomorrow's vote. He said, and I quote, *What helps me, helps you. What hurts me, hurts you.* The men threatened his life and told him to put his man in Los Angeles or find another way to fulfill his promises to their boss."

"His man?" Ma asked. "Who is he trying to replace me with?"

"This is too much," Gung-Gung said. "I don't believe anything you're saying."

I held out the folders. "These are the files I stole from Mr. Lau's office."

Gung-Gung snatched them from my hand and rifled through them. Ma moved beside him so she could see as well. When he reached the end, he closed the cover. "I don't see any wrong doing in these reports."

"But you agree that they are authentic."

Gung-Gung grunted.

"Who is this man those thugs were asking about?" Ma demanded.

I held out my hand. "I'll get to that, but I need to tell this in order so it makes sense."

She leaned back in resignation. "Fine."

I turned back to Gung-Gung. "Since Mr. Lau was concerned about whether I had spoken to Kenneth Hong, I decided to meet with him and see what I could learn. Although Mr. Hong doesn't seem to be involved with this triad business, he did explain some things about how HKIF works and the bi-annual shareholders' reports. Apparently, no one would know if one of you sold their stock until the report comes out next week."

Ma leaned forward. "Are you saying someone sold their stock?" She looked at Gung-Gung with alarm. "Was it you?"

Gung-Gung sighed. "This is not how I wanted to tell you."

"Tell me *what*? You own fifty-four percent of the shares. Derrick has thirty, Raymond has ten, Cecil, Kenneth, and I own two percent each. Tell me nothing has changed. Tell me you still have the majority vote."

Gung-Gung shook his head.

"Even added with mine?"

"Not anymore."

"Oh, Ba. What have you done?"

"I ran into trouble back in 2012. We had moved into the new offices at IFC Two ten years earlier, the same year I hired Kenneth to take over the day-to-day business—six years after I hired you. I was making big investments to cover the expense. Things were going well, but I became over confident. Our biggest client at the time wanted a quick payoff and was willing to take the risk. I found a Chinese stock ready to take off, so good that I invested myself."

Ma gasped. "You told me never to do that."

"And for good reason. At the last moment, China changed a policy. The company lost its deal, and the stock plummeted. HKIF lost its biggest investor, and I lost two million U.S."

"Why didn't you tell me?"

"How could I? No one would have confidence in a financial advisor who loses his own money. I didn't tell anyone, not even your mother."

He poured himself a cup of tea and drank it down like a shot of whiskey.

"I had money saved but not enough. I borrowed one million U.S. from Derrick in a low-interest five-year loan, which would have solved all my problems if I had been able to pay it back on time. Again, politics did not work in my favor. I should have had a big year in 2017 with the twentieth reunion of the British handover to China. Instead, protesters disrupted everything. That was the year that young pro-democracy activist was sentenced to a maximum security facility after serving his community service. Do you remember? The discontent disrupted one of my deals. My late-payment interest with Derrick doubled and then tripled within a month."

"*Tripled*? What do you owe now?"

"Nothing."

"You sold Derrick your stock?"

Gung-Gung shook his head. "Derrick's thirty percent was already too much. I sold seven percent of my stock to Raymond for seven million U.S. Now, he has seventeen percent, and I have forty-seven." Gung-Gung took a breath and let those numbers sink in. "If the board votes to replace you, we would need another shareholder to vote with us to overrule it."

Ma shook her head. "The only shareholder in that room who stood up for me was Derrick Lau. But after what you and Lily have shared, we obviously can't trust him. Triad thugs, double- and triple-interest penalties, and this business about replacing me? These are not the actions of a friend. Don't you see? Derrick is taking over your company."

"It's worse than that, Ma. Derrick Lau ran into his own financial trouble. He borrowed from a triad. When he couldn't pay it back, they forced him to launder their money through HKIF."

"Through my company?" Gung-Gung exclaimed. "How?"

I held up the folders. "Mr. Chu set up shell companies in the U.K. and has been using them to launder triad money through legitimate real estate transactions, an upstart investment fund, and—"

"Those upstarts have very lax due diligence," Gung-Gung interrupted.

"I know, Kenneth Hong told me the same thing, but it's even worse. Mr. Chu is also using triad money to buy stock for another one of his clients and depositing that client's money into the triad shell company's bank accounts."

"That's illegal."

"We'll be liable," Ma said. "They could throw us in jail."

"My company would be ruined."

"We would *all* be ruined."

"Please," I interrupted. "Let me finish."

I poured them each a cup of tea and waited for them to drink and calm their nerves.

Ma settled first. "What can we do about this?"

"I have a friend with a connection to this triad."

"You mentioned that before. How on Earth would you..." Ma stopped herself from asking and shook her head. "Never mind. Tell us what can be done."

I took a moment to decide what they needed to know and what I needed to conceal.

"My friend met with the leader of the triad and told him Derrick Lau was keeping a record of their illegal transactions. He also told them the OCTB was investigating HKIF."

Gung-Gung blanched. "Are they?"

"No. But since one of Mr. Hong's cousins is an OCTB investigator, it seemed plausible. My friend used Mr. Hong's family connection and details from Mr. Chu's illegal transactions to convince the triad leader that your company was no longer safe for laundering money."

"Did the leader believe this?" Gung-Gung asked.

"He's checking."

"In time to stop the vote?" Ma asked.

"Who cares about the vote?" Gung-Gung said. "We could all end up in prison."

"Right," Ma said, and shook her head. "I'm a bit overwhelmed by all this."

I leaned forward and took her hand. "I know, Ma, but I'm going to get you out of this." I didn't have the heart to tell her about Daniel.

"How? We're surrounded by criminals and liars. What can *you* possibly do to save us?"

# Chapter Sixty-Two

As Uncle had suggested, I slept with a kitchen knife beneath my pillow and woke relieved to be alive. I had left my door open in case intruders had invaded to slaughter us in our beds. From the sounds of voices and movement throughout the house, the triad had left us alone.

I checked my phone for messages: two from Daniel, one from Mr. Tam, one from Baba, none from Uncle.

I skipped over Daniel's message and opened Mr. Tam's, notifying me that Jing had made it home safely. Although I'd asked for this confirmation, I had exhausted myself with Gung-Gung and Ma and gone straight to bed without checking my phone. Baba's message had come in five minutes later: an adorable sticker with a puppy saying "Hi," followed by, *How'd it go with Daniel?*

I groaned. I still had to tell Ma and Gung-Gung who Derrick Lau had set up to take her job. I leapt from the bed and froze as my tightened muscles seized. Good thing I had stuffed myself with dinner because I needed a long, hot shower far more than I needed food.

I sent Uncle a quick text. *Any news?*

Lee: *Not yet.*

Me: *We leave for the office in forty minutes.*

Lee: *I'll let you know when I hear.*

I took a scalding shower, dried my hair, and pulled on a muscle tee, stretch pants, and boots. No makeup today. The only thing I cared about was keeping my family safe. I put on a stretch jacket and inserted my phone and other items in my pockets. Ma and Gung-Gung would frown at my all black, body-hugging outfit, but at least I'd have flexibility to fight and skin protection if I was thrown out of another car. Ma, on the other hand, had chosen to wear a defiantly power-red dress.

We looked each up and down and nodded our mutual approval.

"Are you ready," I asked.

"Are you?"

"I wouldn't mind a knife." I patted my side pockets where I'd stashed a few legal substitutes. "Other than that, I'm set."

Gung-Gung looked old and frail in his gray business suit, but Po-Po complimented him all the same. He took her hands and gave them a kiss. "Have a good day, my love. We will return triumphant."

Despite Gung-Gung's bold assertion, he walked somberly to the car.

Ma whispered in my ear. "Any news from your friend?"

"Not yet."

"The meeting begins in an hour. What should we do if this comes to a vote? Exposing Derrick will cause a panic."

I shrugged. "The only one who's still ignorant about everything is Kenneth."

"He's the COO. What if he quits?"

I gave her the classic Baba look.

"I know," she said. "Don't borrow trouble."

I opened her car door and smiled, reassuringly. "It's going to be okay. The triad will pull out, or you and Gung-Gung will tell everyone the truth and tackle the problem as a company."

"You make it sound so easy."

"Not easy, clear." I frowned. "Which reminds me, I never told you who Mr. Lau has chosen to replace you."

"Is this something your grandfather should know?"

"Probably."

"Then tell us on the way."

I walked around to the other door and nodded to Mr. Tam. "Thanks for the text last night."

"Thank you for checking on Jing. Is everything okay with your mother and grandfather? They look serious,"

"They're handling a crisis. They'll be okay."

I slipped into the car and prayed that was true. Legal ramifications were bad enough without a triad gunning for them.

As soon as I closed the door, Ma tapped Gung-Gung on the shoulder. "Lily has more to tell us."

He turned in his seat. "What now?"

"Derrick Lau intends to replace Ma with his nephew Daniel Kwok."

"That snake."

Ma said nothing.

I touched her arm. "You *knew*?"

"I had my suspicions. Ever since Raymond suggested replacing me with someone younger, I started to wonder. The timing of Daniel's visit was too coincidental. Then you and he…" She circled her hand to encompass everything she didn't want to say. "I didn't see the point in bringing it up."

"He betrayed our family. Did you think I wouldn't care?"

"I didn't know for sure. I haven't seen you that happy since your sister was alive. I gave you such a hard time about that college boy you were dating. I didn't want to make the same mistake again."

I stared at her in shock. Ma had sabotaged me and Pete at every turn. It never occurred to me she felt remorse.

"I didn't want my suspicions about Daniel to ruin your chance at true love. Besides, it's only business. Your happiness is far more important."

I took Ma's hand and squeezed it with all the love I couldn't express. Only business? My happiness more important? I didn't know what to say.

Gung-Gung grunted angrily. "All this talk of feelings. Did it ever occur to you that your suspicions would be important for me to know? Derrick was the one who suggested Lily and Daniel should date. I was flattered that he'd want to link our families. I never dreamed he would use his nephew to steal my company."

"Daniel doesn't see it that way. He thinks you'll pass control of HKIF to him and that he would eventually pass it to our son or daughter."

"He proposed?" Ma asked.

"He *assumed*."

Gung-Gung snorted. "He actually thought I'd cut out my own daughter?"

"Wouldn't you?" Ma demanded.

"That's not the point."

"How convenient."

"We're almost there," I said, before their bickering erupted into a full-blown fight. "I told you about Daniel to prepare you in case he shows up at the meeting."

Gung-Gung shook his head. "It's only for the partners."

"I'm just saying…I wouldn't put it past Derrick to bring him along."

"Nor would I," Ma agreed.

"Pull up to the front of the building, Mr. Tam. I want to enter through the main doors."

"Yes, Mr. Wong."

Ma pointed to the maroon sedan up ahead. "That's Kai Ba's Jaguar."

"Hurry up, Mr. Tam. I want to speak with him before he enters."

"What are you going to say?" Ma asked.

Gung-Gung ignored her and muttered to himself in Cantonese.

Mr. Tam turned onto the cement driveway and paused to speak with the security guard at the barrier gate. After a brief exchange, the guard raised the gate's arm and waved us through.

Since the skyscraper occupied the corner lot, there were several entrances. This side of the glass tower faced the wide open event space, the harbor-front observation wheel, and the long elevated footpath that ran above the far side of a five-lane avenue. I had traversed that passage two days ago on my way to the waterfront and remembered the airy feel of the glass railings and open ventilation.

Once through IFC's barrier gate, the driveway turned right and ran across the front of the building. Shallow steps, wider than the length of a city bus, descended toward the street on the right where a drop off zone and bus stop cut into sidewalk. Similar shallow steps rose from the street around the corner.

"What are you going to say to him?" Ma asked again, as Gung-Gung stepped out of the car.

"I'm going to demand the truth."

She grabbed her purse and reached for the door.

"Wait for me," I said, as a phone call came in from Uncle. "What's the news?"

"Keep your mother in the house."

"What? We've already arrived at IFC."

"Then drive away."

"Ma, come back." I scrambled out the door to chase after her. "She's left the car."

"Then drag her back in and get out of there."

"What's going on, Uncle?"

"Saan Zyu has ordered the hit."

# Chapter Sixty-Three

Instead of waiting for me as planned, my mother marched along the driveway toward Gung-Gung and Raymond Ng, arguing beside the maroon Jaguar. Derrick Lau's blue metallic Tesla drove up behind our shiny black Mercedes. Three fancy cars parked in front of an iconic glass skyscraper. We looked like a commercial for a luxury car dealership.

I scanned the area.

No other cars had entered the driveway or pulled into the unloading zone on the street. No men watched us from the sidewalk or approached from any of the stairs. The nerves in my body still fired an alert.

I unzipped the side pockets of my jacket, pens on one side, punch rug needle on the other. Hong Kong had strict policies against firearms and knives, but nothing against carrying office supplies and crafting tools. The needle I had found in Po-Po's rug and knitting bin had a solid weight and a sturdy handle for punching yarn through rug mats. Its handle fit in my palm like an icepick.

Mr. Tam got out of the car. "Is everything okay?"

I called over my shoulder. "Stay inside and keep the engine running."

As I hurried toward Ma, someone else called my name. I looked behind me and saw Daniel rise out of Mr. Lau's Tesla. I stuffed my anger and continued toward Ma, keeping a steady pace so as not to alarm any Scorpion soldiers who might be watching. I didn't want to trigger a pre-mature attack. Better to let them move at their own pace until I was ready to force them into mine.

"Lily, can we please talk?"

I dismissed him with a wave and continued toward Ma.

She had joined the argument between Gung-Gung and Mr. Ng on the tower side of his car. I checked the elevated walkway across the street for a glint of metal or other signs of a sniper.

"Lily, please." Daniel grabbed my arm and turned me around.

I slid my arm down the outside his, scooped up his elbow in a shoulder-wrenching lock, and grabbed him by the hair. Our faces were so close we could have kissed. "I don't have time for you today. Understand? Go back to your uncle, and leave me alone."

The security guard called from the front door. "Are you okay, miss?"

"Fine. Thanks."

I released Daniel from my Musha Dori lock and shoved him away, but when I turned back to Ma, it was too late. A man was charging up the stairs.

I retrieved the heavy-weight pens I had lifted from Gung-Gung's den and flung the first ballpoint dagger at the attacker's throat. I missed and hit his eye. The man screamed and fell to his knees on the steps.

The security guard shouted for us to stop.

The barrier guard shouted to ask security guard what was going on.

Ma yanked Gung-Gung and Mr. Ng behind the car as a second Scorpion soldier charged up the steps from around the corner. Both of us sprinted toward Ma. Since I was running too fast to throw with any accuracy, I pulled out the rug punch needle. When the soldier saw this, he pulled out a knife and switched his path toward me.

Ma screamed. Daniel shouted. The security guard ran to the fallen man and yelled for me and the other attacker to stop.

The clash was quick.

The Scorpion soldier stabbed down onto my neck. I parried his arm, dodged to the side, and thrust the punch needle into his liver.

Ma screamed, no doubt thinking I was the one who had been stabbed.

I yanked out the tool and shoved the Scorpion away, but he wasn't done. He covered the bleeding wound with one hand and attacked with the other, slashing at me with the knife. I leapt back then charged in close as he sliced again,  struck him in the jaw with my elbow, captured his swinging arm, and spiraled him to the ground. Rather than waste time with a controlled Muso Dori arm lock, I knocked him out with a hammer fist below his ear.

The security guard yelled at me to drop the weapon, but since he was armed with nothing more than his masculinity, I ignored him, just in time to see the man with the pen still stuck in his eye attack.

The gruesome sight made me pause. The combat knife in the man's hand spurred me into action. I jumped to the side and landed with a heavy knuckle strike to the top of his forearm where muscles met and the radial nerve was tunneled. The knife dropped from his useless hand.

As the security guard grabbed the Scorpion soldier from behind. I kicked the knife toward the stairs. I didn't want the illegal weapon anywhere near me. I'd have enough trouble justifying the damage I'd done with a rug punching tool and a ballpoint pen.

Daniel ran toward me. Behind him, the Tesla driver opened the rear door and Mr. Lau emerged. He took a few urgent steps in our direction and opened his hands as if to ask what was going on.

"Watch out," Mr. Tam shouted, and hurried toward him from Gung-Gung's Mercedes.

A third Scorpion soldier—the same man who had thrown me off the roof, chased me in the alley, and threatened Mr. Lau in his office—grabbed Mr. Lau from behind and plunged a knife into his back.

The Tesla driver cried out as the Scorpion assassin yanked the blade from Mr. Lau's back and slid it across his throat.

"No," I shouted, as Mr. Tam charged forward to help. But the assassin had done what he came to do and ran.

I looked behind me to check on Ma and spotted the security guard on the ground and the other two Scorpion soldiers running down the stairs.

Doors slammed. The car idling at the bottom of the steps drove away.

# Chapter Sixty-Four

Daniel rushed forward and pulled me into his arms. "My God, Lily, are you all right? What just happened? Who were those men?"

I eased out of his arms. He'd been so focused on me, he hadn't seen what had happened to his uncle. "Daniel, I'm so sorry."

"About what? You're the one who was in danger."

I resisted as he pulled me close. "Your uncle."

"I know, I'm sorry about that. I didn't think of it as betraying your mother. I honestly thought it would be a good thing for all of us if they replaced her with me. Clearly, I was wrong. I explained that to Uncle Derrick on the ride over, but he disagreed."

I pushed him away. "Daniel, stop."

"Why can't you forgive me?"

"Your uncle was attacked."

"What? No."

Mr. Tam, the Tesla Driver, and the barrier guard stood on the walkway behind Mr. Lau's Tesla, bent forward to see or turned away in horror as people rushed out of the building to help. Daniel stood in place, frozen by confusion.

I pushed him gently. "Go."

Lights flashed and sirens blared as Daniel ran to his uncle. Squad cars pulled up to the curb. Officers stormed up the steps and from both sides of the driveway. I placed the bloody rug punching tool on the cement and waited for them with my hands open and my arms held low and away from my body.

"Lily," Ma called. "Are you okay?"

"Stay back, ma'am," the security guard said, and walked forward cautiously.

"What happened here?" an officer demanded in Cantonese.

The security guard shook his head. "These people were attacked by three men. This girl stabbed one in the eye and the other in the stomach."

"Men? What men?"

"They escaped in a car."

I couldn't understand the rest of what they said, but the topic was clear when one of the officers examined my rug punching tool and another searched the driveway for the missing knife.

The officer guarding my weapon rose and questioned me in English. "What is this?"

"It's a crafting tool. It belongs to my grandmother. She uses it to push yarn into a mat."

"Why do you have it?"

"She asked me to buy her another. I took it with me so I wouldn't have to describe it in Cantonese."

He looked in my eyes as if trying to detect a lie.

Ma stepped forward. "This is my daughter. Men tried to kill us. She fought them off. Even the security guard couldn't save us."

"Is this true?" he asked the security guard in Cantonese.

The guard rattled off an explanation as Ma walked around them to give me a hug.

The other officer stopped her then frisked me from chest to ankles. He took my pen and wallet from my pockets. "Is this everything?"

"Yes."

He checked my identification then examined me again. "There's blood on your hand. Are you injured?"

I shook my head.

"Okay. Step over there." He nodded to my mother but remained near the rug punching tool and held onto my pen and wallet.

Ma grabbed my shoulders and checked me for injuries. "Are you sure you're okay?"

"I'm fine, but I don't think Derrick Lau made it."

"I don't think so either."

An ambulance and another squad car arrived. Then another. And another. A murder at Two International Finance Center was a big deal.

After interviewing everyone on the scene, the officers declared it a random attack on wealthy business people— *Look at those luxury cars, after all!* —and concluded, with the combined statement of Ma, Gung-Gung, and me that it was fortunate for all that I had my grandmother's crafting tool in my pocket when the unknown men attacked. That said, they didn't return it.

Neither Ma, Gung-Gung, nor I said anything about the Scorpion triad.

Daniel left before I could give my condolences or even give him a hug, but from the look on his face he wouldn't have wanted either.

I hugged myself and tried not to cry. Although I had been the one to end our romance, the reality of not being with him broke my heart. Despite everything I had said, Daniel had run to protect me. He had admitted his mistaken perception about taking Ma's job and apologized for his actions with sincerity. He had even confronted his uncle in the car, presumably to convince him not to proceed against Ma. I wanted to forgive him. But would he even care?

After Rose's murder, I cut ties with everyone who reminded me of how I abandoned her to live on a college campus away from Ma. I dropped out of UCLA, ghosted my friends, and dumped my boyfriend. I avoided my mother and spent all my time, energy, and resources trying to make up for my failure as an elder sister to Rose by becoming a big sister to other girls and women in need. How could I expect Daniel to react differently?

"Are you okay?" Ma asked, again.

This time, I could only shrug.

"Your grandfather, Raymond, and I are going up to the offices to talk. Cecil and Kenneth are waiting for us to explain what happened. Will you come? We could order in lunch." Ma was obviously afraid I'd run off on one of my secret adventures.

I glanced down the driveway to where Mr. Tam and Mr. Ng's driver had parked the cars. "I'll be up in a minute. I want to check on Mr. Tam."

Ma smiled. "You're a very caring person, Lily. I'm not sure if I've ever told you that."

When I didn't respond right away, she shrugged off the awkward moment. "Join us upstairs when you're ready. We could all use a calming meal."

I watched her leave and marveled at what she had said. A caring person? Ma had most certainly never told me that.

As I walked toward Mr. Tam, I noticed Uncle leaning against a wall on the far side of the steps. When I met his eyes, he nodded for me to come and disappeared into the nook overlooking the sidewalk.

"How long have you been here?"

"An hour."

"Derrick Lau is dead."

"Yes."

"Are they coming for anyone else?"

"No."

"Why attack Ma and me?"

"They were only after Lau. You, as usual, got in the way."

I slumped against the wall. "Did we do this? Did we get him killed?"

Uncle shrugged. "He was doomed from the moment he laundered their money. Saan Zyu would have forced him to continue until HKIF was ruined and Derrick Lau was spent. He would have moved onto the next opportunity and erased any ties. Lau was dead either way."

"What about Cecil Chu?"

"He doesn't know who he was working for, only that he had to do what Lau asked or his career and reputation would be destroyed."

"What did Mr. Lau have on him?"

Uncle shrugged. "Does it matter?"

I considered the situation. The illegal transactions Mr. Chu had done could land him in jail and destroy Gung-Gung's reputation. HKIF would crumble, and everyone working for the company would be ruined. Far better, to secure the company and let everyone keep their secrets and maintain face.

"What about the smurfing and shell companies?"

"Someone will contact Mr. Chu to sell everything and shut it down."

"Gung-Gung will ask him to resign."

"He should."

"So it's done?"

"Yes. As long as you stay out of trouble."

"*Me?*"

"Don't act so innocent. Mind your business, and leave the Scorpions alone."

When I started to answer, he pointed his finger between my eyes. "Listen to me, stupid girl. Everyone you care about is safe. There's nothing you can do about a triad. Enjoy the rest of your visit and go home."

Uncle really *had* been watching me all these years. He knew it would burn my gut to let murders go unpunished. And I knew the triad would wiggle free regardless of the damning evidence I could provide. Derrick Lau had paid a high price for his poor choices. I didn't want Gung-Gung and Ma to suffer from them as well.

"You're right. I'll let this one go. But if the triad comes for *my* family, I'll run a stake through Saan Zyu's heart."

# Chapter Sixty-Five

Mr. Tam eyed Uncle with suspicion. "Is everything all right, Miss Wong?"

"Yes, thanks. This is a friend of mine. I'll be right over, okay?"

He glared at Uncle then nodded to me. "Of course, Miss Wong."

Uncle watched him go with a smirk.

"He's a good man."

Uncle snorted. "So are a lot of stupid people."

I groaned at the dig. "You and I are going to have a long talk back in Los Angeles."

Uncle chuckled. "If you say so, *Miss Wong*."

He walked away with a spring in his step, as if none of this had happened. Is that how it would be in Baba's kitchen? Would Uncle continue to drop his cleaver near my feet and loose sharp projectiles at my face? Would he call me stupid girl and complain about my lack of respect and the slipperiness of the objects that flew from his hands? Or would he interfere with my work and try to help?

Only one thing was for certain: In my mind, Uncle would forever be Red Pole Chang.

I walked over to Mr. Tam and leaned against the car beside him. "You scared me when you ran to help Mr. Lau."

"You scared *me* when you fought off those gangsters."

We locked eyes then chuckled with relief.

"Were those the same men you saw when you were in Mr. Lau's apartment?"

294

"One of them was."

"Will they be back?"

I shook my head. "They did what they came to do."

"Did you tell the police?"

"No."

"Good. What now?"

"I'm going to put this day to bed, spend a quiet Saturday with my family, and fly back to Los Angeles on Sunday. Unless you need help with Jing. Did you have a chance to speak with her last night?"

"I did, along with her mother."

"Really?"

He smiled with amazement. "It's been a long time since we spoke as a family."

"How did it go?"

"Jing acknowledged that she was being used. The activists only wanted her around because she resembles Agnes Chow and could provide them with protest art. Her mother and I explained what could happen to prominent activists if China takes control of Hong Kong."

"Could that happen?"

Mr. Tam shrugged. "We have our own political system for now, but we are still part of Communist China. They have arrested activists in the past. They could easily arrest more in the future. Better to be like water and not stand on a mountain with a target on your forehead."

I smiled at the Bruce Lee axiom adopted by the pro-democracy activists. Be like water applied to so many things in life, not just the fluidity to evade police interference.

"Jing's mother and I also agreed that art is just as important as academics. We are going to enroll Jing in those drawing classes she wants to take."

"That's wonderful."

"She was very happy. Thank you for suggesting it."

"I'm glad. What about the protest tomorrow at Tamar Park?"

"She won't be going." He smiled at my skepticism. "She and her mother are going to the New Territories to visit her aunties. She won't be anywhere near the island this weekend."

"Glad to hear it."

He nodded toward the entrance. "You should go upstairs and be with your mother and grandfather. If I were them, I would want you close."

I entered the tower but stopped in the lobby. It was one o'clock here and nine o'clock back home. I wanted to speak with Baba before he went to bed.

"Dumpling? What a relief. I've been waiting for your call."

"Have you spoken with Ma?"

"Just now. Are you hurt?"

"No."

He exhaled into the phone. "Your mother told me you were fine, but... I heard about Derrick Lau."

"Yeah. He was the target. Ma and Gung-Gung are safe."

"I see." He let that sit a moment then added, "How'd it go with Daniel?"

"Ha. Not so good."

"Well, there are other bulls in the pasture."

"Seriously?"

He chuckled. "You know what I mean."

"What about you? Any more kitchen accidents?"

"Oh for crying out loud, you're as bad as your mother. Hot woks and too little to drink, nothing more."

"And seven stitches."

"Fine. I made an appointment to see a doctor. Are you happy? But he's going to say the same thing."

"Thank you."

"You're welcome. Now go be with your mother."

"How do you know I'm not?"

"Goodbye, my darling."

"Bye, Baba."

By the time I finally made it upstairs, Mr. Chu had left and Kenneth was in his office on the phone looking stressed. A plastic platter of sandwiches sat untouched on Gung-Gung's coffee table beside empty teapots with their lids overturned so Katie would know to replenish them. From the forlorn expressions on Ma and Gung-Gung's faces, that wouldn't be necessary.

I covered the sandwiches with the plastic wrap and picked up the platter. "Come on, you two, it's time to go home."

# Chapter Sixty-Six

I woke up late the next morning feeling calmer and more confident than I had since we arrived. Ma had retained her job, my family was safe, and the triad was out of our lives. My romance with Daniel was over, but although painful, I could live with that. Losing my mother would have killed me.

I padded to the kitchen in fluffy socks and pajamas and found Po-Po refilling the teapot.

"Jou san, Lei Lei. You want tea?"

"Jou san, Po-Po. Yes, please," I responded in the same mix of languages.

My adorable grandmother searched through her cupboard and brought out a slender porcelain cup with a painted bunny face and a raised puff-ball tail. She set it in front of me and smiled. "You remember this cup?"

"You still have it." I picked it up, thumb on the nose and my fingers on the tail. The delicate cup felt so much tinier than it had on my last visit. "Do you still have the other? The one you used to give to Rose?"

Po-Po retrieved a similar tea vessel made of porcelain but painted and shaped to resemble a fat yellow chick. I cupped it in my hands and remembered Rose's sweet chubby face.

"You want to take them home?"

I smiled at her thoughtfulness but shook my head. I had my own mementos of my sister on my altar cabinet and scattered throughout my apartment. Po-Po only had a few photographs.

"I'd rather visit them here."

She beamed with delight, and I could see how precious the cups were to her. "Okay, Lei Lei. I keep them safe for you."

Gung-Gung entered dressed in a light-weight cardigan and slacks. "You finally woke up. Good. We leave in thirty minutes."

"For where?"

"Dim sum banquet with your grandmother's family. We usually meet on Sundays, but since you and your mother are leaving tomorrow, they pushed it up."

"How thoughtful."

"It is. Don't make them wait."

Po-Po poured tea in my bunny cup and handed it to me. "Take this with you," she said in Cantonese. "And put on something nice. I want to show you off to my sisters."

"Yes, ma'am." I hurried to obey and arrived at the front door with minutes to spare only to find Gung-Gung standing beside Po-Po and Ma, tapping his foot with impatience.

"Aiya, Lei Lei. You move slower than honey on a winter morning."

I followed them out of the house and leaned toward Ma. "Did he not see me fighting off those men?"

She shrugged. "One does not affect the other. You know how he is, five minutes early is five minutes late. Don't worry about it, we have lots of time."

Which would have been true, if not for the protesters.

"Why must they block the streets?" Gung-Gung said. "Bad enough they protest during the week. Why must they ruin our Saturdays?"

After hearing how a past protesting incident had caused one of Gung-Gung's critical investments to crumble, I better understood his agitation with the current political climate. Even so, I felt inclined to comment. "Today is the anniversary of the Umbrella Movement."

"You think I don't know that? Thousands of them occupied Harcourt Road and Tim Mei Avenue with tents and barricades. The government had to bring in portable toilets for the encampments they built. Can you imagine? The occupation lasted for seventy-four days, right in front of Central Government, one kilometer from my offices. What if they do it again?"

"From what I've read, they have permits for a peaceful protest in the parks and a rally later this evening. I haven't heard anything about another occupation."

Gung-Gung snorted. "What they plan and what they do are not the same thing." He pointed to the traffic jam. "Can't you drive around this, Mr. Tam? We're going to be late."

Fortunately, Gung-Gung had allotted so much time that we arrived at exactly eleven o'clock—ten minutes late to him but the start of a leisurely arrival for Po-Po's family. Her three sisters greeted her first.

"Yu Ying," they exclaimed, and fired questions in Cantonese too fast for me to understand.

Ma nodded toward a slender woman with a long gray braid. "That's Po-Po's eldest sister, Li Ying, the rounder woman beside her is Po-Po's second eldest sister, Zhi Ying, and the youngest sister with the short black hair and squat legs is Shao Yin. If you forget which is which, call them all Yi Po."

"Good plan." Hongkongers and mainlanders assigned specific words for every relative based on birth order, relationship, and whether they came from a person's maternal or paternal side of the family. Yi Po meant sister of my maternal grandmother.

"The names of Po-Po and her sisters all end in Ying. What does it mean?"

"They are all blossoms—Jasmine, Gardenia, Peony, and Jade."

"Is that why Po-Po named you Violet and you named us Lily and Rose?"

Ma nodded. "Except your grandfather insisted that my official name would be Shun Lei."

"How'd that work for him?"

She chuckled. "Not very well, I imagine."

Giving Ma a name that meant *obedient* had not made her so.

I greeted all of my grand aunties in halting Cantonese then did the same with their husbands, children, and grandchildren as they arrived. We took over the rear section of the restaurant with four round banquet tables, three for my mother's cousin's families and one for Po-Po's sisters, their husbands, and us. My great grandmother arrived last, escorted by Li Ying's husband.

We rose to welcome the matriarch of Po-Po's family and greeted her one by one.

Ma kissed her grandmother's cheek and introduced me in Cantonese. "Ah-Po, this is my daughter Lily, do you remember her? She was very young the last time she visited."

I knelt beside my great-grandmother's chair so I could greet her at eye level. She was so tiny, peeking over the table, her toes barely touching the floor. Pleasure sparkled in her eyes at the sight of me and her wrinkled lips pressed into a smile. She patted my hand and murmured gentle words I couldn't understand.

Ma answered quietly, bent down to kiss her cheek, then led me back to our seats on the other side of the table.

"What did she say?" I asked.

"That you reminded her of her eldest daughter and would grow up to be a strong and determined woman."

"And what did you say?"

"That you already had."

The banquet lasted for four hours with seemingly endless steamers and plates of Hong Kong delicacies, including my favorite sticky rice, bean curd rolls, and black bean chicken feet. I struggled with the fast-paced Cantonese, made everyone laugh by mixing it up with Mandarin, and ended up relying on Ma for translations.

"Wait. Did you say Po-Po's maiden name is Tam? Any relationship to Gung-Gung's driver?"

"Actually, yes. Mr. Tam is the son of your great-grandfather's brother's son."

"What's that, an uncle twice or thrice removed?"

"Think of him as a distant cousin."

"This is so cool. Should I call him Uncle?"

"God no. He's your grandfather's employee. Honestly, Lily, there's not even a specific word for his relationship to you. Please don't make a big thing of it."

"Okay. Just trying to get to know the family."

Although I meant it sincerely, it was an impossible task, especially with all the great-great-grandchildren sitting with my cousins at the other tables. I was the only one in my generation who wasn't married with a family.

I thought of Daniel and checked my phone. Should I send him a message?

*And say what? Sorry I got your uncle killed?*

Better to let him grieve with his family than send condolences about a man I had reason to hate.

Still... I tried to imagine us at one of those tables, Daniel chatting with my cousins in Cantonese as I wondered how the hell I ended up with an infant on my lap and rice stuck to my clothes. I closed the app and put away my phone. Too much had happened. Even if I accepted his reasoning about why he had thought it would be okay to take Ma's job—and I hadn't—we weren't after the same kind of life. I might feel differently one day, but Daniel wanted a wife and family *now*.

Ma leaned against my shoulder. "Don't try to be like them. You have your own path to follow."

"You don't know what my path is."

"And I don't want to. But whatever it is, own it."

# Chapter Sixty-Seven

Cars packed the five lanes on both sides of Gloucester Road while protesters swarmed the sidewalks between Victoria and Tamar Parks.

"Can't you take another route?" Gung-Gung asked.

"I will, Mr. Wong. As soon as we reach the next main street."

I studied Mr. Tam through the rearview mirror. He had Po-Po's round face with high cheeks that bulged into cheery balls when he smiled, but none of my mother's singular beauty. My own features were too mixed up with Baba's Norwegian genes to compare his to mine. It was so weird to think of him as family.

His phone rang from the caddy stuck to the windshield. He glanced at the caller and let it ring.

Gung-Gung groaned. "Answer it. The noise is giving me a headache."

Mr. Tam retrieved the phone so he could speak privately. His eyes widened with alarm and flashed to the rearview mirror to focus on me. After a few more words, he hung up. When I mouthed Jing's name, he nodded.

"Would you guys mind if I got out here?" I asked. "This protest will be part of Hong Kong history, I'd like to check it out."

"Why do that?" Po-Po asked.

"Because she's young and foolish," Gung-Gung answered.

Ma raised her brow. I smiled back innocently. She wasn't buying it. I kissed her cheek and crawled over her lap to exit the car.

"I would have moved, Lily."

"No need. Hold up, Mr. Tam. I want to ask you for directions." I closed the rear door and came to his window as he rolled it down. "Where is she?"

"Tamar Park. She ran away. Her mother only realized it a few minutes ago."

"I'll find her. Call me when you get them home."

"I will. Take the overpass at Flemming to Harbour and follow the crowd."

"Got it."

I waved to Ma and ran.

Ten minutes later, I slowed to a walk, shoulders deep in protesters. I called Jing on the phone. She didn't answer.

Me: *I'm at Tamar Park. Where are you?*

I kept the phone in my hand and followed the flow of people up the broad paved walkways and scanned the grassy areas for signs of Jing.

I called Mr. Tam. "Are you free yet?"

"I just dropped them off. Have you found Jing?"

"There are thousands of people here."

"What are they doing?"

"Sitting."

"That's all?"

"And singing. Look, I know she ran away, but maybe this isn't the time to drop the hammer. Everything looks peaceful and organized."

"Okay, but I want to see for myself. There's a rally scheduled in front of Central Government Complex that she might attend. Will you meet me there?"

"By the Lennon Wall where Jing was almost arrested?"

"Not there, across the street at Admiralty Shopping Center where I rescued you from those violent men."

I coughed out a laugh. Every location in this city correlated to a dramatic incident.

"There's a KFC facing the main road," Mr. Tam said. "I'll text you when I've parked."

By the time he arrived, the sun had set, and protesters had taken over all ten lanes of Harcourt Road. He joined me at the window and watched the crowd grow.

"Those people don't look peaceful to me," he said. "See those piles of rocks and bottles? They're expecting to fight. And if they keep pointing those lasers at the windows, there's going to be trouble."

I messaged Jing again and, this time, received an immediate answer.

Jing: *I've moved to Harcourt Road. You should come.*

Me: *I'm already here. Where are you?*

Jing: *With Matthew, Kris, and Nate. On the street in front of the ramp. Join us!*

Me: *On my way.*

I pocketed my phone. "Don't worry, Mr. Tam. We'll find her."

"How can you be sure?"

"Because it's what I do."

# Chapter Sixty-Eight

The energy of the crowd in front of the Central Government Complex crackled with pent-up rage. These protesters had staked their places early. Instead of walking over from Tamar Park after communing in the sun and singing *Glory to Hong Kong,* they had clad themselves head to toe in black and come laden with backpacks no doubt stuffed with defensive and offensive tools. Most wore surgical masks. Many carried umbrellas to use as shields against projectiles, water, and sprays. Some protected their heads with motorcycle helmets and construction hats. Others wore gas masks hanging around their necks.

Thousands more protesters filled the streets, sidewalks, pedestrian overpasses, and the six-lane flyover ramp emerging from the center of Harcourt Road. They chanted slogans, spread their fingers for the five demands, and waved black flags with *Free Hong Kong* and *Revolution Now* emblazoned in bold white letters.

Camera operators in bright yellow vests hurried through the crowd, capturing footage of the event. Not a square foot of standing space remained except for the sidewalk directly in front of the West tower and behind a white police tanker truck that had recently arrived.

I pointed to the building where protesters sprayed graffiti slogans and others attempted to breach the metal gates. "That's not going to go over well."

Mr. Tam pointed to a circle of men burning the People's Republic flag. "Neither will that."

No sooner had we commented on this than squads of police, dressed in riot gear and holding shields and guns, emerged from and around the government building. They ordered the crowd to stay back and disperse but were met with angry slogans and demands.

Blue and green lasers crisscrossed into the sky and onto the building walls and windows. Helicopters thundered overhead, car horns blared, and thousands upon thousands of people shouted. I looked around us for Jing or her activist friends, but the crowd was too closely packed.

Rocks flew through the air.

Officers raised red warning flags to signal imminent force.

Canisters hit the ground and exploded into clouds of pepper spray. People shouted and covered their eyes. Those with goggles or gas masks grabbed the canisters and threw them back at the police.

I flipped up the back of my jacket to cover my face against the next assault, motioned for Mr. Tam to do the same, and pulled him toward the wall of the flyover ramp rising from the center of Harcourt Road. A woman beside us screamed as a rubber bullet struck her back. She screamed again when a pepper ball hit the man next to her and exploded.

"Over there." I pointed to a group of protesters hanging behind the front line. One of them was a girl about Jing's size wearing a hot pink mask like the one I'd seen her wear at the protest in the Dragon Center mall. Before we could shove our way through, a cannon burst of blue-dyed water blasted into our sides and propelled us into people, backpacks, umbrellas, and more.

I shouted for Mr. Tam over the thundering noise. He called back from the ground. I felt around and clasped his extended hand, helped him to his feet, and threaded a path through the chaos. The farther we moved from the source, the wider the water cannon sprays became. Umbrellas opened and formed walls of protection. Once sheltered from the onslaught, I wiped our faces with the inside of my jacket. The blue dye stung, but at least we could see and breathe.

Mr. Tam cried out in despair, "Where's my Jing?"

People scrambled in all directions. Some ran away from the police and others toward them. They shone laser pointers and hurled petrol bombs and rocks. Officers beat them back with batons and spray.

When an officer pointed his pressure gun at me, a man in black shoved the muzzle up to the sky, swept out his legs, and stomped on his face shield. The plastic cracked, and the officer scurried away from the threat. When the man in black turned, all I could see of his face were cruel eyes and pointed brows. The rest of his features hid behind his mask.

It didn't matter. The way he stood, the hard angles of his body, the wavy hair bound at his neck—I recognized my rescuer. It was J Tran.

He lowered his mask, smiled at me, then vanished like a wraith.

*Why? How?*

I shook my head. All that mattered was finding Jing.

I turned to Mr. Tam and spotted the girl with the hot pink mask run around the low wall and onto the ramp above where he and I stood.

"Was that her?"

"Yes," he cried.

We shoved our way to the bottom of the ramp and up the six-lane flyover highway. The higher we climbed, the safer it became. Protesters around us shouted insults at the police below and shone their lasers at the helicopters above. I cut through the crowd and pulled Mr. Tam in my wake.

We shouted Jing's name, and she waved back with surprise and relief. She threw her arms around Mr. Tam and buried her face in his chest.

"We have to go," I said, and pushed them toward the Admiralty Center side of the ramp.

Once back on the ground, we were shielded from the police and hurried down a side street and into the garage. We didn't stop until we made it to Mr. Tam's tiny car.

"Thank you, Lily." It was the first time he had called me Lily instead of Miss Wong.

I smiled. "What are cousins for?"

"You knew?"

"I found out at the banquet this morning. Why didn't you tell me we were related?"

"It wasn't my place."

"Wait," Jing said. "You're my cousin? That is so cool."

I pulled her under my arm and knocked playfully on her head. "You won't think it's so cool if you run away from your parents again." I let her wiggle free. "I'm serious, Jing. You put yourself and your father at risk."

Tears welled in her eyes. "I'm sorry, Daddy." She fell into his arms and cried.

# Chapter Sixty-Nine

I sat in my usual spot in Gung-Gung's Mercedes, back seat center between Po-Po and Ma, as Mr. Tam drove all of us to the airport. Gung-Gung sat in the front seat beside his driver, my newly discovered, thrice removed uncle. I smiled. This hadn't been the most peaceful of trips, but it had brought us closer together.

"Will you come back for New Year Time?" Po-Po asked.

She was referring to Spring Festival, what we called Chinese New Year, a fifteen-day celebration that began on the second new moon following the Winter Solstice and culminated in the Lantern Festival. It marked the return of Spring and symbolized family reunion.

Ma shook her head. "That won't be feasible. Perhaps, you could visit us later in the year."

"We already came to Los Angeles," Gung-Gung said. "No need to come again."

Po-Po nodded her head in agreement.

I stifled a laugh. So much for family reunion. My mother and grandparents had apparently had their fill.

When Mr. Tam pulled up to the curb, everyone exited the car as if we were late for our plane instead of three hours early. After the week's anxiety, I couldn't blame Gung-Gung and Po-Po for wanting us gone. This had been the most stressful vacation I had ever taken. Even my romantic interlude with Daniel had devolved into a heart-wrenching convoluted mess.

Mr. Tam set the luggage beside me and closed the trunk.

"It was nice to meet you, Miss Wong."

"Likewise, Mr. Tam."

The affection in his eyes communicated the sentiments propriety would not allow him to speak.

"We should keep in touch," I said.

"I would like that. So would Jing."

"Good luck with her. She'll keep you on your toes."

He cocked his head. "Why would she do that?"

I laughed. "Never mind. Just hear her out, okay? Otherwise, she'll rebel."

"You know this from experience?"

I glanced at Ma, eager to be on her way. "Yep. It's a Wong-Tam family trait."

Ma grabbed the handle of her suitcase. "What are you two laughing about? Never mind. It's time to go."

I waved to Mr. Tam, gave my grandparents a hug, and caught up with Ma as she charged inside the terminal. When she saw the long lines to check in for our flight, she flashed me with a satisfied grin. "Good to still have my executive perks."

As we joined the much shorter V.I.P queue, she received a call from Baba. "Hello, darling. We just arrived at the airport. Yes, everything is fine, we'll be home before you know it. No, don't leave the restaurant on our account. I've hired a driver to pick us up at LAX." She smiled at me. "Yes, it's quite a relief to still have my job. Mm-hmm. She's right beside me."

Ma passed me her phone and inched forward in line.

"Hey, Baba."

"How's my Dumpling?"

"Glad to be leaving Hong Kong."

He laughed. "Well, I should say so. Next time, plan to have a more peaceful visit."

"Hey, this wasn't my doing."

"Uh-huh."

"What?"

"You do like adventure."

"Not when it strikes this close to home."

"Uh-huh."

"What? Spit it out."

He heaved a sigh. "I haven't decided if you look for trouble or if trouble finds you. Either way, it turns my stomach in a knot."

"I'm sorry."

"I'm not fishing for an apology. I just want you to be safe."

"Well, I can't get into too much trouble on a plane, can I?"

"Don't tempt fate."

"We're almost to the counter, love you, here's Ma."

I handed off the phone before Baba could expand on his theory.

Sensei and I had discussed my relationship with trouble on several occasions. He believed warrior protectors, like us, opened ourselves to cries for help. He said we projected an energy to those in need and listened for their responses with heightened senses. We noticed what others did not and took action where others *would* not. As a result, we found trouble as often as trouble found us.

Ma put away her phone and motioned me forward. "Your father made an appointment to see a doctor."

"I heard."

"I don't buy all that nonsense about hot woks and too little water. Stubborn Norwegian. He might own a restaurant, but your father is a stoic North Dakota farmer down to his toes."

I laughed. "True enough. When's the appointment?"

"In a couple of weeks. It's probably nothing."

I leaned my shoulder against hers. "I've been worried, too."

My phone vibrated against my hip. "Hold on a sec."

She nodded toward the counter. "Call them back. It's our turn."

"Hello?"

"It's me."

"Uncle? What's up? Are you still in Hong Kong?"

"Are you?"

"I'm checking in for my flight home."

"Can you fly here instead?"

"Where's here?"

"Shanghai."

 "Why would I come to Shanghai?"

"They took my niece."

"*What?* Who?"

"Call me when you arrive."

The call ended.

I shook my head. Trouble had found me again.

## THE END

# Acknowledgments

I had always planned to take Lily Wong to Hong Kong, where her mother had grown up and where Gung-Gung and Po-Po still lived. But my excitement for this idea grew once I visited Hong Kong and met the Hongkonger relatives of our son's then-fiancée. Stopher and Joeye brought Tony, Austin, and me to Shanghai to spend Christmas with her parents. Then we all traveled to Hangzhou and Hong Kong. I am forever grateful for their generosity and this magical opportunity to experience these cities from an insider's point of view.

Joeye's relatives welcomed us into their Li and Ching families—unrelated to my own Ching relatives—and celebrated with us nine months later when Stopher and Joeye married on Kaua'i. As I bonded with those in attendance, I had no idea that Joeye's childhood friend Kenneth Ng would end up beta-reading *The Ninja Betrayed*. My deepest thanks for his keen insights and verification. He helped me make this book as authentic as it could be. Any H.K. missteps are entirely my own.

I am continuously amazed by the overlap between my life and fiction. Our son fell in love with a Hongkonger woman *after* I had created the character of Lily Wong then brought me to her homeland where I was able to research locations and culture for my *yet-to-be-imagined* book. They married in my homeland, introduced me to my future beta-reader, and gave birth to our beautiful granddaughter, Moana. Now my dear mo-'opuna (grandchild) and my feisty protagonist share more than Chinese and Norwegian heritage. They both have mothers from Hong Kong!

Thanks *always* to my incredible editor, Chantelle Aimée Osman, whose skill, judgment, and insights have made every Lily Wong novel the best they can be. I imagine her future notes while I write and rely on her impeccable taste. I'm proud to be part of the Agora Books / Polis Books family and continually blown away by these gorgeous book covers. Many thanks to Chantelle for including me in the process and to Kristie at 2Faced Designs.

Mahalo to my fabulous literary agent, Nicole Resciniti, The Seymour Agency team, and my supportive husband, Tony. I'm a lucky writer to have all of you in my corner.

Finally, my deepest thanks to you, my wonderful readers. It means so much to know you're enjoying the adventures of Lily Wong. You can send me a message, connect on social media, and find book club discussion topics and fun extras on my website: ToriEldridge. com. And if you subscribe to my monthly muse-letter, with insider news and giveaways, you'll also receive a thriller short story for free. Take care, lovely readers. I hope to connect with you soon.

# About the Author

Tori Eldridge is the bestselling author of the Lily Wong series, including *The Ninja Betrayed*, *The Ninja's Blade*, and *The Ninja Daughter*. Her books have been nominated for the Anthony, Lefty, and Macavity Awards for Best First Novel, named one of the "2019 Best Mystery Books of the Year" by *The South Florida Sun-Sentinel*, and awarded 2019 Thriller Book of the Year by Authors on the Air Global Radio Network. Her shorter works have been published in horror, dystopian, and other literary anthologies, including the inaugural reboot of *Weird Tales* and her screenplay "The Gift" earned a semi-finalist spot for the Academy Nicholl Fellowship. Tori introduces another empowered female protagonist next May 2022 in her new standalone DANCE AMONG THE FLAMES.

Before writing, Tori performed as an actress, singer, dancer on Broadway, television, and film. She is of Hawaiian, Chinese, Norwegian descent and was born and raised in Honolulu where she graduated from Punahou School with classmate Barack Obama. Tori holds a fifth-degree black belt in To-Shin Do ninjutsu and has traveled the USA teaching seminars on the ninja arts, weapons, and women's self-protection. Follow her online at:

Website: ToriEldridge.com
Facebook: @ToriEldridgeAuthor
Instagram: @writer.tori
Twitter: @ToriEldridge

CPSIA information can be obtained
at www.ICGtesting.com
Printed in the USA
LVHW022200280921
698964LV00002B/2

9 781951 709365